Hush Little Baby

HUSH LITTLE BABY

SUZANNE REDFEARN

GRAND CENTRAL PUBLISHING

NEW YORK BOSTON

This book is a work of fiction. Names, characters, places, and incidents are the product of the author's imagination or are used fictitiously. Any resemblance to actual events, locales, or persons, living or dead, is coincidental.

Grand Central Publishing
Hachette Book Group
237 Park Avenue
New York, NY 10017

www.HachetteBookGroup.com

Printed in the United States of America

RRD-C

First Edition: October 2013
10 9 8 7 6 5 4 3 2 1

Grand Central Publishing is a division of Hachette Book Group, Inc.
The Grand Central Publishing name and logo is a trademark of Hachette Book Group, Inc.

Library of Congress Control Number: 2013941571

ISBN 978-1-4555-7320-2 (pbk.)

Hush Little Baby

1

The priest stands to the side waiting for the piano to quiet, then walks to the pulpit. I always marvel at his height and wonder if he gave up an NBA career for the cloth, or if perhaps he heard the calling because he was a foot closer to God than most mortals.

I sit between my children—Addie, four, on my right, her white-stockinged legs sticking straight out on the pew, her patent leather Mary Janes swishing like windshield wipers; and Drew, eight, on my left, dressed in his pressed khaki pants, his psalm book on his lap. My husband, Gordon, sits beside him, his eyes intensely focused on the altar, devoutly waiting for the gospel to begin.

We look like the perfect family, and I'm happy to pretend.

Father Kimball looks down at his parish. "Welcome, my brothers and sisters in Christ, beloved children of God..."

Beside me, Drew squirms. Gordon's firm squeeze of his knee stops the squiggling. I take Drew's hand in mine to keep him still. No one in our small clan has an iron bladder. I slide my eyes in a sidelong glance at Gordon. His jaw is set tight. He won't be happy if Drew gets up in the middle of the sermon. Of course, he'll be even less happy if Drew wets himself.

"During the first reading from the *Book of Isaiah*, we heard that the Lord God said, 'Do not remember the former things, or consider the things of old.' When the Lord God spoke these sacred words, He was commanding His children to set aside the past in order to open the door to a better future..."

I sigh. I don't want to hear about forgiveness, not today.

On the cross behind Father Kimball, Jesus poses in His final moment of martyrdom. On His right, St. Catherine, namesake of the church, angelically smiles down on us, chiseled of marble and more beautiful and flawless than she ever could have been in life.

I smile at her as I have just about every Sunday for most of my life. She died almost a decade younger than I am now, but her legacy has lived almost a millennium, an impressive achievement for a fourteenth-century peasant.

Catherine was the twenty-fifth of twenty-six children born into a poor family in Siena. At seven, she claimed to have had a vision of God and, because of the experience, consecrated her virginity to him. She spent the next dozen years in a nine-foot-by-three-foot cell praying, fasting, and scourging herself three times a day until Christ visited her and placed a ring on her finger (visible only to her), and she was told to end her years of solitude and enter into the service of God.

The Dominicans at Rome still treasure her body in the Minerva Church, and her head is enshrined in St. Dominic's Church in Siena.

Below Catherine's image is an engraving of her writings: *If you will wreak vengeance and justice, inflict them on me, poor wretch, and assign me any pain and torment that may please you, even death.*

I believe that through the foulness of my iniquities many evils have occurred, and many misfortunes and discords. On me then, your poor daughter, take any vengeance that you will. Ah me, father, I die of grief and cannot die!

I stare at the holy face peering down on me and think, *Today you would be diagnosed as a delusional bipolar narcissist with a masochistic streak who probably became that way because you were the twenty-fifth child and your parents were exhausted, and therefore, you didn't get enough love or attention, and you would still be given a cell in which to pray and starve yourself, but it would have padded walls.*

This is what happens with all the unlikely stories of the Bible—my over-rational brain dissects and reassembles them until they make sense and hold no magic or mysticism at all: *The walls of Jericho tumbled down because of an earthquake; Jesus was actually walking on a patch of floating ice common in the Sea of Galilee; Mary was naughty and didn't want to confess.*

Yet, even with that much cynicism, I believe. I clasp my hands tight and pray for guidance and mercy. When I see the ocean, I attribute it to God. I aspire to create in His vein, trying feebly to emulate His perfection. He haunts my decisions, and the rules of His church guide me. And I have faith He will help me.

Drew's hand moves from mine back to his lap. His legs are crossed, his knees knocking together.

Father Kimball is still going strong with no sign of slowing. The ardor of the audience rising with his words, each amen growing in fervor until the parish almost sounds Baptist.

"Go," I whisper in Drew's ear.

Gordon's eyes shift. Drew looks from me to his father, and his fidgeting stops.

I sneer at St. Catherine.

Maybe she wasn't insane. Maybe she was brilliant. A master manipulator and con artist who, recognizing her lowly status in life, realized at a young age the perfect escape and, preying on the superstitions and fears of her brethren, masterfully elevated her lowly stature as the twenty-fifth child of a peasant to that of a saint.

I return to my churchgoing pose—eyes on the pulpit, lips moving in sync with the audience—while inside I think of Drew holding tight beside me and pray for the sermon to end.

"...I am He who blots out your transgressions for my own sake, and I will not remember your sins. Amen."

A glorified united "Amen" from the audience and the pews begin to empty into the day. Drew runs ahead of the throng and into the anteroom before everyone else. I gather Drew's sweater and trail behind Gordon and Addie.

St. Catherine's is set into the hills of Laguna and overlooks the Pacific. The morning is quintessential Southern California–spring gorgeous—the ocean stretched to a seam of blue sky, a light breeze gently swirling magnolia and jasmine in the air.

Gordon herds us to the car. He needs to sleep. He works tonight and Drew has a Little League game this afternoon, which only allows Gordon a couple hours to rest.

Frozen smiles, polite nods, a few princess waves and we're in the car and on our way.

A beautiful day. A beautiful family.

I'm happy to pretend.

2

Gordon's home.

Like a silent alarm, I jolt awake, alerted by a presence I don't see or hear. Nine years have honed my senses, so I'm aware of him even before he pulls onto our street or into the garage.

The door to our room, left unlatched so he won't wake me, pushes open, and the smell of beer and something feminine that's not me haunts his almost silent footsteps. I peer through slits to see the numbers on the clock—six, five, eight.

His shift ended an hour ago. The drive takes twenty minutes. Familiar disappointment and hurt well behind my veil of feigned sleep.

I struggle to keep my breath even so I won't feel compelled by pride to confront him or humiliated by shame when I don't. Though the shame decimates me just the same.

The safe opens, and his gun and holster clunk softly as they're laid inside, then the dial clicks secure. His watch, wallet, and badge are placed on the bureau. There's a sigh as he sits in the chair beside the dresser and removes his Bates boots. My eyelids glow with soft light as the closet door opens and the boots are placed in the precise row of shoes beneath his hanging clothes. The toes are pointed out and the tips aligned. Across the spread of carpet, my shoes mirror his, aligned just as precisely—men's shoes and women's shoes faced off in perfect ranks, prepared to advance against each other in an epic battle.

His trousers and shirt slide down the dry-cleaning chute, his undershirt, boxers, and socks down the laundry chute. The door closes, and despite my efforts, my heart pounds. If the drawer opens to retrieve his pajamas, it will be okay.

Naked footfalls on the carpet. I can't tell which way they travel.

The sheet pulls open, and as the draft whips across my skin, my mind races. I need to decide whether to resist. It's a complicated question. One for which there isn't time.

He grunts more than speaks his disapproval at my grotesqueness, and already, tears fill my eyes. Then, before I can blink them away, his hands grab beneath my arms and I'm half carried, half dragged, from the bed and dropped to the floor.

I land on my knees and palms, but fall flat when my pajama bottoms are wrenched from my hips. With one hand, he rips them from my ankles, with the other, he rolls me to my back.

My eyes blink rapidly to bring the moment into focus. He's on his knees, his chest looming over me. His beard, blonder than his rusty hair, breaks the smooth line of his jaw. His mouth is set in a sneer, and I wince at his hatred. His eyes, during the day, light as glass, are dilated and dark and scan my body to assess how much more I've disintegrated.

"Gordon, please," I manage, my hands instinctively flying in front of me to cover my face. They're too slow, and heat rises to fill the void where the sting of his palm was a second before.

I bite back the next protest and the hurt and every sound in between as he enters me, his erection at half-mast—the alcohol, my repulsiveness, and the fact he performed minutes earlier with someone else making the encore challenging.

"Fuck with me and you get fucked," he says as he pounds against me.

My mind spins to figure out the offense I've committed. For three months, he's been good; we've been good. I've been so careful.

It hurts.

His hands wedge beneath my butt to assist the hammering. "Fat. Disgusting and fat," he says as he grabs my excess skin so hard I cry out. I grasp at him to dislodge his grip, my left hand latching on to his shoulder, my right swiping his cheek below his eye with a nail before finding his chest.

The reaction causes him to pinch harder, turning the flesh in his clamped fist.

I remove my hands, bite back the next cry, and pray for it to end.

He slips out, and fear pools in my throat. I reach to reinsert him, but it's too late.

"Fucking, disgusting cow." The blow to my ribs is much harder than the one delivered to my face, which is how I know he realizes what he's doing. A bruise beneath my shirt won't be seen.

I roll and try to curl, but his left hand cuffs my wrists above my head and his right clamps down on my neck. I gag and my eyes bulge, and the memory of a year ago returns with sheer terror. He grins more than smiles, lightens his grip slightly so air whistles into my lungs, and with renewed strength, thrusts violently back into me to finish the job.

I lay gasping for air, but otherwise unmoving.

When he's done, he removes himself, delivers a brutal departing kick to my thigh, and stumbles toward the bathroom. A second before the door closes, something light and hard is thrown beside me, the corner nicking my ear.

"Lie to me again and I'll fucking kill you," he says. The latch clicks, and the shower starts.

Tears and semen drip as I push my trembling body to sit.

The thin morning sun through the shades allows just enough light for me to understand. Beside me on the floor is an empty tampon box.

The box had been hidden in the toiletries bag of my workout duffel. It had concealed three doses of Next Choice, otherwise known as the morning-after pill. It's the contraceptive I've used for the past six months. Unlike birth control pills, I can get it over the counter, and there's no record of it for Gordon to find.

He wants more. I can't handle what I have.

I stumble from the room, lock myself in the guest bathroom, and try to wash the past half hour from my body. The red bruises on my ribs and thigh and the finger streaks on my butt can't be washed away, but the other evidence—my tears and his seed—I scrub until the skin is raw.

The metallic tang of blood touches my tongue, and I realize my lip is bleeding. I press a tissue to the wound to staunch the flow.

Gordon's shower stops, and I squat in the corner, stare at the door, and wait. I rock, hugging my knees to my chest—scared, nauseous, exultant—grateful I'm alive. I obsess on my beating heart, the blood pulsing in my veins, the oxygen filling my lungs.

Until you've almost died, you don't appreciate the tenuous tether you have to life, but when you come within a breath of your mortality, suddenly you become very aware of its precariousness. And as insane as it is, and I acknowledge it's insane, I'm never so grateful for my life than the moment I realize Gordon didn't kill me.

My ribs throb, and I'm cold. I wrap a towel around my bare bottom and continue to wait.

Fear does a strange thing to time—a minute or an hour, I can't be sure—but a door different from the one I'm listening for opens, and I leap from my huddle and dash into the hallway.

"Mommy..."

My hand slaps over Addie's mouth so hard my towel disengages and drops to the floor, and instantly, my baby starts to cry. My hand muffles the noise, and I pray Gordon doesn't hear. I carry Addie back to her room and mule-kick the door closed. I run to the far corner where her stuffed animals crowd on a beanbag and set her down, pulling her to me to calm her.

"Shhh," I soothe, as I pray she won't begin to wail. Her eyes are wide with hurt and fear.

"I'm sorry, sweetie," I say, and stroke her red curls.

She whimpers, and my heart breaks.

"Why you do that?" she asks.

I shake my head, unsure if the gesture is because I can't explain, or because I'm too ashamed to explain, or because the explanation is too burdensome for a four-year-old.

"I didn't want you to wake Daddy," I answer honestly.

Her head tilts slightly, then rights itself, satisfied with the explanation. "I need to go potty." Her tears have stopped, and she seems to have already moved past the moment.

I take her hand and lead her silently back to the bathroom, retrieving my towel sarong as we go.

I sit beside her as she does her deed.

She looks sleepily at my face. "Why you bleeding?" she asks, her shoulders sloped in boredom as she waits for her bladder to remember why it woke her.

A question with no answer.

3

Eat," Gordon says. "You need to be out the door in half an hour."

My body protests as I push to sit up against the pillow. He hands me a plate with a slice of whole-wheat toast and a soft-boiled egg.

He doesn't mention the reason I'm in the guest bedroom and neither do I.

It's moments like these I wonder if I'm the one who's crazy and if maybe the nightmare didn't actually happen.

He pats the comforter over my abdomen, and my battered ribs flinch at his touch, reminding me with no uncertainty that the nightmare was, in fact, real.

"Morning, son," he says with a celebratory grin, as though his earlier performance were a glorious triumph of baby-making to be rejoiced. On his cheek is a red scratch barely an inch long, a pitiful testament to my lack of resistance.

This is how it goes, an unexpected explosion after months of calm. Always, just as I start to relax and believe I'm safe, just as life resumes its hum and I'm lulled into believing it wasn't as bad as I remember or that it isn't going to happen again—that he's changed, I've changed, we're good now—bam! It happens again, worse than I remember, always scarier and worse.

Addie bursts into the room. "Daddy, youw're home!"

Gordon scoops the galloping four-year-old into his arms, plants a kiss on top of her red curls, then twirls her back to the ground.

Addie's feet touch the carpet, and she spins to me. "Mowrning," she says as she jumps onto the bed and wraps a hug around my neck, then pulls back, her freckled face widening into a huge grin. "I got you a bewrthday pwresent." And as quickly as she appeared, she vanishes.

Gordon sits on the bed beside me and places his hand on my belly. "I'd be happy with another girl as well," he says, and I will myself not to tremble.

Addie's back. In her hands is a lump wrapped in taped-together magazine pages.

"Open it. Open it," she says, her energy buzzing like a hornet in heat.

I peel off the wrapping.

"I made it myself."

I hold up the long strip of yellow-and-blue-plaid flannel. It's about five feet long and varies in width from a few inches to a foot. I recognize it as a piece of one of Addie's baby blankets.

"It's beautiful."

"It's a scawrf."

"Oh."

"For in case you get smudges again."

Addie's eyes sparkle, Gordon's recede, and mine fill as I swallow the emotions back inside. I didn't think she remembered. I hoped she'd forgotten.

Scotch tape patches the edges of the scarf where it frayed.

If I speak, the tears will escape, so instead I nod and wrap the soft gift around my neck as the memory replays—almost exactly a year ago, my life darkening as Gordon strangled me. Then after, the "smudges"—swollen red, bruised blue, vermilion green, then jaundice yellow—a month of color changes ringing my throat before they disappeared.

"How you get smudges?" Addie asks.

Gordon pats his thigh, and Addie climbs on board and wraps her pink arms around his neck.

"Sometimes, Ad, someone gets real mad or real sad," he says, "and by accident they hurt themselves. And that's what happened to your mommy, but then your daddy showed up and stopped her, and she got all better."

A thousand jolts of electricity couldn't shock me more.

I stare at my husband as he spins his horrible tale, my fear and shame teaming up to squelch the pride and outrage that rise like a fist in my throat.

Your father strangled me. Your father tried to kill me. Your father is insane. The smudges are from his arm wrapping around my neck and squeezing so hard I couldn't breathe.

My mouth doesn't move.

Addie sits on his knee, her left hand on his massive shoulder. Her right pokes the dimple on his chin, and she studies him with a hero worship that can't be shattered with the truth.

Dragging footsteps, then the shaggy head of Drew appears, followed by his spindly body.

He plops himself onto the foot of the bed.

"Mowrning, Dwrew," Addie says. "You see what I got Mom for hewr bewrthday?" She points to the scarf as I start to unwrap it.

"Youw're not gonna weawr it?"

"Of course I am." I rewrap the boa, my neck sweating in protest.

"It's a cut-up blanket," Drew says.

"It's a scawrf."

"It's stupid."

"At least I got hewr something."

Drew sneers at her, his muscles tensing.

"Time to get dressed," I announce, shifting the tides. Addie trots off, and Drew shuffles behind her.

"Eat," Gordon says. "Eating for two."

With another kiss to my belly, he follows them out.

This is how it goes, the initial shock absorbed like a wave, disappearing in the chaos of the day—ignored, pushed aside—remembered in every breath and bruised movement, but overwhelmed by the responsibilities of life, buzzing in the shadows of my mind and creating a cloudy numbness that, by day's end, will progress into paralyzing fear.

The pattern's so familiar it's like déjà vu before it's happened.

For the next few weeks, I'll obsess on preventing another attack, catering to Gordon like he's a king—loving him and worshipping him with abject devotion. I will work out, wear sexy lingerie, attempt to be more beautiful than I am. I will smile and purr, forsaking my dignity, my pride, and any sense of self that remains, all in a vain attempt to prevent it from happening again.

Like now, though I'm nauseous, my system wrecked, and in no condition for food, I force the breakfast Gordon's given me down my bruised throat in an effort to please him.

This will go on for a while, perhaps a few weeks, until exhausted, I give up in despair, slipping into an antipathy so deep that a chill shudders my spine to remember it. Waking up, breathing, existing, becomes a chore—bathing, grooming, eating, out of the question.

It is a dangerous time—a time of feeling nothing, wanting nothing—a time when I'm no longer afraid. So I tempt fate, taunt Gordon and my mortality with sloven disregard, inviting and inciting my own destruction.

Two years ago, I accidently-purposely left the stove on and nearly burned down the house. Another time, I half-intentionally released my parking brake, taking out a parking meter and the trunk of my car. And a year ago, I had an affair—Russian roulette with five bullets in the chamber.

I choke down the last piece of toast, closing my eyes and willing it to stay put.

If I survive, if I don't destroy myself, eventually Addie and Drew will bring me back from the ledge, and thoughts beyond the present will begin to break through as I think of their future and what will happen to them if I don't pull it together and figure out how to make things right. And as the bruises fade, my resolve will grow, and I will become determined to reclaim my life.

Gordon senses this, instinctively knowing when I begin to regain my strength.

As we lie in bed, my head spinning with thoughts of escape, he will turn to me. "Jill, you know how much I love you."

I will nod.

"And if I ever lost you..." His voice will trail off and he will shake his head, then he will look at me fully so I can witness the veracity in his eyes. "...I'd go crazy."

He is crazy. I already know this.

"You won't leave me," he will say. "You wouldn't do that? Do that to me and the kids?"

And my heart will twist in terror for Addie and Drew.

This is how it will happen. This is why I have stayed.

I set the empty plate on the nightstand, and numb and sore, hobble toward our bedroom.

I limp as I walk and try to force my left leg to bend, but the battered muscles refuse to cooperate.

Each step aches. My pelvis is bruised, and my ribs pulse so acutely I wonder if they're broken. Halfway there, I stumble into a gimpy run, lunging for the bathroom and getting there just in time to vomit my efforts into the bowl.

I flush away the evidence and, my head spinning, pull myself to the seat. I rest my forehead against the cool edge of the vanity. Below me, the trash can holds the empty tampon box, and the pain intensifies as my breaths deepen with despair. I can't be pregnant. I'm already at my breaking point.

Gordon's hand on my neck was a warning, its loosening, a show of mercy. I close my eyes and feel his fingers tightening, the thin stream of air whistling to my lungs.

If I stay, he will kill me. If I leave, he'll destroy Addie and Drew. This is the impossible catch-22 I'm left with.

There's a third possibility, but I pretend I don't recognize it. Like an itch I'm afraid to scratch for fear it will fester and grow, I turn from it, close my ears to it, drape it in a sheet, but like an elephant in the room, it cannot be disguised—it smells, it bellows, it takes up too much space.

NO! I scream. I refuse to acknowledge it, consider it. I push it back. It doesn't budge.

I pull on my clothes and turn on the faucet to drown it out.

Run, it whispers.

I apply my makeup, a heavy coat of foundation and a deep shade of lipstick to conceal the truth.

Take the kids and run. Hide where he can't find you.

Leave my job, my home, my parents?

I can't . . . I won't . . .

He'll kill you; he'll destroy them.

"Jill, let's go." A holler from downstairs.

Mercifully, the choice will have to wait. Like all the times before, at this moment, my focus is on survival—survive this moment, this hour, this day.

"Jill!"

On shaky legs I stand; my time to decide is up.

Drew's lunch is packed and sits on the counter above his Angels backpack that sits on the floor.

Gordon walks from the hallway wearing the off-duty uniform worn by most of the cops in the department—white T-shirt, dark Levi's 501s, and a blue windbreaker that conceals his Glock.

He pulls a banana from the stainless steel banana hanger and walks to the door. He's going to work out, then he'll return to sleep a few hours before spending the rest of the day with Addie. And this afternoon, he'll coach Drew and the Laguna Beach Indians.

"Game's at six," he reminds me, his tone laced with warning.

I nod.

The door closes behind him, and I breathe.

I comb Addie's red curls, though they spring instantly back to an unruly mop, and finish just as the front door opens, letting in the crisp morning air along with my mom.

"Morning," my mom says, and that's all it takes.

Addie bolts to my leg, and the tremor before the eruption begins. The quivering starts with her lip, then moves outward to her chin and cheeks, culminating in a bloodcurdling wail as she clings to my skirt to prevent my departure.

Drew pulls on his backpack and watches unimpressed. When we get in the car, he'll rate it on the Addie Richter scale. Friday was mild, only a six. Today's revving up to be a nine.

My mom walks past us and pours herself a glass of orange juice. Tantrum consoling isn't in her job description nor in her skill set. She sits at the counter sipping her juice and paging through the latest edition of *Redbook*.

I pry Addie's hands from my skirt and almost escape, but she lunges back, sending a jolt of pain through my injured ribs.

"Damn it," I snap.

My mom scowls, annoyed that my expletive interrupted her reading.

"Addie, honey, you know Mommy needs to go to work." I try, though my stressed voice hardly conveys the sympathetic plea I was going for. My ribs throb, and the clock ticks.

Addie latches on tighter and screams louder, and I don't have time for this. Drew's going to be late; I'm going to be late. I wrench myself free from my sobbing daughter, grab Drew by the hand, and drag him out the door.

As we drive, the stress ebbs, and I glance in the mirror to see Drew sitting quietly in the backseat. His mop of sandy hair hangs past his forehead and curls around his ears. His blue eyes are like Gordon's, his long eyelashes are mine. Since he turned eight, he no longer sits in his car seat, so my view of him is limited to his eyes, which stare solemnly forward toward the road and the reluctant destination of school.

"Morning," I say.

He smiles for the first time of the day, an anemic grin with no teeth.

"Red or blue?" I ask.

"Red."

He always picks red, because red almost always wins.

We start to count. This morning blue cars are in fashion and I pull to an early lead, but then I miss a few, and when we pull into the drop-off lane of his school, we are even. He unbuckles his seat belt as a teacher drives past in a small red Mini Cooper.

"You win," I say.

4

I enter the glass and steel tower and ascend to the fourteenth floor, where the executive offices of Harris Development are housed. Harris is the third-largest design-build firm in the country with close to a thousand employees and six offices throughout the world. Last year, we did over a billion dollars in projects, ranging from prisons to housing developments. I've been with them since I graduated sixteen years ago and have risen through the ranks quickly to become the youngest vice president in the company and the CEO's right-hand man (woman), a position I relish and defend with pride. My mantra is *Anything you can do, I can do better, and make it look as though I'm not even working hard to do it.* And achieving it requires not yawning, eating, or peeing.

As soon as I step through the ten-foot glass doors, my world shifts, and for ten hours a day, five days a week, I escape.

Sherman McGregor sits across from me as he has a dozen times in the past year, but today will be the last time. In a few minutes, he and I will shake hands and our firms will merge and we will part.

He's twice my years and with ten times my accomplishments, so I allow him these last moments. He will accept, but I also understand how much he doesn't want to.

"Better for who?" he says.

"For everybody," I answer.

"But more better for Harris?"

"Probably."

Sixty years have brought him to this, a lifetime of passion, sweat, and achievement diminished to a sale of it all to his lifetime nemesis for a small fortune he won't have time to spend. He knows, as do I, that before the ink is dry, he will be reduced to an old man, once great, now no longer relevant.

With a silent breath, he straightens in his chair and says, "Jillian, I'd say you're worth your weight to Harris in gold, but since you only weigh three pounds, that would be a gross understatement."

"I used to weigh more, but then McGregor Architects came into my life."

The humor fades with the mention of the company that bears his name.

"Three sons, five grandsons, and not a single one wants anything to do with the business that's paid for their lives," he says, his great jowls shaking.

We've had this conversation before. Sherman's old-school—work hard and earn what you've got. His kids are a new generation—play hard and spend what you've got.

My children are decades younger than his, but I feel his disappointment. Until you have kids, you don't realize that their worlds and ideas won't necessarily reflect yours and that their paths will be their own.

With the thought of my own family, I glance at my watch.

The day's just begun and already there's too much to get done.

"I'll have Connor draw up the papers," I say.

Sherman groans. "Harris's shark."

Connor Enright is Harris Development's in-house counsel and my best friend. He's the only employee who makes more than me, and he's worth every penny. He earns his healthy salary ruthlessly negotiating Harris's business dealings as well as cleaning up Harris's personal messes, of which there are plenty. And for the past two years, he's been a thorn in Sherman's side, wreaking havoc on the battalion of attorneys Sherman's employed to negotiate this deal.

"You have some great whites on your side as well," I say.

He nods and sticks out his hand. It's been a noble battle—the takeover not friendly, but ultimately necessary for both companies' survival.

"Jillian, there's no one I'd have rather waged war with."

"Likewise." I take his large veined hand in both of mine.

And with his shoulders slightly more stooped than they were when he entered the office, Sherman walks out the door.

5

I walk through the maze of cubicles inhabited by the draftsmen and architects who draw the three-dimensional future in two dimensions.

Too many eyes. Too many shy smiles.

Shit.

There are over a hundred employees at the western office of Harris Development, and it seems every birthday is an excuse to stop working and traipse everyone into the cafeteria for a "surprise" celebration of their aging.

Beyond the sea of gray boxes, I spot the blond head of Connor, "the shark," working in his glass-walled office, and take a quick detour.

"Connor, call it off."

His head lifts from his reading, and he smiles without teeth—a grin that probably as a kid got him into more trouble than he actually caused.

"Call what off?"

"Whatever spectacle of distraction has been concocted on behalf of my birthday."

"It's your birthday?" he says as he reaches into his drawer, retrieves a silver envelope, and holds it out, his smirk widening.

On the outside of the envelope in beautiful penmanship is Connor's pet name for me, "Jinks," lovingly given to me for my Velma from Scooby-Doo looks and smarts. I pull the card from its shiny envelope.

On the front is a middle-aged couple playing tennis; beneath the cartoon it says, "Love 40."

Inside it reads, "New balls please."

Clipped to the inside are two tickets for *Wicked*.

My heart swells. Why can't all guys be this good?

Because then they'd all be gay, procreation would stop, and the human race would go extinct.

"Take me, take me," he says, bouncing in his chair with his hand in the air.

I walk around his glass and chrome desk and hug him. "Who else would I take?"

"Well, I thought you might feel obligated to take that hunk of a caveman you call your husband."

"Seeing women and men singing and dancing in tights isn't exactly Gordon's thing."

"Mine, neither," he says. "I prefer singing and dancing without the tights. Big plans for the big event?"

"Just a night out with my parents on Wednesday. Nothing too big or sexy."

"Well, be on notice, when I turn the big four-oh, I'm expecting big and sexy." His hands spread over his head to about fourteen inches. "Really big."

"Ouch."

He delivers his beaming smile, and his eyebrows rise and fall twice. "Speaking of which, gorgeous brown eyes, nice teeth, and good hair is coming in today, and I'm supposed to tell you to play nice."

"Don't I always?"

"Jinks, I mean it. We need this."

"And the kids we're building the school for deserve windows."

"Do you like my shoes?" he asks, turning his crossed leg to and fro in order for me to see his finely polished Prada. "Because I do. I like my shoes, my BMW, my condo, my Sports Club membership. It's insanely superficial and utterly selfish, and I've beaten myself up repeatedly for my shallowness because you're right, the little kiddies living in war-torn Compton should have the benefits of light and air. But let's be reasonable. If we lose this contract"—he looks forlornly at his foot—"no more shoes."

"I'll play nice."

"Good, then off with you. I have a few more things to take care of before I'm beckoned to participate in your spectacle."

"Just kill me now."

"The plebeians need these small moments of levity and continual doses of useless calories and sugar to keep them sane."

"Are you responsible?"

"No way. Over-thirty birthdays are like gas, better passed in private."

6

I'm very good at smoothing out trouble. I roll over it like a steamroller without paying the emotions around it any mind. It's a special talent I have, and it's why I get paid the generous salary I do.

But this afternoon, the trouble is in the form of Jeffrey Wheeler, and I'm afraid my talent might fail me.

"Morning," Jeffrey says, standing and extending his hand. I go along with the nonchalance and shake it as though he's any other client, any other man. He looks good—his thick brown hair a little longer than last time I saw him, his chocolate eyes smiling.

Tina, my assistant, has set out the drawings and sits with her pad and pen ready. Asian and efficient without an ounce of entertainment value, she's been with me a year, and I'm dying for her to move on.

"Water?" she asks in a clipped accent.

Jeffrey nods, and she skedaddles from the room.

Kelly, the project architect, sits across from Jeffrey, her thick arms wrapped around herself as she holds in her anger. I vaguely remembered that young cockiness—an ounce of talent and the optimism that you could change things, leave your mark, become the next Le Corbusier. The difference is, Kelly has more than an ounce of talent, and unlike me, she might just turn out to be the next revolutionary architect of her time.

Kelly's nose begins to flare with short huffs, and this means her voice isn't far behind. I get there first. "Jeffrey, it's not that we don't understand the security concerns. It's just classrooms without windows, it's, well, it's..."

"Inhumane and stupid."

I glare at the girl, whose Irish face, normally flush, is now entering Pink Panther territory.

Jeffrey laughs. Not a mean, in-your-face laugh, but the I-love-your-chutzpah-but-it's-not-gonna-change-my-mind kind of chuckle.

And that does it. With great theatrics, Kelly pushes from her chair, teetering it, but not achieving the dramatic topple I'm sure she was going for, and storms from the room.

I roll my eyes, first at the back of Kelly's wide booty as it exits, then at Jeffrey.

"What?" he says with a shrug. "She's cute. I love the spunk."

"She's whiz-bang talented."

"So are you, but you're cuter."

I feel my own flush, but unlike Kelly, my Italian skin conceals more. "Jeffrey, don't."

"Don't what? Tell you you're cute?"

A small smile escapes, and he ricochets it back with a big one that shows all his teeth. His grin is lopsided, and the eyetooth on the left a smidge too far forward, giving him an almost canine appearance.

I lower my eyes to the drawings and set my mouth to serious.

"So you're standing by your no-light-or-air-for-the-children position?"

"I miss you."

My face tightens, my focus moves in and out, and I close my eyes a second too long as I swallow my thoughts one by one: regret, humiliation, attraction, and back again. And when the past is buried back where it belongs, in the recesses of a memory a year old, I take a deep breath and lift my face to meet his. "We need to fix this."

"Yes, we do."

"This," I say, losing my strength and lowering my stare back to Compton's new middle school.

He continues to examine me without excuse. "No windows, that's the order from the school board. Too much vandalism and too many break-ins. They're tired of dealing with it. I like your hair that way. It shows off your neck."

The perfect lines on the bright vellum blur again, and I blink rapidly to keep the emotions in check, from traveling back to the time when I was the craziest I've ever been, when for a brief, wonderful, dangerous while, Jeffrey was more than a client, more than a friend.

Outside the conference room, a phone rings, snapping me back to the present.

"Please, Jeffrey," I manage. I want to tell him how hard this is, this day in particular, my body and resolve freshly bruised, my resistance weaker than it's been. Instead, that's all I say.

"Okay," he says with a sigh I feel more than hear. "Compton Junior High. Jill, I want you guys to have this, but the board's getting impatient. No windows or no contract. That's the bottom line."

My hand traces the elevation in front of me, an edgy prefabricated box with ribbons of glass striping vibrant blocks of blue, white, and yellow in a Mondrian abstraction.

I lean back and pull my attention away from one attraction to focus on the other. "Will you at least read the research?"

He holds up the sheaf of papers Kelly prepared detailing the numerous studies that have been done purporting the benefits of fresh air and natural light in everything from factory production to animal fertility.

"She does have moxie," he says.

"And she has a point."

Jeffrey's head shakes, and he gives a repeat performance of his not-serious laugh.

"Read it, then laugh," I say.

He runs a thumb along the thick ream, and his eyebrows seam together in dread. "All of it?"

"Just until you're convinced."

I move to his side of the table to shake his hand, and he looks at my extended paw like it has six fingers.

"A hug is out of the question?" he asks.

I nod and keep the hand in place between us.

He takes my fingers princess style and lifts them to his lips. His breath brushes my knuckles as the callused tips of his fingers slide into the pocket of my palm, then, the instant before contact, my hand is turned, exposing the pale underside of my wrist. Light stubble graces the heel of my hand as his lips whisper across my skin.

"I miss you," he says again, then turns and walks out the door.

7

The latch clicks, and I collapse into my chair.

The touch of his lips lingers on my wrist, and my fingers move to the cross around my neck, my guilt resurrecting itself like locusts waking after winter. In the glass of the conference room wall, my warped reflection stares, and my hand moves from the gold talisman to massage the neck he complimented.

I look tired. I am tired.

I turn away from myself, gather the drawings in my arms, drop them at my office, then leave for my appointment—my annual gyn exam, postponed three times, which landed it on my birthday and I had too much shame to postpone it again.

I'm fifteen minutes early and the doctor's running an hour behind.

I settle in with my laptop.

An hour and a half later, my phone buzzes. Caller ID says it's Melissa Williams, Drew's room mom. My first instinct is to ignore it.

No, I can't make cupcakes for the bake sale.

No, I'm not available for the field trip.

No, I don't want to be a part of the PTA.

On the fourth ring, I answer.

"Hi, Jillian, it's Melissa. How are you?"

Not as chipper as you. "Fine."

"I'm calling because I'm concerned about Drew."

I don't even know the name of her son, nor do I have the slightest concern about him.

"This is the third time this month he's come to school without lunch."

Shame blindsides my irritation as the brown bag sitting on the counter at home etches into my brain. I close my eyes and bite my lip.

The door to the inner sanctum of the doctor's office opens. "Jillian, we're ready for you," the nurse says at the exact moment Melissa says, "Jillian, are you there?"

As I stand to follow the nurse, my laptop slips and I juggle the phone, and when I recover, the phone is off. I just hung up on Melissa. I power it on to call her back, but the nurse stops me and points to the sign, "No Cell Phones."

Drew has no lunch.

"So you might be pregnant," the nurse says, scanning my updated medical questionnaire and smiling. "Congratulations."

On the way back to the office, I stop at the drugstore and buy a box of Next Choice, irrationally scanning the store for Gordon as if he might be watching. I swallow the pill in the restroom and dispose of the evidence. It's still too early to know whether or not I'm pregnant, and if I wait, it will be too late.

I can't handle what I have.

8

I look at my family in the sterling-silver frame on my desk—we're at an Angels' game. Addie wears a sunhat with daisies, and her smile fills her face. Drew has on a blue cap with an A embroidered on the front and holds up a giant foam hand with the finger extended that says, "Go Angels!" Gordon's arm is around my shoulders, and I look happy.

I put my head on my folded arms on my desk.

Addie crying without a good-bye.

I feel bad.

Drew, no lunch.

I feel bad.

Gordon. Jeffrey.

I feel bad. I feel bad. I feel bad. The chorus beats with my heart.

"Mr. Harris would like to see you in the cafeteria."

I wake myself to look at Tina, who stands expressionless in the doorway, and make a mental note: *Tina is a brilliant liar.* Her flat, expressionless features betray nothing as she invites me to my birthday glorification.

"SURPRISE!"

Fifty forced smiles face me, and I force a grin back as a few risk glances at their watches. A bouquet of balloons floats from the center table, the inflated "40" rising above the other rainbow orbs.

"Thank you, you really shouldn't have." *They really, really shouldn't have.* "But since you did, and since the cake looks delicious, let's celebrate my old age. Dig in."

The group breaks into the smaller groups of the office—the twenty- and thirty-something singlettes, the future up-and-comers, the over-the-hill, just-trying-to-maintain-status-quos, and the power brokers who are already making their way toward the door. The cake is dissected and passed around, and a few more watch-glancers stealthily slip out the door.

Tina walks up, her dark bob bobbing, and hands me a piece of white-frosted yellow cake with red filling.

"Thank you," I say, wondering how long I have to endure the tribute before I, too, can slip away.

"Would you like a drink?" Tina asks.

A stiff one. Saying that to Tina would almost certainly cause the girl's fine-teased brows to furrow, and then she'd probably spend the next hour searching for a way to stiffen my fruit punch. Sarcasm and humor are lost on her. "No thank you," I answer instead.

"I sure could use one," the familiar baritone of Bronson Harris interrupts from behind us, "a double, dry, straight up."

He kisses my cheek as Tina and her furrowed brow scurry off with a "Yes, sir," in search of a solution to her new crisis of making a double-dry-straight-up fruit punch for the big guy.

"I hear congratulations are in order. You finally slayed the dragon."

"Actually, I think Sherman just got tired and ran out of fire."

"I'm still going to call you Dragon Slayer, at least for a week."

Tina reappears. "McGregor's back," she says.

"Speak of the devil," Harris says, looking concerned. "Want me to go with you?"

I shake my head a little too emphatically. Harris and Sherman have locked horns too many times in the past.

"Damn bastard, you're right. Don't know how you do it, Jillian. That man brings out the Irish in me."

"Sherman's like my dad," I answer, smiling. "I have forty years' experience in how to negotiate a proud man into doing something he doesn't want to do."

"Go get 'em, Dragon Slayer."

9

Sherman sits in the same chair he occupied earlier, his thick body filling the armchair and his powerful anima filling the room.

I take my seat across from him.

"Hello again," I say.

"I need a favor."

I tilt my head.

"I've changed my mind."

I don't breathe. Like the Compton school, we need the McGregor deal.

Without the two, I might as well start updating my resume. Harris Development is two jobs away from going belly-up like a thousand other developers that have been wiped out in the last three years. Already we've suffered layoffs, bonus cuts, and salary freezes. Compton Middle School and the Sherman merger will ensure our future for the next five years.

The old man raises his hand. "Not about the deal."

I let go of my breath and wait for the rest.

"About the sale," he says, "the firm is yours, but I don't want the sale made public."

I tilt my head.

"For two months," he continues, "for two months Harris needs to continue as you have for the last two years, as though we're still negotiating, then you can announce the merger."

"Why?" But I know why and it makes me sad. How did it get to the point where it is? I wonder for a moment about my own marriage and if Gordon and my wounds will poison our children as well, if the future is looking at me.

He shakes his liver-spotted head. "The money needs to be transferred, but the sale needs to be kept quiet for two months."

"That's going to be difficult."

"Difficult is your specialty."

The deal we already made was difficult. Sherman fought to protect the people who work for him and that made things complicated. He negotiated that McGregor Architects remain sovereign for three years after the merger to guarantee, or at least hopefully guarantee, that his employees would have a chance to survive the merger and then either prove their worth to Harris or move of their own accord.

"Sherman, difficult is one thing, but do you really want to do this? This morning, we were good to go."

"The future is not what it used to be."

"Now you're quoting Valéry?"

"Smart and beautiful. Where were you when I was younger?"

"Studying Valéry."

His smile is sad. "They're not getting any of it, and I don't want them to know. I don't want my last days to be a war with my children attempting to declare me incompetent."

"Sherman, they're your family."

His head bends to his chest, causing two chins.

In the two years we've been discussing the merger, histories have been revealed. Sherman knows about Addie and Drew and that Gordon is a police officer and that my dad recently suffered a stroke.

And I know about Sherman's three failed marriages, his older son's struggle to find success, his middle son's struggle to find sobriety, and his younger son's struggle to find anything of meaning at all.

"I called Tom," he says, his eyes still on the carpet, "to tell him I'd closed the deal, but before I could tell him, he interrupted to tell me he was getting another divorce and that I was calling at a really bad time.

"I couldn't call Kyle because he's in lockdown, so I called Jordan, and in the background, I hear him tell his girlfriend to tell me he wasn't home."

He raises his head, his yellow eyes slashed with rage and hurt. "Not a penny, Jillian. Not one red cent."

"Sherman..."

His hand stops me. "Don't feel sorry for me. I don't deserve it. I did this. God, country, family. For me it was my ego, my business, a dozen mistresses, then somewhere down the list was my family. I did this, but I'm done paying for it. Sink or swim. They didn't have the nurture, but by damn it, they have the nature. If there's a single one of my genes in those boys, they'll make it. But not on my dime. This is my way of making it right."

Right as a two-headed nickel.

Genes don't cut it. I'm living proof. I come from one of the world's greatest men and one of the world's most tenacious women. Sink or swim, and I'm sinking fast.

"Two months?" I say, the lump swelling in my throat. He

looks better than he has in months, but only because he's not fighting anymore. In two months, it will be over.

He stands. "Two months."

"You're sure about this?"

"This is my last gift to them. They won't see it that way, but it is. I can't protect them anymore, and in the end, we're all destined to disappoint."

His sorrow is so complete that it weights the air, and I think I don't want to live to be old…or rather, I don't want to live to be old alone.

I stand and walk around the desk. "I'll see what I can do," I say, though I'm completely unsure how I can convince Harris to hand over eighteen million dollars but keep the merger under wraps, knowing the sale will be questioned when it's disclosed and that the one man who can explain will be dead.

Sherman lingers half in, half out the door. "I wish I'd had a daughter." Then he's gone.

I check my watch, 5:43. *Game's at six.* Gordon's voice from this morning resounds in my head.

My phone buzzes. Harris wants an update.

10

Gordon stands in the dugout door, its frame dwarfed by his size. His hands are relaxed at his side, a congenial mask of encouragement on his handsome face. My glance moves to Drew standing on the mound. His chin, my chin, juts forward in determination. His eyes, his father's eyes, focus on the catcher's mitt forty-six feet away.

Every fiber of my being wishes for a strike.

Drew sets, his feet come together on the rubber, his right hand grips the ball inside the glove. His thin arm hammers high over his head as his leg rears up, and with all fifty-three pounds, he hurls the white sphere toward its destiny.

Crack.

My wish worked, a perfect pitch right down the middle.

Worked too well. The ball soars into right field, and the outfielder fumbles it, and for a split second, I hate the child. The runner rounds the middle base and heads for third. The outfielder overthrows his cutoff, and the runner scores. The game is over.

Around me, people shuffle and chatter, the moment that was so important a minute before absorbed into the present like the backwash of a large wave.

"Hi, Jillian."

I turn to see Michelle Garner, an almost-friend, and it takes a second too long for my required smile to find my face.

"You okay?" she asks.

"Yeah, fine. Good game."

Michelle's not who I want to see. I never want to see her. Solid, genuinely nice, and with a terrier-like acuity—I try to avoid people like Michelle as much as possible.

Her brown eyes study me as she says, "Shame they lost. They were so close."

I smile and nod. "Win some, lose some, but the boys played well," I say, while marveling inside at how well I've perfected the language of saying the pointless things humans say to each other all day long.

Before everything changed, there was a possibility Michelle and I would become friends. Drew and her son, Max, are the same age, and, when they were babies, we'd gone to lunch a couple times and had met at the pool.

"Pizza at Gina's, right?" she asks.

I'm bone tired, and the idea of pizza with the team as the parents discuss the intricacies of eight-year-old baseball makes my throbbing head swell.

"Perhaps another night. I've got some work to catch up on."

Michelle's head tilts slightly and her pupils dilate and recede a flicker as she discerns the lie, then she offers her own short smile and says, "Well, maybe next time."

I continue past her toward the restrooms, avoiding her perceptive eyes that look beyond the veneer and recognize more in my superficial platitudes than our acquaintance and polite protocol allows.

In the dugout, eleven of the twelve Laguna Beach Tigers are trying to dislodge a ball that's burrowed into the fence behind the dugout. The twelfth player, my own young Tiger, quietly gathers his equipment.

For ten minutes, I sit on the toilet with my face in my hands, and when I'm certain the postgame lag time of small talk is almost done, I return to my neighbors and friends.

And family.

My mom is ahead of my dad and approaching fast, her dog, Martha, a yippy terrier mix, beside her. The two of them leave my dad literally in the dust with his walker as he tries to negotiate the uneven park without being hit by wayward children, balls, and skateboards.

My mom wears a bright red Nike sweat suit that clings too tight to the extra flesh around her hips that no amount of exercise can correct, and like a mother duck with absolute entitlement, she waddles toes-out toward me.

"Jill, what took you so long? We've been waiting."

I ignore her and continue past her so my dad won't have to continue his struggle to get to me.

I lean in to give him a gentle kiss on the good cheek that can still feel me, the half of him his stroke didn't destroy. "Good game, Pops, didn't you think?"

He nods, and his eyes twinkle. Baseball is his passion—on the field when he was a young man and in the spectator seats when he could no longer play. For six years, he was a designated hitter for the Orioles. When his bat got unlucky, he retired and bought his first restaurant. He used to joke that he was a better ballplayer than businessman, which wasn't saying much, since his career average hovered around .225.

Thirty yards behind my dad, Gordon talks with some of the other dads. The men dissect each minute and congratulate each other on each play as though they were the ones who played the game and as if world peace were determined by the outcome.

My dad turns to look with me, and the twinkle leaves his eyes.

"Come on, Pops, I'll walk you to the car."

"And we'll get to dinner by breakfast tomorrow," my mom says. "Just get him to the curb. I'll bring the car around."

She marches off with Martha at her heels. My dad begins to shuffle in the direction of the parking lot. I shuffle with him, happy to have him by my side.

"Mommy!"

A redheaded pirate with an eye pencil mustache, a backward ball cap, and more freckles than anyone can count is holding me at sword point with a twelve-inch twig.

"I surrender," I say, my heart swelling at the sight of my girl.

"Mmmeee toooo," my dad gurgles beside me.

Addie doesn't laugh. Her mission is too serious. "Mommy, I want to go. We've been hewre foooowrever."

Three hours is forever to a four-year-old.

"I'm just going to walk Papa to the parking lot and then we'll go."

"Okay. I'll help," she says, and takes her spot on the other side of her grandfather to help him avoid holes and uneven spots with his walker. A job she takes very seriously until a stray ball crosses our path and she takes off after it.

"Jill."

At Gordon's voice, I stop, and my dad pushes forward at twice his previous pace. Nine years and I'm still between them.

"Hello, Nick," Gordon says as he walks past me and in front of my dad, extending his hand.

With some difficulty, my dad accepts the outstretched palm.

Gordon's mood appears light, considering the loss.

"Jill, the team's headed to Gina's. We need to get going."

I glance at my dad, who has continued his struggle up the ramp to the parking lot. Gordon's already turned and is walking the other direction, fully expecting me to follow.

The walker sticks in a crack, and my dad struggles to dislodge it. With a deep breath, I move toward my dad, help him out of his jam, then continue beside him toward the parking lot at the pace of a proud man who's had a stroke and needs to use a walker, but won't stoop to any more assistance than that.

Gordon's eyes are on me, but I don't look back.

We're twenty yards from the curb when Addie appears on the left.

"Mommy, Daddy says we got to go." Her voice is too tense for a little girl.

I nod, and my dad stops, which I don't want him to do. Suspicion fills his eyes, and I feel his concern and his blood pressure rise.

I force my face into an easy smile and say with what I hope passes for nonchalance, "Tell your dad I just need to say goodbye to Papa and Nana."

Addie looks uncertain, but turns to deliver the message, and my dad and I shuffle on, no longer worried about hurrying.

The damage has been done.

11

Gina's Pizza is Laguna Beach Little League's second headquarters. Gordon's team and the opposing team and at least two other teams fill the red, white, and green landmark. Team photos from three decades cover the walls, and pennants for every team west of the Mississippi fill in the holes.

Beside the restaurant is a drugstore, its glass storefront blazing with fluorescent light. My eyes slide guiltily through the windows to the pharmacy counter where hundreds of boxes of Next Choice are kept, then shift to the dim interior of Gina's.

Gordon drinks beer at a table, completely absorbed in his conversation, his hands gesticulating a story of grand proportions.

His eyes pause, find mine through the window, and I shiver with fear.

He knows my thoughts. He always knows. He possesses superhuman powers—ESP, radar, incredible intuition. No matter how small the deceit, he catches me, and the punishment is always so much greater than the crime.

Gordon's eyes find me again, staring twice as long as the

moment before, and I walk away from the light and into the darkness to join the team for the celebration, hoping this time I get away with it, manage to deceive him, survive another day, knowing it's only a matter of time before he catches me.

"I'm glad you decided to come," Michelle says, stepping up beside me. "You don't join us often enough."

I offer my patented smile as my eyes slide more than I intend to wander to Gordon's beer glass. Four or five, hard to know exactly because it's being refilled from endless pitchers on the table.

Beside him, Claudia Rousseau, a petite pale predator with large accoutrements and bird eyes that never meet mine, laughs too loud at whatever Gordon's saying. From twenty feet away, I smell her scent, the perfume that so often lingers on my husband. The emotion evoked is unclear—sorrow, jealousy, pity, gratitude, relief—a combination of all of the above.

Michelle misinterprets my glance. "You're a lucky woman," she says. "Gordon's so great with the kids. I wish Bob doted on Max the way Gordon does on Addie and Drew. Fifteen minutes a day's about his tolerance."

Michelle's husband, Bob, sits half a table down completely immersed in the Lakers-versus-Orlando matchup on the screen above his head. He's so typical that, although I've known him for years, there's a chance I wouldn't recognize him if I ran into him outside of baseball or church.

Gordon, his instincts honed like a lion's, notices me looking Bob's way. My eyes slide to his, then return to Michelle.

"Or looked at me the way Gordon looks at you," she continues. "He's crazy about you." Something in the way she says it is a question.

The pitcher rises and falls again from Gordon's glass, and Claudia's laughter bubbles over like champagne, as though my husband is the next Rodney Dangerfield.

"Excuse me," I say. I walk from Michelle and out the doors to the throng of players and siblings playing tag on the pizza parlor's patio.

Addie runs past me in hot pursuit of a child two years older. Unbeknown to him, he's seriously outmatched. Addie's flaming red hair is matched by her lightning speed.

I look around for Drew. He isn't there.

I wander right toward the parking lot, see nothing, then retrace my steps to the left and into the service drive.

Full darkness has settled into a moonless night, but four street lamps provide halos of illumination down the hundred yards of pavement. In the distance, the slow trickle of water whispers from the runoff channel that runs behind the strip mall.

Under the third halo of light, three young heads squat around something in the middle of the road.

My footfalls are concealed by the boys' whispers and nervous giggles. Max, Michelle's boy, is closest to me, his round figure unmistakable. To his right is Travis Burk, catcher for the team, a scrawny, shy boy who I like very much. To the left is Drew. All three still wear their uniforms, though their caps are gone and their cleats have been traded for sneakers.

Three feet from them, still in the darkness, I stop, and the pizza crawls up my throat.

"I think we should leave it alone," Max says.

"Yeah, I think we're killing it," Travis stutters.

Drew continues to spin the helpless toad on its back, stopping every few seconds to see how it's responding.

It's not responding very well.

"Drew," I say.

All three boys look up, Drew glancing only for a blink before returning to his work. The other two boys stare, eyes wide, a combination of fear and relief in their young faces.

"Drew," I say again stronger.

"What?" he answers, still not interrupting his stirring.

I step between the other boys so quickly that both fall back from their haunches to their butts and scuttle back on the pavement. I grab my son's arm that still holds his stirring stick, a Big Gulp straw, and he looks at me with annoyance. "What?"

"Stop it."

His arm tenses against mine, but he's still only eight and I'm still stronger.

I glance at the boys on the pavement. "Go," I say, holding on to my anger so they won't witness it.

Both spring to their feet and sprint away.

When they're out of sight, I kneel to the ground and examine my son's handiwork. The toad, an unsightly spotted brown blob a few inches tall and wide, is laid out helpless on its back. Its arms and legs splay from its round body as it twitches against the pavement, its small heart rapid-firing through its parchment underbelly.

I snatch the straw from Drew's hand and roll the beast right side up. Its legs fan flat from its body, and its eyes are closed.

I nudge it gently, but it remains inert.

My eyes squeeze tight, and I swallow hard.

Drew is beside me, but he isn't looking at the poor creature, he's looking at me. I raise my eyes to his.

"Why?" I ask.

For a moment he says nothing, just stares at me with his icy blue gaze that always receives so many compliments—long, dark lashes that frame irises the color of a robin's egg.

Then he answers. "Why not?"

And I feel the tears rebelling again.

"Jillian?"

Michelle walks toward us. "Max said there's a hurt toad?" she asks quizzically, unsure the eight-year-old's message was relayed correctly, "and he wants me to help it."

I inhale my emotions and stand to face her. "I'm afraid it may be beyond help."

Michelle looks at the small mass at my feet.

"I suppose I'm a bit relieved," she says. "Giving mouth-to-mouth to a toad might be a little beyond the call of duty."

I force a smile.

Drew stands and walks past us and, without a glance back, heads toward the party.

Michelle and I fall in behind him, Michelle filling the air with a boys-will-be-boys anecdote that I lose track of after the first sentence.

We return to the patio where the families have gathered and are beginning to make their exits.

Gordon and Bob stand together on the curb, their backs to us.

"Nasty scratch," Bob says, looking at the red line beside Gordon's eye. "Bad arrest?"

Gordon chuckles and shakes his head. "Mad wife. Let's just say Addie doesn't get her temper from me." The words stop my footsteps and my blood.

Michelle stops as well.

Gordon turns and sees us. "Speak of the devil."

Michelle moves to stand beside the men, and her eyes slide to the red slash on Gordon's face.

Gordon puts his arm around my shoulder and pulls me to him.

I smile and take hold of his fingers draped around my neck, my pulse quickening.

"We should get going," I manage. "Addie's getting tired." At the far side of the patio, Addie runs from the child that earlier she'd been chasing. She looks anything but tired. "Give me the keys, and I'll get the car. You can drop me at my car in the morning."

He's drunk, but not so inebriated as to not notice the manipulation. "I'll get it," he says.

"Maybe you should let Jillian drive," Michelle says, her eyes fixed on the scratch.

"Nothing better than a beautiful chauffeur, I always say," Bob adds in support of his wife. Gordon smiles as he digs into his shorts for the keys. Only I see his eyes pulse.

Bob grins at me with approval as I take the keys from my intoxicated husband. He errantly believes I don't want Gordon to drive because I'm a conscientious mother.

I adjust the seat and rearview mirror in Gordon's Cayenne to accommodate my smaller size. My vision won't focus past my own eyes. Gordon's hand squeezing my throat was a warning, a reminder of a year ago, and it worked.

It was a night similar to tonight. Gordon had been drinking, and we'd been fighting.

It was half an hour after I'd picked him up from jail, the second time in a year he'd have gotten a DUI had he not been on the force. It was also the day I found out he'd bankrupted us.

We were in our bedroom. I still wore the sweats I'd thrown on when I'd gotten the call to come and get him. I stood near the bed, and he stood near the closet unbuttoning his shirt. Gordon's side of the bed was unslept in, the sheets tucked tight, the pillow plumped and unused. The clock on the nightstand said it was 3:02.

"Get out," I said, surprised the words were in the air, unaware, until that moment, I intended to say them.

Gordon looked at me, unsure, a rare moment of humility, the day of failings reaching his soul. He'd failed in every part of his life—his business was a bust, he'd been arrested by his brethren, he'd broken his oath not to drink, his wife stood before him hating him.

Emboldened by his dejection, I clarified, "Out of the room, out of the house, out of my life."

The diffidence evaporated, transformed into a smile, and then he chuckled, his mouth screwed up in a toothless grin, his eyes dancing like we were having some kind of friendly repartee.

And when he moved, it was so quick that I didn't react. I braced for a blow, but was entirely unprepared for my body to be spun and my neck to be trapped in the crook of his elbow, my throat crushed, my feet lifted off the ground. Everything happening so quickly that I didn't have time to take a breath.

My eyes bulged, and my tongue gagged out of my mouth as I clawed at his arm to break free, my strength draining as quickly as my air.

"Tell you what," he seethed, his beard chafing my cheek, "we'll go together, you first, then the kids, then I'll take care of myself."

And in that instant, several things became clear: Fear overcomes anger quickly; time moves slower when it's running out; when you're going to die, you'll do almost anything to live; and it takes less than a minute to snuff out a life.

"Dad, stop." Drew was in the room.

I tried to scream, but there was no air. I swung like a ragdoll as Gordon turned toward the voice, my toes dragging across the carpet, then his arm released and I dropped to the ground. My throat took a second to open, then I was gagging and coughing and gasping for air as the world pulsed back from blackness.

Drew was in front of me, my frantic breaths blowing on his small toes, and I reached for him, but before I could touch him, the toes were lifted and carried away.

I'm still uncertain if Gordon would have killed me—if Drew saved me or if Gordon stopped himself. And worse is the uncertainty of whether, as I fled from the house into the night, I considered Drew or Addie at all.

I close my eyes, wishing I could clear away the memory, but the scene is always in my mind. It plays so often that it's like a chronic hiccup I can't cure, an unwanted infliction continually interrupting the rhythm of my life.

A siren screams in the distance, and my eyes fly open, and for a moment, I'm trapped between then and now. I scan the parking lot, blinking rapidly, until finally, the air returns and the memory recedes.

I'm not a good person, a conscientious citizen, a concerned mother worried about her husband driving drunk. I'm just scared. That night changed so much—the insults, slaps, punches, and kicks diminished to minor offenses.... *You first, then the kids, then I'll take care of myself*—escape and survival rising paramount, the only things that matter.

Could he? Would he? Addie and Drew?

His threats were no longer rhetorical bluffs. He could kill me . . . would kill me . . . so easily.

That night I ran to my father, the one person I knew would believe me and protect me. And just as I hoped, my dad took one look at my bruised throat and tear-streaked face and charged. He collapsed before he reached the door, suffering a massive brain hemorrhage that nearly killed him.

My dad doesn't remember that night or the stress trigger that caused his stroke, but he struggles each day because of it.

I pull from the parking spot, my hands clenched on the steering wheel. I'm just scared, a coward terrified of history repeating.

12

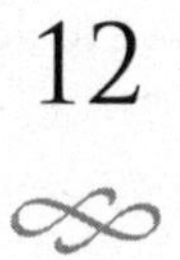

We drive home in excruciating silence. The day and my multitude of failings fill the air between us like a pressurized chamber. Addie fell asleep the moment the car began to roll, Drew stares intensely out the window, and Gordon sits beside me rigid and unmoving.

I roll into the garage and hit the remote to lower the door.

Gordon climbs out and bundles Addie in his arms to carry her. Drew bolts ahead of them and is through the door before I manage to climb from my seat, an obvious avoidance tactic. He knows I won't confront him about the toad in front of his father and is hoping to be in bed and "asleep" before I manage to find him alone.

As I climb the stairs, I hear Gordon singing Addie a lullaby from *Tarzan*, his voice slightly off tune, but in perfect pitch, a soft tenor that always takes me by surprise coming from such a large man. "...I will protect you from all around you, I will be there, don't you cry..."

I continue past to Drew's room. The sign on the door says, "Do Not Enter. Keep Out. Danger Zone." I ignore the warnings.

Drew's Tigers uniform has been stripped to his T-shirt and boxers, and he's beneath his blanket feigning sleep. Beside him, on top of his Spider-Man bedspread, is a shoebox with a shoelace bow holding a folded lined sheet of notebook paper that says, "Mom."

The card is typical Drew. He doesn't mince words. "Happy Birthday Mom. Love, Drew."

I pick up the present and sit beside the pretend sleeping body.

The box is light and shakes like a tiny maraca, making me wonder.

I slide off the ribbon, lift the lid, and whisper the word out loud. "Hollyhocks." Like vermilion, the name is half the attraction, the way the syllables roll off the tongue.

Forgetting he's supposed to be asleep, he asks, "That's right, isn't it?"

And my anger disappears. The gift so beautiful, it destroys me. Tears leak from my eyes and the small package drops to my lap—an act of torture, a perfect present delivered with such tenderness it makes me believe I can still change things.

"You okay?" he asks, sitting up and putting his small hand on my back. I pull him into my embrace and kiss his warm head that smells like sweat and boyhood.

Four months ago, a tour of Frank Lloyd Wright homes in Los Angeles prompted the family outing. Aline Barnsdall's home was the third on the tour, but the only one I really wanted to see.

Addie thought the Barnsdall home was creepy. Drew thought it was like a medieval castle and he was almost right. Mayan castle was closer, but the Mayans are rumored to have learned from the Spanish Moors, so the vernacular was similar.

"This is youwr favowrite?" Addie asked, wrinkling her nose at the musty smell.

I nodded. "The owner, Mrs. Barnsdall, was a lot like me, and I wanted to see what she created."

"She was?" Addie studied the small portrait in the brochure. "She doesn't look like you."

Mrs. Barnsdall was twice my weight, lived at the turn of the nineteenth century, and was well past her prime when she endeavored to build her opus.

"Nope, but our hearts were the same. She loved architecture and her favorite flower was the hollyhock, and in this house, she combined both. I always wanted to see how it turned out."

"So what do you think?" Gordon asked, obviously about as impressed as his daughter.

I turned a full three-sixty in the main living space, a sunken cavern with deep recessed highlights framed by massive carved pillars that supported a soaring, coffered ceiling.

"I think sometimes combining the things you love just doesn't work."

Addie nodded.

"She never ended up living here," I mused. "She spent ten years building it, spared no expense, hired the greatest architect of the time, and yet, when it was done, it just didn't work."

Drew stood near the giant fireplace trying to look up the chimney.

"I guess the lesson is..." I took Addie's hand to lead her back to the sunshine. "...hollyhocks bloom once a year, they're a fleeting glory, and they just don't work in concrete."

I hadn't even thought Drew was listening.

13

Bravely I walk from Drew's room to my own.

Gordon waits. He stands bare-chested in his pajama bottoms between the door and the bed, his hands behind his back.

My heart thumps wildly as I face him, my eyes on the carpet between my feet.

"Happy birthday," he says, and when he whips his hands from behind his back, I fall back a step and cower away from him.

"Jill, here. Your present. You okay?"

Again, it's as though I'm the one who's crazy and my reaction was completely irrational. I reach out, my hand trembling, and take the silver Nordstrom box with the pretty, pink satin bow.

He's smiling, excited to give me my gift.

I pull off the lid, and like a few minutes earlier with the present from Drew, tears fill my eyes, my heart unable to reconcile the beauty of the gift with the previous pain.

Swirling layers of silver and teal sit on the bed of cotton. For months, I've admired the Chan Luu wrap bracelets at Nordstrom, each handmade and unique, polished stones woven in an abstract web of wire and glass. Somehow he knew, somehow he picked the perfect one.

"Do you like it? I couldn't decide between the turquoise and the hematite. I almost bought both."

He's like a little boy eager to please. It's not an apology, but an overture of his love that says, despite what he did, he loves me.

He pulls me into an embrace and kisses the top of my head. "Happy birthday, babe." Something in the tone lets me know that, in addition to the bracelet, his mercy tonight was part of his gift.

14

The alarm buzzes, and I roll across the empty bed, hit the snooze, sneer at the fifty-seven frozen men and women who laugh and smile at me from across the room, then put the pillow over my head to return to sleep. There's a bare spot in the middle of the wall for the five porcelain partiers still missing.

Gordon's already up, probably gone for a run.

My mind returns to the memory the sculptures inspire as my predawn dreams have every morning for the past twenty years.

In my memory, my dad is already old, gravity and too many Wild Turkeys making his face sag. I'm young, and the prettiest I will ever be.

It was the spring of 1990, and we'd already rock hunted in Quartzite, ridden mules into the Grand Canyon, and watched Dale Earnhardt bring his Chevy into the victory lane at the Phoenix International Raceway.

My dad drove with his left arm out the window, the palm of his right on the top of the Jaguar's mahogany wheel. My hair, long at the time, whipped in the wind. Sometimes I tied it back. Most of the time, I didn't.

The great saguaro cacti kept us company as they reached for the sky at the painful pace of an inch a year. Most of our drive was quiet, accompanied only by the wind and the jazz from the CD player. A few times we talked, but most of what we had to say had already been said. At one particularly long stretch, my dad told me a story. When I was little, his fantastic tales were frequent. As I got older, there was less time or maybe he had less inspiration.

"I ever tell you the one about the lion who was in love?"

I shook my head.

"The maiden was beautiful, not much more than a girl, the father old and ugly, but still wily."

I smiled. The story was about us.

"But because the daughter was a bit too much of a smartass for her own good," he paused and gave me a toothless grin, "she chased off all her suitors."

The story was definitely about me.

"The father worried there was no man brave enough or strong enough for his beautiful daughter and prayed for the gods to bless them with a worthy soul who would provide for her and protect her."

I rolled my eyes.

"Not that she wasn't completely capable to fend for herself," he amended, "but as a father does, he worried that should something happen to him, she would be left with only her mother, who was not so good in the ways of the world."

"Pops, really?"

"What? I'm telling a story."

"Whatever."

"Then one day, not so long after he made his wish, there was a knock on the door, and the father opened it to a shocking sight.

On his porch was a lion, a magnificent beast tall as the father and with a mane that filled the frame."

"A lion who knocked?"

"Shhh."

"You're kidding?"

"It's a story."

"Fine."

"And the lion said..."

"The lion talks?"

"It's my story."

"Fine."

"And the lion said, 'Kind sir, if you would please do me the honor, I've been in love with your beautiful daughter since she was a child, and now that she's of age, I would like to ask for her hand in marriage.'

"The father was terrified. The lion had teeth like sabers and claws like... well, like... well, like claws."

I laughed.

"He didn't want to insult the beast, but how could he possibly agree to betroth his precious daughter to this wild animal? The lion, while noble and beautiful, was... well, he was... he was..."

"A lion?" I finished for him.

My dad didn't laugh, but instead flicked an annoyed look at me, pulled out a cigar, lit it, and began to puff.

"Well?" I said, irritated.

"So you want to hear the story?"

"Yes, tell your story."

"No more sarcasm?"

"No more sarcasm."

"Fine. So the father explained that he would be terrified for his daughter to be the lion's wife; one accidental swipe or slash and she would be killed.

"'But I would never hurt your daughter,' the lion explained, 'I love her.'

"Not intentionally, but in a rage or by accident you might. Your teeth and your claws are so sharp.' As the father said this, an idea came to him. He was in quite a pickle. If he denied the lion's request, the lion would kill him and his daughter, and if he agreed, his daughter would be married to a dangerous lion.

"'Perhaps if you had your claws and teeth removed,' the father suggested, 'maybe then I would allow you to marry my daughter.'

"The lion eagerly agreed and, a week later, returned with his teeth and claws gone. 'Kind sir, now may I have your daughter's hand in marriage?' he asked.

"The father laughed and shook his head. 'Now you may go. You have no teeth or claws and I am no longer afraid. Leave my daughter alone.'"

My dad puffed on his cigar and turned up the music.

I turned the music back down. "That's it. That's your story?"

"Yeah, that's my story. Get it, the father tricked the lion into defeating himself. It was brilliant."

"It's horrible."

"What do you want? It's a story."

"I want a different ending. Here's my ending. The father tricks the lion, but it's too late. The daughter's already in love because no one's ever made such a sacrifice for her, so she goes with the lion. And they live happily ever after and never see the father again. The end."

"That's a terrible ending."

"It's a better ending than yours."

We drove the rest of the way in silence, and the story was forgotten by the time we reached our destination, Frank Lloyd Wright's winter home—Taliesin West. The sun was low as we pulled into the parking lot. The fading orange light and long shadows concealed the compound's age, same as my dad's, and the masterpiece looked almost new. That was Frank Lloyd Wright's genius; like a fortune teller or a time traveler, he created the future before it happened, or maybe, it's arguable, he simply created the future.

Our tour guide was a woman with gray hair, a wide nose, and a name tag that declared her "Edna." And when she warned us in a firm voice not to leave the group and not to take photos, my dad winked at me.

At the entrance, Edna pointed out a porcelain diorama of five Chinese men painted in garish teal and plum and blue, and I couldn't decide, looking at the laughing men, if they'd won a war, won a game of Cujo, or had won nothing at all and were simply drunk. Wright had bought the piece along with eleven others from the clearance basement at Macy's in San Francisco. He got a great price because the sculptures were damaged. The dioramas were sprinkled throughout Taliesin and showed Frank's admiration for Asian art. They also illustrated how broke the architect was at the sunset of his life.

When the group moved on, my dad and I set off on our own. Our quest was never mentioned, but we both knew we were going to find the other dioramas. Of course, this was easier said than done. We needed to avoid the tour group, avoid security, and avoid the resident architects who lived and worked on the site. We found four before we got caught the first time, then another three before we were chased by a fat security guard to our car.

The first diorama of my own set was given to me by my dad a year later on my twentieth birthday. It's the third scene and not one of the ones we found during our visit. It's one of the more perfect pieces; only a small chip is missing from the second column of the pagoda.

I found a pair a year later on eBay after looking through at least ten thousand pieces that weren't what I was looking for. And together, over the past two decades, we've found the other eight, along with three duplicates my dad keeps at his house. The last, the seventh in the set, has been elusive, and each day, my dad and I discuss where our search should travel next. I almost hope we never find it, that our quest never ends.

My eyes slit open, and the clock beside me blurs into focus. And though the world only barely glows with the promise of morning, I've used up my time for dreaming. I push to my feet, say good morning to the fifty-seven Chinese revelers, and move to the bathroom to get ready for the day.

15

Connor's office is like mine, except he prefers color and I like silver and black. No clutter, sharp oranges, kiwi greens, and lots of glass.

I sink into a retro velvet wing chair and swivel on its chrome base to face him.

"Did you kiss and make up with Jeffrey?" he asks with a Cheshire grin.

"He's reviewing the information Kelly gave him, and he'll get back to us."

His smile widens. "But did you kiss?"

Connor is the only one who knows about my marital misstep with Jeffrey, and he loves to bring it up, though I trust he'll never tell.

I sneer at him, and his smile turns into a mocking frown. "So he's not firing us?"

"Not yet."

"Good, because these beauties come in an amazing gray suede." He holds out his foot again for me to admire. My laugh is lost somewhere beneath the weight of the world, and when I don't respond, Connor drops the banter, and in his lawyer voice, which is both serious and soothing, says, "What's up?"

It takes several seconds for the words to find their way to my mouth, and when they do, they're strangled. "I think I need a divorce."

Last night, as I lay beside Gordon, his arm draped around my waist, my beautiful bracelet on the nightstand beside me, three things became clear. The first is I'm not crazy. The second is Gordon is crazy. The last is, and here's the surprise, I realized that if I leave him during a calm, not during a storm, it might work.

There's always a period after the violence when a precarious balance lingers between us, an aftermath of restraint, a time when we're both trying to do better. If I'm good, if I don't rock the boat, I might be able to take control.

This morning, when I got to work, I called the bank to get an accounting of our finances, and now, calmly, rationally, while things are stable, I'm going to find out the best way to go about getting a divorce.

Connor nods. "Okay, why?"

"Does there have to be a reason?"

"There doesn't, but usually the ending of a nine-year marriage that's resulted in two kids has some basis. Did he find out about Jeffrey?"

The words slap me with apoplectic terror at the thought of Gordon finding out about me being unfaithful.

Connor shakes his head at my reaction. "I'll take that as a no. He doesn't know about Jeffrey."

I shake my head.

"But he knows about the divorce?"

This new thought is as horrifying as the first, exploding my synapses or neurons or whatever it is that connects in your brain to create logical thought.

He will kill me. He will kill me. He will kill me.

My throat constricts, throttling itself in anticipation of Gordon's reaction.

What was I thinking? That blurred state between sleep and awakeness can do that to you, enable you to believe things are better than they are, make you think you're more capable.

As sure as I'm alive, I will be dead—it will be an accident, but it is certain.

"Jinks..."

I hold up my hand and swallow hard to regain my composure. "Connor, forget it. Never mind. I don't know what I was thinking. Forget I ever came in here."

His face is as serious as I've ever seen it. So serious, he almost looks straight.

"What's going on?"

I shake my head and manage to stand.

"Talk to me," he says.

"I can't."

16

I leave the building and drive ten miles to the beach. Work is piled on my desk, and I have a zillion things to get done, but I can't focus and I can't breathe and I need a time-out.

The wind gusts like dragon's breath swirling the sand and the sea. While overhead, gulls and pelicans float on the breeze as though inflated with helium, the air pregnant and billowing with the promise of spring.

A pair of lovers sits on a blanket to the right, so I walk to the left, sink to the ground, and dig my toes into the sand to find the coolness below.

My head and heart throb.

I'm a fool. I'm a coward. I hate myself for what I've become, and I'm so afraid.

How have I let it get to this point? Why have I stayed so long?

Fear.

Yes, but the fear, real fear, came later. I stayed even before I was too scared to leave.

The truth makes me want to rip at my skin with self-hatred,

the reasons I've stayed so asinine that I'm loath to confess them even to myself.

Pride, obstinacy, vanity, arrogance.

A pelican dives from the sky, changing course a moment before impact to skim gracefully across the water, then rises again for the sky.

The phantasm I've created of my life is a masterpiece of deceit, easy to believe because most of the time it's real. I look at the bracelet on my wrist—love. I feel the bruise beneath my shirt pulse with my breath—insanity. One flaunted, the other concealed.

I rest my head on my knees and stare at the grains of sand between my feet, each completely different from the next, but completely unremarkable.

A squealing giggle causes me to lift my head. A mother chases a toddler toward the water. The mom grabs the girl's hand and together they flee with a shriek from the wash running up the beach. The girl looks something like Addie, same light skin and bird-boned body. The girl hesitates at the edge—she's not like Addie. The mother pulls her back toward the froth laughing. And I'm not like the mother. It's so effortless for her. Over and over she runs with her daughter from the water, completely content with the tediousness of the game.

I couldn't do that. I don't want to do that. Gordon's the one who plays, runs, romps with the kids. He loves doing dad things—volunteering in the classroom, helping with projects, coaching. He's better at packing their lunches, organizing their activities, wiping their noses.

I love my kids, but I get easily bored doing kid things and mom things. It's horrible to admit, but my favorite moments of motherhood are when they're asleep, when I can stare at them and cherish them without having to tend to them or pretend I'm enjoying myself. When they're not demanding and I'm not failing. Of course, I allege the opposite, lament how I wish I could spend more time with them and rave about our wonderful weekends and how quickly they flew by. While, inside, I'm so relieved to be at work I'm almost giddy. But here, with only the seagulls and the sand, I don't pretend to be anything but what I am—and I am not like the mother in front of me; this ugly, shameful truth is in part why I've stayed. I don't want to have to be like her, to go it alone, be a single parent, not be able to escape.

I always assumed motherhood was something that descended naturally as soon as you had a child. Then after Drew was born, I thought it came with time. Now, I've given up. I don't know how other moms instinctively know what their children need and how to care for them. I don't know how to relate to my kids, how to play pretend, how to live in their world or roll around in the mud. I didn't get excited when Drew went potty for the first time or Addie said her first word. I'm happy for them, but these are their accomplishments—milestones I take for granted they will have. After all, eventually don't we all learn to walk, talk, and poop in the toilet? I don't take any more credit for those achievements than I do for Addie's curly red hair or Drew's blue eyes.

I'm not a good mother.

I try. I do the requisite duties—I make sure they're fed, clean, and well provided for. I take pride in my role as a provider, that I make a good living that pays for a nice life for them, but this is not a sacrifice. I work because I like what I do and because I'd go insane with the banality of motherhood if I didn't.

The little girl says, "Again, again."

"Mommy's done," the mother says.

The little girl grabs the woman's hand and pulls her toward the water. The mother reluctantly relents and runs toward the perilous edge for the thousandth time, and for the thousandth time, squeals with pretend panic as they run from the froth.

Mothers sacrifice for their children, throw themselves in front of trains, lift cars with superhuman strength to save them.

I do nothing. Drew has glimpsed Gordon's temper. He was there when Gordon nearly killed me. He's been subjected to Gordon's demand for perfection, has suffered the consequences of not living up to his impossible standards.

He knows his dad has hurt me. He's heard the slaps and the thumps at night, has been woken by my involuntary gasps and yelps, has heard the sharp intake of my breath when he hugs me too hard the next day.

Yet I stay.

My mind drifts to the first time Drew and I were alone. It was the day after he was born, and he was cradled in the rook's nest of my arm, his tiny lips opened and closed, glubbing around his toothless gums, and his newborn eyes, barely slits, opened around their pale blue centers to find mine.

"Hello, little man," I said.

At my voice, his mouth rooted for my breast. He knew me.

Although he'd just fed, I opened my gown, and he latched on again, a lackluster effort more for comfort than nutrient. That moment lives in my heart, the moment he was all mine, when life was still perfect and I could give him everything he needed.

Now, when he needs me most, I'm failing.

My cell phone buzzes. It's probably Tina wondering where I am. I ignore it.

I need to protect them. I just don't know how. I can't keep

Gordon from hurting them any more than I can keep him from hurting me.

I need to leave, but I stay.

Scared, yes. Lazy, maybe. Weak, definitely. Exhausted, always.

When the mother and daughter pack up, so do I. Attending to the calamity of my life will have to wait, because today, like yesterday, and a thousand yesterdays before that, there's too much to be done.

As I walk to my car, I play the message that was left on my phone. It's Gordon. Addie's having some friends over so I need to pick up Drew from after-school club on my way home from work.

17

My detour to the beach created a backlog of work, and the afternoon whirls by in a hailstorm of catch-up. Four hours later, when I leave the office, the sun's already begun its descent and I'm still texting, phoning, and dictating as I walk to my car.

My daily odyssey is so familiar I barely notice it as I drive on the endless freeway that leads hordes of cars like ants toward their destinies, the landscape around me a redundant scene of industrial buildings, apartments, box stores, minimarts, and car dealerships.

When the last fire of the day is stomped out, I speed-dial my dad.

We rehash Drew's baseball game, then I tell him about work. He grunts his approval at Sherman finally acquiescing to the merger and his disapproval at the man's decision to hurt his sons as his final act.

His laugh, one of the few things not compromised by the stroke, fills my heart as I recite the joke on the birthday card Connor gave me.

My blinker signals my exit, and I merge onto Laguna Canyon Road to travel through the preserved strip of wilderness that leads to the Pacific. Twisting native oaks, sycamores, and coastal sage paint the canyon green and gold, and splashes of wild mustard and artichoke thistle add spots of yellow and purple. This is my favorite part of the journey.

"I might have found it," my dad says. The consonants aren't there, but I fill them in. In the past year, I've learned to interpret my dad's speech like a translator, and the language is no longer foreign.

My excitement grows with my dad's as he tells me about the granddaughter of Lucille Montagne, a woman who bought a set of the Chinese dioramas around the same time Frank Lloyd Wright bought his.

"The granddaughter's been out of the country, but she's sure her grandmother still had them when she died."

"So where are they now?"

"She thinks in storage."

"And she has the one we're looking for?"

"She's not sure, but maybe. Her grandmother had four of them. I described the one we're looking for, and she asked if it looked like the woman was falling down the steps."

"That's it! That's the one."

His smile resonates through the phone.

I turn onto the twisty-turny street that leads to our neighborhood. The ocean sprawls behind me. On my right, houses burrow into the hills. Below, on the left, is the wedge of golden canyon I drove through minutes before.

"When will she know?"

"She said she'd check next week."

"Where does she live?"

"The Bay area."

I pull onto the road that will take me to my home.

"I wanted to get it before your birthday."

"Close enough."

The search for my gift has occupied my dad since his stroke. It's been a godsend, his days filled with the quest and forcing him to recover. Each day, for hours, he struggles through web searches and pecks out e-mails with his one good hand, all to find our missing piece.

"I think I'll call again tomorrow. Maybe she can go earlier so we can celebrate tomorrow night at dinner."

My heart swells as it always does when I talk with my dad. No one will ever love me the way he does.

I pull into our driveway, and the garage door slides up so I can pull my Land Rover in beside Gordon's Cayenne.

"Sayonara, Sister," my dad says.

"Adios, Amigo," I answer. It's been our signoff for thirty years.

I click the garage door closed behind me, but stay in the car, the conversation with my dad radiating hope, allowing me to believe somehow I'll find a way to make things right.

My phone buzzes. I've been texted. "I have an idea how to solve our problem. Dinner on Thursday and I'll explain. Xoxo, Jeffrey."

My heart pounds, and I stare at the letters until they blur. When the panel goes blank, I step from the car, and with a deep breath, walk into my house.

The kitchen is empty, but the backyard is full. Through the sliding glass doors, there's a party.

Four bathing-suit-clad adorable princesses, three moms, and Gordon. The girls run through a helicopter sprinkler, squealing and screeching with delight. The moms lounge on our patio furniture, sipping refreshing-looking pink concoctions, and Gordon leans against the barbeque regaling them with an apparently hilarious anecdote.

Addie takes a running slide through the mud, her bottoms not skidding as fast as the rest of her to reveal her white heinie, and my heart smiles at the sight of my girl who I haven't seen in twelve hours.

I never realize how much I miss my kids until I see them.

I set down my briefcase and walk out to meet our guests. Gordon introduces me to the women, but the names immediately blur together—Jen, Jan, June, Jackie, Janet, Greta, or Fred—or maybe, the truth is, I just don't care.

As I walk back through the sliding door, I feel the judgment in their stares and imagine what they're thinking.

Bitch.

Doesn't keep herself up very well.

Can't believe that's Gordon's wife.

She didn't even say hello to her daughter.

I turn heel and step back through the doors.

"Hi, Addie," I say through the swirling water.

Addie either doesn't hear me or ignores me.

The women's eyes and Gordon's watch.

"Hi, sweetie," I try louder.

Addie has her friend, a gangly dark-haired girl, by the hands, and they're jumping over the stream of water.

"...eleven, twelve, thirteen..." they chant in unison.

"Addie." I step closer but still out of the water's reach.

She glances at me, and her lapse in concentration disrupts the rhythm, and the water sprays against her shins.

"You lose," a heavy girl standing beside the hose yells.

Addie, still standing in the spray, glares at me.

I glare back.

"Addie, come say hello," I say.

"Go away," she answers, the spray still whipping around her.

"Come here now."

Her nose wrinkles.

She only wants to have fun with her friends.

See how Addie doesn't listen to her?

She has no control over her daughter.

It's no wonder; she never spends any time with her.

I walk through the fracas, no longer concerned about the damage the water will do to my Joan & David pumps or my Anne Klein blouse or my Tahari skirt, and my irritation rises with the destruction and the wetness.

I take Addie by the arm to pull her from the whirling stream, and she pulls back.

"Leave me alone," she yelps.

She's slippery and impossible to hold, so I change tactics and wrap my arms around her in a bear hug, half dragging, half carrying her from the sprinkler.

"Let me go," she screams, her legs and arms flailing.

I slip and fall to my butt in the mud as I continue to hold my tantruming daughter.

"Addie, stop it. Say hello and say you're sorry for not saying hello, and I'll let you go." I'm painfully aware of our audience and the humiliation this is causing both of us, but I refuse to let go. She just needs to say hello.

Two hands, large and strong, reach in and divide us, then lift the despairing four-year-old from my grip. Addie grabs on to Gordon's neck and cries into his shoulder. He pats her back and carries her back to her friends.

I push my wrecked self from the ground and stumble past the mothers, who no longer look at me as I pretend not to be humiliated, returning to the shelter of my house and away from my display of maternal failing, completely wrecked, wishing I could undo the last ten minutes, wanting to apologize to Addie, knowing I can't.

A moment later, the phone rings. Drew's after-school club ended an hour ago. He's been waiting outside the school with the director for me to come and get him.

I forgot about my son.

18

I curl on the couch staring at the silent, blinking television as it shows four amateur cooks trying to create an appetizer from a basket of random ingredients—marshmallow spread, cinnamon candy, and artichoke hearts.

I turn at the sound of Gordon's feet descending the steps. He raises his clasped hands over his head in triumph—both kids are asleep—a miraculous feat of parenting worthy of celebration. I smile, both understanding his sense of accomplishment and in gratitude that he took on the colossal task tonight.

He sits beside me, lifts my feet onto his lap, then begins to rub them the way I like them to be rubbed. If I were a cat, I would begin to purr.

"Artichoke cinnamon s'mores, yum-yum, what a delectable combination," Gordon jokes, and I laugh. "The one on the left's going home; never trust a skinny chef."

I look with him at the pencil-thin man who at the moment is freaking out because his spatula is glued to the skillet by his melted cinnamon candy caramel. The spatula breaks away, and the pan goes flying, nearly taking out the chef beside him.

"That's one way to eliminate the competition," I say.

"Speaking of which, how's the Compton project?"

"Still struggling. We might lose it. They really want us to build it without windows." I tell him about the meeting and Kelly's melodramatic exit.

"You won't lose it," he says. "You're the best architect in the state."

"Yeah, right. More like the finest bullshitter. I haven't picked up a pencil in years."

"I still tell everyone you're the best."

The thin man sobs on the screen; he's been chopped.

Gordon continues my foot massage. He loves that I'm an architect, and I love that he loves that I'm an architect.

We watch as another contestant is eliminated, my eyes getting heavy, and as I drift away, it occurs to me all the small things I'll be giving up if I leave—nine years of shared memories, habits, routines, a shared vocabulary of life and experiences. Never again will I lie on the couch with Gordon rubbing my feet and asking about my day.

I must have fallen asleep because Gordon's carrying me up the stairs. I wrap my arms around his neck and curl into his familiar smell, safe and warm, the way I used to feel in the beginning.

He tucks me beneath the down comforter we chose together on a road trip we took up north, a year after Drew was born. In those early days, our life included weekend adventures on Gordon's motorcycle—the wine country, architecture, treasure hunting—discovering the coast and each other. As the years went on, the trips became less frequent.

I try to remember the last one we took. It was years ago, before Addie.

I'm certain I didn't realize it was the last one. At the time, the trips were so precious that it would have never occurred to me we wouldn't be taking another. I would have thought we're just stopping for now, for a little while. As soon as things settle down, we'll start again.

Then I must have stopped thinking about it. And now, as I snuggle into the comforter we chose together on one of those amazing weekends, I can barely remember.

"Good night," Gordon whispers, and he leaves me to sleep, which I do, deeply and peacefully, warm and protected in my bed, in my home, with my family.

19

I'm finishing my hair when Gordon walks in from his shift, the sun rising through the window.

He still wears his uniform—navy with a silver badge over his heart and five ribbons of color above it, commendation for meritorious acts. A shadow of beard lines his jaw, and the crow's feet etched at his temples squint with fatigue, but his eyes sparkle, the scintilla twinkling between glass and sky, the stench of sweat and death surrounding him.

He reaches over my shoulders, wraps his hands together over my breasts, and brushes my cheek with a kiss. I will myself not to stiffen at his touch and twist around to kiss him the way he likes to be kissed. His breath tastes like beer, but this morning, there's no perfume.

"How was your shift?" I ask.

His eyes blaze as he stares at my reflection. "Rough night," he says, his gaze leveled on mine in the mirror. "Shotgun deaths are brutal."

I don't want to react and didn't think I did until I realize the brush is frozen in my hand, suspended mid-stroke. His eyes dance as I pull it through the rest of the way.

He kisses my neck. The odor of putridity is overwhelming. The scene must have been awful.

"I still need to give you the rest of your birthday present," he says.

I nod. It's all I can do.

He turns me to face him, peels my robe from my shoulders, and it slithers to the ground.

I want to turn off the lights or drape a towel around my waist. My hips are beginning to resemble my mom's, my thighs bulging like jodhpur riding pants. But his eyes aren't on my swollen quarters; instead, they're intensely focused on my face.

With one hand, he cradles my chin so he can kiss me, with the other, he closes the door. I kiss him back knowing this is what he expects.

Shotgun deaths are brutal.

His lips didn't move. It was only my imagination that he said it again.

20

On the way home from work, I stop at the drugstore. My heart pounds as I irrationally scan the parking lot for Gordon.

He expects me to get pregnant, and if I don't, he is going to become suspicious, and when he discovers the truth, which he will, he always does . . . a shiver shudders down my spine . . . a second defiance this large will send him over the edge.

I swallow. He's going to find out. If not today, then in a month or in a couple of months. He's going to find out.

I can't have another baby. I can't.

My eyes fill with tears.

My petrifaction makes me think about the stories I've read of victims of genocide marching to their deaths. I've always wondered why they didn't make a run for it. They were going to die anyway. Why not at least try? But I understand. It's because fear paralyzes. It replaces logical thought with a numbing inability to alter your destiny.

With a deep breath, I walk into the store, buy a dose of

Next Choice, a thirty-five-dollar solution to an otherwise lifelong mistake, and swallow it in the bathroom, a lifetime of regret averted...for the moment.

When I pull into the garage ten minutes later, Gordon's Cayenne is gone.

At the door, I pause, take a deep breath, then with a smile pasted on my face, step into my home.

The kitchen is empty. I dump the smile and my pumps in the shoe basket next to the door and slide the briefcase into the small cabinet designed for just such a purpose.

"Hello," I call.

No answer.

Through the sliding door, the yard is empty. The yellow swings on the cedar play set that rarely get used sway slightly in the breeze, and in the distance, the last light of day rides the golden hills in the canyon.

I move to the notepad beside the phone where we leave our messages.

J., Bank called. I took the kids, G.

I stare, unsure how to interpret the words. *Bank called*—does this mean he knows I called about our accounts? *I took the kids*—to the market, to the park, to another country?

I brace myself against the counter.

A second later, the front door flies open.

"Mommy, Mommy, I made something else for youwr bewrthday."

I catch the sweet bundle hurling toward me, squeeze her tight, and bury my nose into her little-girl smell—strawberries and the slightest remnant of baby.

Addie squirms from my arms, darts to the refrigerator, and yanks open the door.

A second later, she reappears balancing a plate loaded with brown disks in her outstretched hands.

"Happy bewrthday again," she says.

I grab one of the strange-shaped, almost brown, almost black morsels and bravely take a giant bite. The taste is something akin to cardboard baked hard with cinnamon on top. "Mmmm, mmmm, delicious."

Behind Addie, Gordon and Drew enter the kitchen. Drew's in his practice uniform and his brow is damp, and guilt wraps my gut like a tourniquet. Drew's cherub face is even more sullen than usual. He's probably been "practicing" since he got home from school. I was forty-five minutes late; that means forty-five more minutes of practice.

Gordon has a new baseball training ritual that borders on child torture—Drew needs to make a hundred throws and catches in succession or they need to start over. A week ago, Drew threw for three hours and never achieved the goal. Finally when the light gave up, so did Gordon.

Together, Gordon and I go upstairs to get changed for our dinner out with my parents.

As I zip the back of my boots, I say, "You can't keep riding Drew the way you do."

Gordon smooths his hair into place in front of the full-length mirror. "He's fine."

"He's not." I don't tell him about Drew's bout with toad-sadism at Gina's or the difficulties he's having in school, too afraid of what his reaction might be.

"He's fine," Gordon repeats, the tone leaving no room for debate.

"Gordon, please? He's only eight. You can't expect him to catch and throw a ball a hundred times without dropping one."

"Don't question how I raise my son."

Our son. "I'm not questioning your intentions, just your technique."

I'm being reckless and stupid, and perhaps this is deliberate. Suddenly I'm impatient for things to change, for things to either get better or worse, no longer willing to allow them to stay the same. Completely contrary to what I told myself I was going to do—be rational and deliberate, take control—I do the opposite, and like a car careening toward a cliff, instead of slamming on the brake or veering out of the way, I drive straight toward the abyss and stomp on the accelerator. "You need to back off."

Our eyes lock, and I'm actually feeling proud of myself, until his gaze moves over my shoulder, and suddenly I realize the mistake I made.

I don't turn. I know what's behind me. I feel the drunken smiles and squinting eyes of the hundred-year-old Chinese revelers naively partying and celebrating their good fortune, utterly unaware of the sudden danger.

Life needs an undo, a reset button. Desperately, I'd like to rewind the last minute of my life, but like so many things, it's too late.

I make a superhuman effort not to react, but I know I have by the smirk on Gordon's face.

"Go put on your makeup," he says. "Go on, Jill, everything's fine."

He steps toward me and brushes my cheek with the back of his hand, tracing my jaw, then my neck, his hand coming to rest on my shoulder.

I eye him warily, my heart thumping.

"Gordon, I'm sorry. You're right, I shouldn't have said anything about Drew."

He kisses me on the forehead. "Don't worry about it. Everything's fine. Go on now."

"You're not mad?"

"Jill, I'm fine."

I feel the faces behind me. "You're not going to do anything?"

"Jill, go get ready. It's forgotten."

He's lying, and I'm terrified to move.

My preoccupation with lying goes back to when I was a kid and the ridiculous game of Truth or Dare. Being painfully shy, it was imperative I become a very astute player of the perilous game.

What I discovered was that everyone has a "tell" when they lie. Most fibbers are betrayed by the obvious—their eyes slide or stare unnaturally long, or their posture shifts, becoming defensive or stooped, or their voice changes, or their smile becomes frozen or forced. The subtle tells are more interesting, small ticks that anyone with a conscience has. My mom talks fast and repeats herself. My dad is brusque and abrupt. Harris rubs his forefinger and thumb together—he does this so often that he has a callus.

The most difficult lies to detect are those the liar believes. For example, if I ask my mom if her ridiculously expensive sunglasses are new, she'll lie and rapidly tell me several times she's had them forever when she only bought them that day—she repeats the answer and says it very fast and I know she's lying. But if I ask the same question the following day, she'll tell me the same thing and the lie is undetectable. She'll have convinced herself that a day qualifies as forever.

Gordon's the best liar I know, and before we were married, I believed he was simply unwaveringly honest. His expression never changes, his posture never falters, his voice is always even. He also believes everything he says.

It's only after years of study that I've discovered his tell. It's subtle and inconsistent, but if you catch it, you know he's lying. It's in the phrasing of his answer. If he uses your name, he's lying.

"Drew, I have no idea where you left your glove." It was in the dumpster because Gordon wanted him to use the new one he'd bought.

"Bob, great car." It was a Dodge Caravan.

"Jill, I'm sorry. I would never hurt you on purpose. You know I love you."

He kisses my forehead and gives me a loving nudge toward the bathroom.

"Go on, Jill, everything's fine."

The first diorama hits the floor as I put on my foundation. The sound chills my blood. I tremble and listen as the other ten follow, unable to help, unable to save them.

When I stumble from the bathroom, Gordon's gone, and porcelain pieces cover the floor, broken figurines and smiles among the rubble.

I kneel before the pieces, crying in near silence, my head resting on the broken shards. And since I'm already on my knees, I pray.

I believe in God, but not in the superhero version. He has larger issues to attend to than the mortal messes of fools like me. My prayer is more of a plea. I pray for some divine inspiration to strike me, an epiphany of how to set things right, to save myself and Addie and Drew.

Instead of inspiration, my mind fills with the impulse to flee, of leaving for work in the morning but driving to the airport instead. Just leave. If I cash in my retirement, I'd have enough for a fresh start. I'm only forty; there's still half a life waiting for me.

Guilt rushes over me like a tsunami until I'm drowning in self-loathing. I'm a terrible mother, a terrible daughter, a terrible person. What kind of sick sociopath has such easy thoughts of abandonment?

My hand reaches to retrieve the head of a singing man with a Fu Manchu mustache, but before I reach him, I'm distracted by a noise outside the window.

Thwap.

Pause.

Thwap.

Again, and again—thwap, pause, thwap, pause.

I don't need to look. The sound is unmistakable, leather slapping leather. Gordon and Drew are in the backyard playing catch.

As always, I've made things worse.

21

Sapphire is the latest, greatest culinary delight in Laguna Beach. Housed in an old pottery factory, the structure is rustic twentieth-century barn and the flounce is twenty-first-century hand-blown glass and leather.

"Mom," kiss, kiss, "Pops," hug, slightly longer than standard.

He smells of Partagas cigars and coffee. I turn into it, my eyes closing in comfort as I breathe it in so it will stay with me. It's my dad's smell and reminds me of my childhood.

"You look tired," my mom says as Gordon holds the chair for her. I reach beneath the table and rest my hand on my dad's good leg, and he taps it twice with his good hand to assure me I look fine.

The server arrives, curly blond with celery eyes. Sapphire is famous for good food and young male waiters who look better than they serve. It's why my mom likes the place so much.

"Gibson," my mom says before the young hunk opens his mouth.

"Actually, ma'am, my name is Henry."

In one sentence, Henry's committed two sins, and the boy's

tip diminishes before my eyes. He doesn't have a clue what a Gibson is, and one more use of the m-word to my mom and he'll be lucky to get ten percent.

Feeling bad for the kid, I try to help out. "A martini with an onion instead of an olive."

He writes what I said in his notepad, then turns from me to my mom. "And for you, ma'am?"

Beside me, my dad groans.

"I'll have what she's having," my mom says.

I don't want a Gibson. I hate martinis. What I want is a glass of wine, but my dad's already ordering his drink, so I let it go.

"She's not drinking," Gordon says beside me and nodding in my direction. "So only one martini."

My mom's painted-on brows rise, and my dad's single brow that works descends.

The blood leaves my face completely. I forgot I'm pretending I might be pregnant.

"That's wonderful," my mom says as she ignores me and kisses Gordon on the cheek.

Henry, our server, still stands beside me waiting.

"I'll have a Perrier," I say, and he scuttles off. Desperately, I'd like a glass of wine. An evening with my parents and Gordon without alcohol—a tooth extraction without Novocain would be less painful.

My mom and Gordon chatter on about the grand news of our expanding family, then about the kids, then about his job. Her adoration always teeters on flirtation and always sits wrong with the other two of us at the table.

I tune it out and turn to my dad. Since his stroke, he's self-conscious about talking in front of others. It tears me apart. I miss his company.

But he still knows me. "Dessert first?" he asks, the T's not quite making it.

When I was a little girl, if I was dragging, he'd always say, "What my girl needs today is a little dessert first," and he'd take me out for dinner, starting with brownies or ice cream at the old soda shop in Orange before moving on to a second restaurant for the main course.

I offer a small smile. I want to nod and take him by the hand, as I had when I was seven, and run from this ridiculous restaurant and straight into the nearest diner to order us both apple pie a la mode followed by two greasy burgers. And tell him everything until I'm so full and empty that suddenly the world is right again.

"Nick, did you say something?"

Both Gordon and my mom have interrupted their dynamic dialogue to attend to ours.

Thankfully, Henry returns. He hands my mom her drink, then gives Gordon and myself our Perriers. Gordon's working tonight, so he's not drinking.

"Oh, God! Vodka, yuck!" My mom thrusts the offensive drink back onto Henry's tray and the kid almost loses it, but in a graceful dancer spin, manages to recover, only losing a few drops.

"Gibsons are made with gin," my mom barks.

Beside me, my dad's hand tenses in mine. Married forty-two years in a month, and for the last twenty-five of them, he's suggested, requested, pleaded, and argued that my mom should just order a gin martini with an onion instead of an olive. But Grace Cancelleiri is who she is and so Gibson it is.

Henry delivers the rest of the drinks, then speeds off on the verge of a breakdown. "Excuse me," I say.

Gordon, always the gentleman, stands to help me with my chair.

I pretend to move toward the restrooms, but instead make a quick detour to the bar.

I slip a twenty in front of Henry, who stands at the well staring blankly at the computer order screen. "This will pay to replace the martini with a Gibson," I say. "A Gibson is a drink, like a martini, but always made with gin, and it comes with an onion instead of an olive."

His hands fly over the screen, and he points. "There it is," he says.

He's young, probably twenty. I glance at the bartender who he sent the order to. He could be Henry's twin.

"You might want to tell him." I thumb my hand at the boy behind the bar, who squints at the screen with the same perplexed look Henry had a moment before.

"Thanks," he says, walking past me to the bar so he can explain the drink.

My BlackBerry buzzes. I continue to the restroom, hiding the cell from view and glance at the text. "Looking forward to tomorrow. Pick you up at seven? xxx, Jeffrey."

My heart beats too hard as I fumble with the pads. *"Absotootely."* Stupid. I erase it. *"Tomorrow, tomorrow, I'll love you tomorrow."* Even worse. *"Dinner and dessert, wink, wink?"* I don't even bother to type it. I feel my own desperation; so much was broken tonight, so much more than the sculptures. *"Sounds good."* Send.

I return to the table, and the conversation has moved to dangerous territory, the tension thick enough to taste.

"I've got the space picked out and am shopping for the equipment now," Gordon says.

My mom is oohing and ahhing in all the appropriate places.

"Who pays?" my dad says. It comes out, "Who hays?" and I feel my dad's blood pressure dangerously rising.

This night was a very bad idea.

I try to put my hand back on my dad's knee to calm him, but in its place is a tightened fist.

Gordon takes a moment to sip his water before answering.

"Are you referring to the initial capital?"

My dad nods.

Twice before, our life savings has been obliterated by Gordon's grand ideas, and Gordon's mishandling of money was the reason I gave for leaving him a year ago. The stroke erased my dad's memory of that night, including the strangling, and all he remembers is that the day he had the stroke was the same day I left Gordon, and the reason I gave was that Gordon had spent our savings.

"The up-start's minimal," Gordon says. "That's the beauty of it..."

"Who hays?" my dad repeats.

Across from me, my mom fidgets with her bread, moving the butter around in circles.

Gordon smiles, then does the unthinkable; he turns from my dad. "So, Grace, as I was saying, the way it will work..."

Stress will kill him.

The doctor's repeated it so many times in the weeks following the stroke that I dream about it in my sleep.

"Gordon," I say, "my father was speaking to you."

Bad move. The only thing worse than being ignored by his son-in-law is being rescued by his daughter.

With great difficulty, my dad stands, the trembling taking over his whole body, the left and the right. He reaches for his wallet.

"Pops, please," I say as I stand to steady him.

"Nick, sit down," my mom adds, still rooted in her seat. "What are you trying to do, kill yourself?"

Gordon watches with a hidden grin on his outwardly concerned face.

My dad lays too much money on the table, and with his walker, hobbles toward the exit.

My mom, in no great hurry to assist him, takes another sip of her now-perfect Gibson, kisses Gordon on the cheek, frowns at me, then moves to her husband's side to support him out the door.

22

Gordon savors his dinner at a painful pace as I count down the morsels left on his plate. He makes conversation about the wine, the weather, and the food as though we are enjoying a perfect birthday dinner.

When dessert arrives, a strawberry panna cotta with mascarpone, he says, "How much is in our four-oh-one-k?"

My blood freezes. *My 401(k).* Since I was twenty, I've steadily contributed to my retirement with the hope I wouldn't have to work past sixty. It's the only savings we still have.

I sip my water to keep my mouth closed.

"I figure it's enough to get things going then we can borrow if we need more."

More? How much more?

His idea is a crackpot concept about elite training for young athletes—conditioning kids to reach their maximum sports potential. Even if enough fanatical parents exist to fill the memberships, the business has limited upside potential considering the investment required and the liability involved.

"Call tomorrow and let me know how much there is and when it will be available."

I'm still not talking, but my head shakes back and forth.

Gordon's head tilts, and his features darken.

Henry's "Happy birthday" slices through the moment. "Enjoy the rest of your evening," and he smiles as he drops off the bill.

Gordon pays the check, and I manage to stand, nod good night to the hostess, and we walk into the darkness.

The chasm moves with us from the restaurant, down the street, and into the car. Gordon doesn't mention the money again, but instead whistles softly as he drives, perfectly content.

He's up to something, and as always, he's a step ahead, and I'm left stumbling to catch up. The only thing for certain is that I will pay for my dissension and that somehow he'll get the money.

We drive toward our home, toward the wreckage that still litters the bedroom floor, and as we get closer, the truth rises like the sun, glaring with such intensity that by the time we pull into the garage, it can't be ignored.

"I need to leave," I say, not necessarily to him.

He holds out the keys. "Pick up some milk while you're there. Addie drank the last of it this afternoon."

"Leave you," I clarify.

"Oh." He pulls back the offering and stares at the steering wheel, mulling over the idea. He hasn't been drinking, so as I wait, I'm only a little scared.

"Have you taken a pregnancy test?" he asks.

The question throws me, and it takes a second for me to process the words.

Unable to figure it out, I shake my head.

Something's wrong. *The future is not what it used to be.*

He returns to his contemplation as I sit beside him, unsure what's turning in his head.

A year ago, he would have killed to keep me.

But time passes, and each new moment replaces the moments before until so much has changed, you can't remember what was so important or why it was important at all.

I'm uncertain what's changed for Gordon, but something has.

He's concerned if I'm pregnant, but doesn't care if I leave.

Without a word, he opens his door and steps from the car. I follow, and we meet at the tailgate. The Land Rover key has been pulled from his key ring, and he holds it out.

Still not understanding, I take it, then follow him toward the house. Before I make it through the door, it closes, and the lock bolts.

Confusion confounds me as I try to understand what just happened.

Our babysitter walks from the front door and saunters down the street toward her home half a block away. I recoil into the shadows so she won't see me in the garage.

I consider knocking, but that makes no sense since obviously he intended to lock me out. I could pound, but that would only wake the kids. I could call the police—and say what?—my husband's agreed to allow me to leave him, but now he won't let me into our house.

Instead, I climb into my car and pull from the garage, unsure where I'm going.

For an hour, I drive aimlessly, then stop at the grocery store to pick up a toothbrush and a cheap pair of tourist sweats advertising Laguna Beach.

At the Best Western on the Coast Highway, the clerk slides

my credit card, then hands it back. "I'm sorry, there seems to be an issue with this card."

I hand her a second, then a third, then my ATM.

"Insufficient funds," she says, no longer apologetic.

Gordon must have the credit card companies and the bank on speed dial.

When I return to my car, it's almost ten. Gordon works tonight. He can't leave the kids alone. I drive back home.

I expect my knock to be answered by my husband; instead the chain allows the door to only open a sliver, and what it reveals boils my blood—every part of me on fire, from my face, to my chest, to the palms of my hands.

Claudia stares at me. She wears an oversize USC sweatshirt and boxer shorts that show off toned, smooth legs that testify to a privileged life of working out and lounging at the spa.

Her scent washes over. "Let me in," I seethe.

Her beady eyes grow large, her head shakes twice, then the door closes and the bolt locks.

23

Life is one thing, then it's another.

Claudia's in my house watching my children. I wonder where her own son is.

I hate her and feel sorry for her at the same time. She has no idea who Gordon is, thinks she's won the love lottery. He has a way of making you believe that, the way he looks at you in the beginning like you're the only woman in the world, making you believe you're more beautiful, more special, than you are.

A honking horn snaps me back to the present, and I realize I've stayed too long at the stop sign. I rub my eyes with my hand and focus on the road ahead.

The recollection of my own fairy tale turned Grimm nightmare hurts to remember.

Even now, I'm surprised at the depth of his cruelty, amazed how irrelevant I've become. Even as I hate him, I'm hurt by him, and a perverted part of me wants him to still love me.

I check off my options: hotel—no, no money; my parents—

after what happened a year ago, definitely not; Jeffrey—I pause, consider his embrace and love, but tonight I can't deal with any more emotions. I turn the car around and head to Irvine, to the only option that remains.

∞

I'm relieved that the light still glows beneath the door, then mortified when a man other than Connor answers it. The bronze-skinned Adonis in the doorway wears nothing but God's gifts and a pair of boxers, and he's so beautiful that he looks air-brushed.

"Jinks, that you?" Connor says, squeezing between the stud and the door frame to greet me. "What are you doing here?"

The specimen steps aside and I follow Connor into the condo.

"Jinks, this is Pete."

My hackles rise, and immediately I hate the man. For a year, Pete has yanked Connor's emotions around like a yo-yo.

Pete smiles, and it's such a sweet smile that, although I don't want to, I hate him a little less.

Connor wraps his arm around me and leads me to the guest room. I carry my pathetic grocery bag of clothes and toiletries.

"Sleep," he orders. "We'll talk in the morning."

Despite my exhaustion, my sleep is haunted. First with Claudia, then Gordon, then with Michelle's infuriating, knowing, sympathetic face. She nods with concern, confused as to how I ended up this way.

It wasn't always like this, I try, then amend it to *I wasn't always like this*.

Michelle's wise eyes squint. *You're sleeping in your best friend's guest room in grocery store sweats, locked out of your house by your husband, while your husband's lover sleeps in your bed.*

I nod.

She doesn't understand.

No one would understand.

24

It's seven in the morning. I stumble from the guest room wiping dried tears and sleep from my eyes. My head is full of cotton, my body and emotions numb—too many circuits misfiring.

Connor sits at the kitchen counter, alone, reading the paper. I plop down beside him, and he pours me a cup of coffee from the carafe in front of him.

"Where's Pete?"

"Went home last night."

He sets down the newspaper and offers a sympathetic frown.

"Looks like I need a divorce after all."

"Okay."

"And I need sole custody and one of those things that keeps Gordon away from me and the kids."

"A restraining order?"

I nod.

His eyes narrow. Then I don't know what they do because all the courage I mustered to get out of bed this morning has evaporated and I can no longer look at him.

"Has Gordon hurt the kids?" Connor's normally smooth voice is tight.

I shake my head, and my hands twist in my lap.

"But he's hurt you?"

My head reverses direction, stopping with my chin against my chest.

"Christ, Jinks. For how long?"

I snivel and my shoulders quake and I bite my lip to keep the impossible truth and the shame from tumbling out.

"That son of a..."

It's no use. I can't breathe; tears and mucus run together and my chest and stomach spasm and I double over with my fists pressed to my eyes, everything I've been holding in for nine years pouring out like demons exorcised from my soul.

"Okay, shhh." Connor stands from his stool and hugs me to his chest, his hand rubbing my back. "It's okay. We'll figure it out. Are Addie and Drew okay?"

My skin prickles at the thought of them, and my collapse intensifies. I wonder if they will ask about me this morning. I wonder what Gordon will tell them. I wonder if Claudia will make them breakfast, get them dressed, pack Drew's lunch, drive him to school.

I gulp air, sucking in broken breaths, attempting to regain my composure. "He won't hurt them," I stammer, "but I need to get them away from him. He...he's...I..." My voice trails off, the truth of the nightmare I've lived behind closed doors impossible to put into words.

Connor continues to placate me with soothing, empty promises that it will be okay.

Mortified by my breakdown and feeling very sorry for Connor stuck beside me, I command myself to pull it together, swallow the hysterics, straighten myself, and pull away. "I'm okay." I sniffle.

He stands and leans against the counter. "Do you have proof he abused you?"

I seam my shirt up my ribs to reveal the yellow splotch beneath my bra. "It's from a few days ago. There's also a bruise on my leg."

"Is the bruise on your leg worse?" he asks, obviously not impressed with the wound, and for a moment, I almost wish my olive skin didn't conceal so much.

My head shakes. After years of marriage to Gordon, I've become an expert on bruising, and what I've discovered is, the harder the blow, the less I bruise; the damage is deeper and the evidence doesn't reach the surface. It hurts more, but shows less. The worst visual damage Gordon ever caused was when he choked me. For weeks, my neck was ringed with the imprint of his arm and my eyes bloody from the capillaries exploding. But with his blows to my ribs or legs, the pain lasts for months but the bruises on my skin are faint and fade within weeks.

"Okay. One step at a time. Let's get your affairs in order, see what's what, then we'll figure out how we can get you out of this mess."

"Thank you." I gulp, incredibly grateful he believes me.

"Do you want me to go to your house and pick up a few of your things?"

My head moves rapidly side to side. "You need to stay away from him," I yelp. "If he knows you're helping me, he'll kill you."

Connor laughs. He thinks I'm joking.

I raise my eyes to his. "He. Will. Kill. You," I repeat without exaggeration.

"I was a DA for eight years. I can take care of myself."

My chin drops back to my chest, and Connor lifts it with his finger. "Jinks, if you want to keep Gordon from the kids, eventually we're going to need to confront him. I know it's scary, but ROs aren't just handed out. No judge is going to keep Gordon from the kids without something more than a couple barely-there bruises that won't show up in a photo and which you have no way of proving Gordon caused."

"So what are you suggesting, you knock on the door and ask him whether he's been beating me up for the last nine years and hope he confesses?" My voice is shrill, my hands flailing.

Connor is calm, but stone serious. "Not exactly, but yes, we need to hope he gives us something, because if you want custody, we're going to need some evidence."

"The only evidence Gordon's going to give us is my dead body or yours."

Connor's smile is patronizing, like I'm exaggerating or being overly dramatic, making me realize that though he believes me, he has no idea how bad it is.

"Well, don't go there," I say. "For now, can you just loan me a few bucks so I can buy an outfit for work? Gordon emptied our account and froze our credit cards. I'll figure out how to get my things another time."

He fishes out his wallet and sets three crisp hundred-dollar bills in front of me.

"Go. Shop. I'm going to work, and when I get there, I'll call a friend of mine who specializes in icky divorces."

Icky divorces. The words stick like a burr.

He grabs his briefcase and starts for the door. Halfway there, he stops and turns.

"Last night, Jinks, when you told Gordon you were leaving,

why didn't he hurt you?" It's said sweetly, but underlying is the interrogation.

I shake my head. "I'm not entirely sure. In part, it's because he wasn't drinking, but I also think it's because he was expecting it, like he was waiting for it." I hesitate, embarrassed to confess the rest.

"And?"

"And I think it might be because he thinks I'm pregnant."

"Are you?"

I shake my head.

"And what happens when he finds out you're not?"

I lay my head on my forearms, which are crossed in front of me on the counter. "I don't know. He might leave me alone, but if I try to interfere with the kids, who knows?"

25

I'm at Target browsing the aisles for a suitable outfit for work. My phone rings the *Grease* tune "We Go Together," my dad's ringtone.

"Hi, Pops." I try to sound normal.

"She found it."

It takes more than a second for me to realize what he's talking about, our seventh diorama, the last piece of our twenty-year quest.

It feels like a lifetime ago that I was kneeling among the rubble of the other eleven.

"Did you hear me?"

"That's incredible." I put as much enthusiasm as I can muster into the response.

"She's going to send it today. It should be here in three days. Can I come by the house tonight so we can hang the shelf?"

With his excitement, the dam breaks, and in the underwear aisle, between a clearance rack of polka-dot thongs and bunny slippers, I collapse to the linoleum and sob.

"Jill?" he asks, and the tightness in his voice transforms my grief to worry.

"I'm fine."

"What did he do?"

I give up pretending. "I left him."

"About time."

I breathe.

"Where are you? Come home."

I shake my head. "I'm getting my own place."

"The kids are with you?"

"Not yet."

"So I can't hang the shelf?"

"Not tonight."

"Okay. Wow, what a day. Two incredible turns of fortune, the final diorama found the same day you leave the moron. I should buy a lottery ticket."

"Pops."

"I'm just saying, 'Good riddance.'"

"Adios, Amigo."

"Sayonara, Sister."

I wish I could share his optimism.

26

"Your conference with Drew's teacher has been canceled," Tina says as I walk into the office wearing my Target finds, a Mossimo dress that's surprisingly chic and a pair of wedge sandals—the entire ensemble cost me sixty-eight dollars.

I nod, relieved that I won't need to leave early after getting to work late in order to meet with Mrs. Kramer. And because, truthfully, I don't want to hear whatever it is Mrs. Kramer has to say. Kindergarten, I made the excuse Drew was just young for his age, not ready for the discipline of school. First grade, I blamed it on his teacher. Now he's in second grade and I'm out of excuses.

Drew's a bright boy, highly intelligent, but he's not working to his potential.

Have you been helping him with the worksheets I've sent home and utilizing the incentive plan we implemented?

Perhaps if you volunteered one day a week, you could see him in the classroom. . . .

No conference—another day's reprieve from facing the fact

that my son is failing elementary school. It turns my insides that he does so poorly. I never got anything less than an A in my life, and Gordon, though not as educated, is brilliant.

Earlier in the year, I actually hoped for a diagnosis of ADD so we could implement a quick fix of dosing him a chemical cocktail of Ritalin or Concerta or Adderall, and suddenly Drew would be the perfectly attentive, overachieving student I'd always assumed he would be. But the problem isn't one of too much energy, it's much more serious—Drew simply doesn't care. Scantron tests are turned in with only his name or with an inventive pattern of dots filled in to make an X or a face. Ask him to write a story and he'll make a paper airplane. Ask him to recite the alphabet and he'll count backward from a hundred.

He spends most of his time in the principal's office or sitting in the hall so he doesn't corrupt the other kids. I minimize the extent of Drew's transgressions to Gordon, fearing the retaliation Drew will receive if Gordon finds out the truth, and I wonder if, in part, this is why Drew does it. It's the only time I protect him.

I'm relieved the conference is canceled. I don't want to deal with it.

I put my purse in my desk, then walk to Connor's office for a briefing on my life.

I plop myself into the chair across from him and listen as he screams bloody murder into the phone to whoever's on the other end of the line.

"...well, you can't have your cake and eat it too."

Squawking screeches through the receiver.

"Damn right I'm the cake, and that tart you're nibbling is the tasteless 'eat it too.'"

He hangs up the phone with great aplomb. "Men. Impossible."

"Pete trouble?"

"For being as smart as I am, I'm an idiot. I need to use my head and stop getting involved with these imbecilic boys."

"You were. Your little head."

He laughs. "You're right, and my little head hath very little brains."

"You do seem to have serial bad taste."

"Perhaps, but at least none of my fervent flubs are as bad as the monolithic boner you made when you married Prince Charming."

His face shifts to sympathetic.

"That bad?" I ask.

"Worse. I spoke with Gordon."

"You called him?" I gulp.

"I figured it was the quickest way to figure out what was what. I didn't say anything about the abuse, just asked him how he felt about you leaving and about the kids."

"And?"

"And he doesn't give a damn you left, but he's gonna fight you for Addie and Drew."

"Well, he can't have them."

Connor holds out a stack of printed sheets.

"What's this?"

"Petition for divorce. It was faxed over a few minutes after I hung up with him."

"Already?" Along with the bank and the credit card companies, Gordon must have his divorce lawyer on speed dial.

"How long until it's final?"

"Assuming you can come to an agreement on terms, six weeks."

I'm stunned. Nine years—vows, promises, a life together, kids—and in less time than it takes for a sprained ankle to heal, it's over—like it never had any weight at all.

Nine years—almost my entire thirties—so much invested and shared. It's hard to imagine that in such a short time all our experiences, our achievements, our inside jokes, our sentimental moments, that everything we've shared will be reduced to a history remembered separately and alone.

This morning on my way into work, an Indian motorcycle a few years older than the one Gordon used to own cruised by, its driver decked out in black leather and strapped to the saddle by a *Baywatch* babe in a bedazzled helmet that said, "Indian Squaw," and my first thought was, *I need to tell Gordon about this*. Then it occurred to me that I would not be telling Gordon anything like that again—not about motorcycles, baseball, anecdotes about the kids, updates on the projects I'm working on that he listens to with such pride, the stupid knock-knock jokes that make only him smile.

The ink on the paper blurs. I knew this was coming, I asked for it, but the fact that he filed so quickly slaps me, as though I've been discarded like a toy a child's outgrown or an outfit that's no longer in style.

"It's what you want," Connor reminds me.

I nod, but my emotions won't agree. What I wanted was for Gordon to love me and honor me and cherish me and to actually be the husband he vowed to be, the husband everyone thinks he is, the husband he pretends to be.

I turn the page past the line that asks for my signature, and my brow pinches. "What's this?" I scan the first of the three pages attached to the divorce petition, and before my eyes reach the middle, I can hardly breathe.

"Gordon's declaration of why he thinks he should get sole custody. He's coming at you with both barrels blazing."

The metaphor takes the last of my breath, and I need to put my head between my knees to still the dizziness. The papers are a summary of my life—a bombastic list chronicling every error, oversight, and blunder I've ever made as a mother and as a person.

"How long were you in the hospital?" Connor asks.

I lift my head. "What?"

"Your hospitalization last year, how long were you there?"

I rear back as the blood leaves my face. No one at work knows about the collapse I suffered following my dad's stroke—the day after I left Gordon, the day after he nearly killed me, the day after I had fled to my parents intent on calling the police, filing charges, getting custody, restarting my life.

Instead, I ended up at New Beginnings Treatment Center in Los Angeles. The first week I was heavily medicated, the second I was numb. There's not much I remember of my time there other than it's terrifying when you lose your mind.

When they released me, it was with a prescription for Xanax and a warning that I needed to change the circumstances that had driven me over the edge.

The first was easy, the second not so much.

The psych report inside my case file states that I tried to strangle myself, and Gordon stopped me. It says that at the time I was admitted, I was a danger to myself and possibly to others. It's a very damning report, as is the story Gordon told them of my breakdown. I never refuted any of it.

Everyone, except Jeffrey, believes I'd taken the time off to help my father.

"Two weeks," I confess.

"And you're still on the Xanax?"

I shake my head. I stopped taking the pills a month after I got home.

"It's not like it's heroin," I snap.

Connor frowns.

"And last year, when Addie broke her ankle and you brought her to the hospital, did she have bruises on her arm?"

The blood returns in a torrent at the insinuation that I could hurt my daughter. "She wouldn't get in the car seat. I needed to get her to the hospital. You know Addie's temper. She bruises like a peach. Are you kidding me?"

His face is stone, completely lawyerly.

Connor squats beside me, his hand on mine—every dirty little secret of my life promulgated in black and white, from the pills I took to cope with the fact that my husband's insane, to every time I've been late picking Addie up from preschool.

I force myself to sit up.

Connor looks like a doctor delivering a terminal prognosis.

"I'm going to lose them?" I say.

"All this stuff is true?"

I shake my head, then reverse direction, the tears flowing with the confession. It's all true, every word. Most of it not my fault and all of it out of context, but all of it true.

"I'm going to lose them," I repeat.

Though Connor's hand has returned to comforting me, the strokes are less sympathetic. Even he's convinced I don't deserve them.

27

Tina follows me into my office and hands me a stack of messages neatly filled in with the date, the time, and the message of each. The seven messages are in addition to the dozen voice mails that blink on my phone and the sixty e-mails that fill my inbox. I'm a day behind, and the day is only half over.

I get to the fourth message and buzz for Tina.

"You told me Drew's conference was canceled."

She nods. "It was. Gordon called this morning, told me to tell you it was canceled. But there must have been a mix-up because then the teacher called wondering why you weren't there."

I dismiss her and dial the school, then the extension for Mrs. Kramer.

I'm surprised when she picks up.

"Hello, this is Jillian Kane," I say. "Drew's mom."

Irritation buzzes through the receiver. "You're calling to reschedule?"

"I'm sorry, Mrs. Kramer, but I thought the conference was canceled."

"Really? Why would you think that?"

She thinks I'm lying. I open my mouth to tell her Gordon

caused this, but before I speak, I catch myself. It sounds as insane as it is. Why would Gordon do that? Instead, I do what I always do when these things happen.

"I'm sorry, Mrs. Kramer, I must have gotten the conference confused with another meeting I had that was canceled. Should we reschedule?"

"No need. I called your husband when you didn't show. Gordon came right away and we discussed the issues Drew's having, and I'm confident he's going to deal with them."

Before I can respond, she hangs up.

Gordon's message is clear: The kids are his. He will challenge me on everything, and he will win. A shudder runs down my spine as I wonder how he'll deal with Drew's issues. He won't hit him, but the punishment will be severe—no dinner, locked in the bathroom for a night, write your name three hundred times, clean the floor with a toothbrush.

I put my head on my hands.

For a year, I've responded to Drew's report cards and worked my schedule around his teacher's constant requests for phone calls and meetings to improve Drew's attitude. I've secretly cajoled, bribed, and threatened him, and we've had some modest, though limited, success. For a year, I've lied to Gordon, keeping Drew's issues away from him to protect Drew, but now the jig's up, and once again, I've failed my son.

I remember when Drew was born. Ten fingers, ten toes, and perfect marks on the Apgar scale. I was so proud. Perfection.

No way but down from there. I reprimand myself for being disappointed in my eight-year-old boy whose failure is probably my fault to begin with.

I need to stay one step ahead, anticipate what Gordon's going to do. We've been married nine years. How hard can that be?

28

I wear the same outfit I wore yesterday to my birthday dinner with my parents. So much has happened in the past twenty-four hours it feels like a lifetime ago.

"I should cancel," I say as I walk from the guest room.

Connor is drowning his relationship problems in a carton of Java Chip Häagen-Dazs.

"Great boots," he says through a mouthful of ice cream.

"Can't I just stay here and eat ice cream with you?"

"Jeffrey's a client, and besides, sitting here moping with me isn't going to get you anywhere that alcohol and a gorgeous man won't get you faster."

"You're a gorgeous man, and you've got alcohol and ice cream here."

"Shoo," he barks, and throws the back of his spoon at me. "I want to wallow in self-pity alone."

I leave the building, and Jeffrey is waiting for me at the curb. He wears jeans and a button-down black shirt with silver embroidery on the left shoulder.

"You look great," he lies as he holds the door ope
Audi.

The radio is set to classic rock, and Stevie Nicks c
one-winged doves, and despite myself and my circ ...nces,
my heart lightens.

"So," he asks, "are we being secretive or is there another reason I'm picking you up from Connor's place?"

"I've left Gordon." It sounds so simple.

Jeffrey's hope fills the car, and for the moment, I pretend I feel it as well.

Sid's is a watering hole on the periphery of town, reputed to have the best steaks and rudest service in the state. There's no sign, no salt and pepper, and you're only allowed one napkin per visit. Sid, the owner, lives in Las Vegas, where he fled a decade earlier to avoid arrest for building code violations.

The motto on the door reads, "Stop looking for it, you've found it."

Jeffrey leads me to a table in the corner and orders us each a glass of wine—the selection limited to box red or box white. I choose red.

The steaks are delivered juicy and unadorned, caramelized carrots and garlic mashed potatoes on the side. The food is delicious, and the wine smooths out the edges.

"I asked you to dinner under false pretenses," Jeffrey says. "I do have an idea about the project, but I can't discuss it until I know more."

"Then take me home this instant," I mockingly demand.

"Not a chance. Tonight you're mine."

My body tingles before I have a chance to stop it. He's a client. My life's a mess. I straighten the emotions.

We talk about everything and nothing. Jeffrey has strong opinions and enjoys a good debate. Tonight he talks about the upcoming presidential campaign and what strategy the beleaguered Republicans should employ to have a shot. I mostly listen, but being a staunch Republican, defend my side as best I can. I'm outmatched because I'm not nearly as well read, and halfway through our steak, I admit defeat and surrender.

The air stills with the pause in our banter, and even the music slows. He sets down his knife and puts his hand on mine. I should pull it away, but it's warm and familiar and at this moment, the last thing I want to do is what I should.

"Jill."

I raise my eyes to his.

"What happened?" There's so much pain in the question that my heart aches. The time we spent together was insanely intense. When I returned from New Beginnings, I was so lost and broken. At first Jeffrey was a client, then a friend, then for a brief wonderful time, he was more—gentle, kind, funny, fun—my lover, my confidant, my love. I fell into the relationship like a gasping fish thrown back into the sea—desperate, needy, every free moment spent in his arms.

Gordon didn't know. My father's stroke was my excuse for why I continued to stay at my parents. I told him I needed to help my mom, to take care of things at the house for them, help with my dad. Though, the truth was, I couldn't bear to be around my parents. The damage I'd caused was too much to bear. Seeing my dad struggling for life, knowing I was responsible, shattered me each time I saw him. Jeffrey became my rock, my escape, my crutch, and so much more.

Jeffrey was just as hungry. A bachelor of forty-two sounds glamorous, but for Jeffrey it was just old—for twenty years he'd been searching for a deeper connection and he thought he'd finally found it with me. He wanted to spend the rest of his life with me. I thought I wanted that, too. We made promises. Declared our love. Then I left.

My eyes turn to my half-eaten meal, and I shake my head. "I can't explain other than I just needed to go back."

His fingers wrap around my hand. They're warm and so gentle I almost want to cry with relief that I'm not completely ruined, that I can still trust a man's touch.

I pull my hand away.

"Jeffrey, there's something I need to tell you."

"Those have to be the seven most dreaded words in the human language."

I nod, and with great difficulty, tell him about yesterday and today. I tell him everything, including the entire list Gordon maligned me with this morning, certain that when I'm done, any love Jeffrey thought he had for me will be annihilated.

When I finish, he's looking at me hard, his eyes fierce.

"He can't do this," he says.

And suddenly I'm scared.

Even in the dark, the heat in Jeffrey's face shows and his pulse pounds in his neck, testosterone and caveman instinct coursing through him.

I take his hand, which is now a fist. "Jeffrey, look at me." He's looking at the door as though he wants to bolt through it and straight to Gordon to confront him in a duel. "Don't get involved. I know you want to, but this is my problem and I'm dealing with it. Connor is helping me, and we'll figure it out. You need to promise me you'll stay out of it."

His eyes are stone. He has no intention of staying out of it. Like Connor, Jeffrey believes me, but he doesn't truly understand. He thinks he can fix this in a civilized manner, talk to Gordon or report him. Jeffrey is a civilized man.

My lips on his interrupt his thoughts. "Please," I say as I pull away, "promise me you'll let me handle it."

He draws me into another kiss, his hand wrapping around my neck and pulling me into him, his tongue filling my mouth as his hungry lips strain to be gentle. He tastes of wine and caramel carrots, and I fall into the moment, forgetting yesterday and tomorrow, escaping into the easy love I remember and miss.

Outside Connor's condo, Jeffrey slides his arms inside my coat, and the heat of his palms soaks through the thin cloth of my shirt and into my skin.

"You going to be okay?" he asks.

I nod.

His kiss is long and hungry, and I consider inviting him up to the condo with me, but something stops me. Even in the dark, away from my home and my family, I feel like Gordon's watching. Jeffrey pulls away, taking the warmth with him.

"I'm here if you need me," he says.

And I believe him.

29

I watch Jeffrey's taillights fade and wonder if it's possible, if second chances for happiness really exist—a husband who loves me, who I trust and feel safe with.

As I wait for the elevator, I think how different my life would have been had I met Jeffrey first, how different I would have been.

But then there wouldn't be Drew or Addie, so I banish the thought and alter it to a wish for tomorrow instead of yesterday. I pray for a future as blessed as tonight, but which includes my children. And for a moment, I believe the wish has a chance.

I walk into the condo to find Connor and Pete cuddled on the couch watching a movie. I smile at their reconciliation and Connor's happiness.

"Jinks," he says, stopping me before I've made it past them.

He sits up, disengaging himself from Pete's arm.

"I spoke with my divorce lawyer friend and sent him a copy of the crap Gordon sent over, and it might not be as bad as it seems.

Family court's pretty forgiving of past mistakes. Keep your nose clean, and you're gonna be fine."

I hug him so long and hard, Pete interrupts, "Can I have him back now?"

I practically dance to my room. Before the door closes, my phone buzzes. I smile at the thought of Jeffrey calling to say another good night, then cringe as caller ID reveals it's my mom.

"Where are you?" she snaps.

"Why?"

"Because Gordon said you were going to pick the kids up at ten and now it's eleven."

My mind spins. It's Thursday; Gordon's working again. He must have asked my mom to watch them and told her I'd get them. I'm confused, but overwhelmed with relief. There's a rush in my bloodstream, the swift realization that things might not turn out as dismal as I believed.

"I'll be right there," I answer.

"An apology might be nice."

I'm sorry, I think, but don't give her the satisfaction of saying it out loud. The apology isn't for her anyway. It's to my kids. How did I let it get to this point? How did I allow this to happen? No more mistakes—how hard can that be?

Before I climb from the car to retrieve my family, my phone buzzes.

How is it possible I miss you this much this soon? Jeffrey.

My heart smiles as I skip toward my mom, who stands, arms folded, in the doorway.

"Thanks, Mom."

"What are you so happy about?" She whirls back into the house, and I follow her.

Addie's curled on the couch, her chipped pink toenails peeking out beneath the chenille throw that's draped over her, her mouth gaped open and drooling—in such a deep sleep, I envy her. Drew dully watches the blinking television across from him. His eyes slide to where I am, then settle back to a catatonic stare on the cartoon.

My heart swells so quickly at the sight of them, I'm certain it will explode.

"Hey," I say.

"Hey," Drew says back, and I read too much into the tone—anger, disappointment, fear.

How many more chances will he give me to get it right? He's eight and already I've let him down more times than I can count.

He stands sleepily and stumbles over to me. I kneel down, and he falls into my arms, his head nestling into the curve of my shoulder. I inhale his boy scent and kiss his soft neck.

At least one more chance, he's giving me at least one more shot to get it right.

"Come on, big guy, let's get you and your sister to bed."

He nods and picks up the bag that holds their belongings while I pick up Addie. Her thumb moves to her mouth, and I wonder briefly when she started sucking her thumb again, and whether the recent upheaval caused the regression.

I strap them into their seats and debate where to drive. With no other option, I drive toward our home. A block from the house, flashing lights appear in my rearview mirror. I pull to the curb and watch in the side mirror as the officer approaches.

"License and registration."

I recognize him. He was at the Orange County law enforcement gala that honored Gordon and others for their heroic acts over the last decade. Gordon received special commendation for pulling a family to safety during the Laguna Beach floods. There's a three-inch scar on his shoulder, a remnant of the gash he received when a piece of debris sliced him as he carried a six-year-old from a floating truck to higher ground.

The officer's name is Craig or something. I look at the brass plate above his pocket. G. Lackey. Gregg. His name is Gregg, and his date was Laura. She complimented my dress; I complimented her shoes.

"Hi, Gregg," I say.

"License and registration," he repeats, and the glimmer of hope I had is snuffed out as I recognize instantly in his posture, the set of his jaw, and the twitch in his cheek, the setup.

I reach for the documents.

"Have you been drinking?" My heart fills with dread.

The thought of my name in the local police blotter along with the urinating drunks and purse snatchers swirls in my overfull brain.

"Mommy."

My head jerks to Addie in the backseat. I forgot they were there, and suddenly, what started as humility turns to panic. *Child endangerment.* The words tick like a bomb not allowing for any other thought.

My head shakes back and forth, and I begin to see red. How is it I continue to underestimate my husband?

He knew I had a client dinner. He knew I'd be drinking.

"He told you to pull me over," I say, the documents between me and the officer, my hand not willing to release.

"Ma'am, I need you to step from the car."

I hold tight and wait for his eyes to find mine. "Don't do this," I say. "It's not right."

"Neither is trying to take a man's kids." And he pulls the paper from my hands.

30

I blew a .085—officially, legally drunk—and because the kids were with me, the charges include child endangerment.

"Supervised visits," Connor says. We're in his office, and he's relaying his friend's opinion of the most I can hope for based on my latest debacle. "I'm sorry," he says. He looks almost as bad as I feel. He didn't fully believe me when I first told him what Gordon was capable of, but he's beginning to. Last night, when he bailed me out, he found out Gregg Lackey is Claudia's cousin. Not that it makes a hill of beans of difference. I was driving, and I was legally drunk.

"Supervised visits, what does that mean?" I ask.

"It means your history combined with what happened last night gives Gordon a strong case for sole custody. And chances are, if you want to visit them, the visits will need to be supervised by an approved provider."

"Like a babysitter?" I'm mortified beyond words and numb with disbelief. "He set me up," I mutter lamely. I'm a fool, an utter fool.

He nods, his expression a mixture of anger and defeat. "Looks like he's been setting you up for a while. We could try and fight," he offers.

"Based on what, my word?"

"Based on the truth and because you can't let him have Addie and Drew."

My head nods in agreement as I argue against him. "Good morning, Your Honor, I'd like you to award me custody of my kids and issue a restraining order against my hero husband, because although there's not a shred of evidence to prove it, he's violent and insane. Oh, and by the way, the mountain of evidence he's compiled against me and my deficiencies as a mother, and my criminal record, I'd appreciate it if you could just ignore that."

I'm crying now, sobbing actually, and Connor's arm is around me, and tears leak from his eyes as well. "I'm sorry," he says.

And I know he is.

I return to my office, close my door, and put my head on my desk. Last night, when I was arrested, Drew was terrified. It's the second time in less than a year he tried to save me.

As I was being led to the cruiser, Drew managed to get himself out of the car. He ran toward us and kicked and punched at the officer. Gregg held out his hand to fend him off, and Drew stumbled. I whirled to put myself between them and fell to my knees as Drew righted himself and charged again, this time throwing his arms around my neck.

"It'll be okay," I said.

"Don't go."

"I have to, but I'll be back. I'm not going to leave you." Even as I said the words, I knew they were a lie. "Daddy's on his way. He's coming to take you and Addie home."

With incredible courage, my boy let go and watched as I was led away.

I lift my head and stare at the picture of my family on my desk until the phone interrupts.

"Why would I want to renew the policy early?" I say to the insurance rep on the other side of the line.

"I asked your husband the same question when he called today, but he was very insistent, said he wanted to extend the policy for another year."

My mind spins. Gordon's up to something, but I'm unable to solve the riddle.

The agent continues, "I'm calling because I didn't realize when I was talking to your husband that you're forty now. Before the policy can be renewed, you need a physical."

The puzzle snaps into place, and I wish I were still confused. Gordon's the beneficiary. If I die, his money problems will be solved. Nausea rises like a fist in my throat.

He's hedging his bet in case I'm pregnant. He needs to extend the policy in the event he needs to wait before I can die.

He's going to kill me.

∞

My first thought is to flee.

My second is such reprehension for my cowardice it's impossible to breathe. A good person's first thoughts would have been of Drew and Addie.

I drive to the minimart, then back to work.

In the restroom, I crouch on the toilet and wait.

The test is glaringly negative—not a partial, not a maybe, a very clear, red minus sign.

And just like that, my time is up.

31

I leave the office grateful for the distraction from my life.

Sherman lives in the wealthy suburbs of Anaheim Hills, in a neighborhood of expansive lawns and marble porticos, regal houses standing in dignified repose from the street and their neighbors.

I follow a friendly nurse to the master bedroom. The room is the size of an apartment, with deep sculptured cornices and heavy swags of drapery over arched windows that open to a miniature Garden of Versailles.

Sherman sits in a damask Queen Anne chair that looks uncomfortable. I take the more demure seat next to him and set the sheath of lawyer-ese on the table between us.

Harris is panicked that Sherman's going to end-run us, but I'm unconcerned.

This man has no reason to do that. He'll sign away his life's work, donate the money wherever he believes it will do the most good, deprive his children of what they will see as their birthright, and he will die, if not in peace, then at least with the same mettle with which he lived.

We fill the air with a few minutes' preamble, and when we're both bored, I ask, "Have they visited?"

"Each one, every day. Haven't seen them this much ever. Vultures, the lot of them, circling and counting the minutes until I croak."

He smiles.

"But their visits make you happy?"

"They're all I have."

I think about my own small tribe—Addie, Drew, my mom, my dad—so little tethers us to this earth.

"Reconsidering?" I ask, hoping he is.

His smile widens. "Wouldn't that make your life and Harris's life easier?"

I shift my eyes to the mountain of papers Sherman needs to sign. "It would make your life easier as well."

"Nope. Not reconsidering. Time for the fledglings to fly."

In the last year, I've met Sherman's boys; none resemble their father in the least.

"Or to fall to a macabre death," I say.

"They won't." The terse tone unsuccessfully masks his doubt.

From the side table, I pick up the book that's facedown, *Death in the Afternoon*, by Ernest Hemingway. Morbidly appropriate.

I'm uncertain what compels me, perhaps it's the peacefulness of the moment, or maybe it's because I'm in no hurry to return to the calamity of my life, or maybe it's the way Sherman looks at me, but I settle in my chair and begin to read aloud.

When Sherman's breath settles into sleep, I show myself out.

32

By the time I return to the office it's close to seven, and everyone's gone for the night. I sit and stare blindly at the heap of work on my desk, amazed at how inconsequential it's all become.

I lay my head on my arms and watch the shadows grow long on the carpet until they disappear, leaving only the fluorescent glare. My thoughts spin and go nowhere.

Soft tapping on the door lifts my head.

Jeffrey's Snoopy smirk fills his face.

"You look like you swallowed a mouse," I say.

"Come with me."

I tilt my head with skepticism as my heart picks up its pace, and I realize how happy I am to see him and how desperately lonely I've been, not only for the past two days but for the past year, and the eight years before that.

To anyone looking from the outside, it would seem like I'm racing into things with Jeffrey, when in truth, I've been denying my heart and waiting for years.

"Come on," he says, almost jumping in place, causing me to smile for the first time all day.

I follow him through the barren labyrinth of cubicles to the glowing conference room. Three large sheets paper the far wall, and as I get closer, I recognize them as renderings of the new Compton Middle School.

My eyes squint, then widen.

"Approved," he says, his smirk beaming. And in his excitement, I glimpse the boy he must have been when he was young—sweet, rambunctious, and a little goofy—the kind of kid who probably ran for class president and was elected treasurer.

I step closer.

The facade is identical to Kelly's earlier drawings with the exception of the small squares at the intersections of the larger ones, which are now reflective.

"Windows?" I ask, pointing.

He nods. "Too small to crawl through. The panes slide into the walls to open."

I run my hand over the lines. The elevations depict a Mondrian masterpiece in three dimensions, and the new random perforations create a depth that's mystifying.

"Your idea?"

He shrugs humbly. "Kelly made it sing."

I tremble knowing I'm witnessing something great. I can already see the publications and awards. In a single master stroke, Harris Development is going to become the frontrunner of educational architecture firms.

Jeffrey's beside me. Then we're looking at each other and smiling.

It's uncertain if I move first, or maybe he does, but I'm in his arms, his tongue diving into my mouth, his left hand twining into my hair, his right pressing against the small of my back as he pulls me to him.

We're against the conference table, then he's lifting me onto it.

I unbutton his shirt, and he studies me as I work, his eyes drinking me in with desire as his muscles tick and tremble.

"I missed you," he rasps, his hands inching my skirt up my hips, then my shirt is being opened, his hands running up and down my sides.

The conference room phone crashes to the floor as I dig my fingers into his chest and bury my face in the soft indent below his ear. I inch my hands down his waist, my fingers burning against his skin.

He pushes me farther onto the table and peels off my skirt and my panties, his eyes never leaving me.

The moon through the window crazes our bare skin blue as his tongue traces my jaw, the curve below my breast, the inside of my thighs.

He hesitates.

"Don't stop," I say, fully aware of what I'm doing.

It's all the encouragement he needs.

His hands roam with his lips. They run down my ribs, push my hair from my face, surveying my body like a blind man, tracing every curve and dimple.

I feel his restraint, his struggle to be gentle, his concern not to scare me. And when we come together, it's so fully, I want to cry out, and in that instant, I know he's waited. For a year, he waited for me to return.

∞

My head is on his chest as his hand caresses my shoulder. We're mostly dressed except for our shirts, and we sit together in one of the chairs. Through the plate glass window, the sprawl of Orange County stretches below, lights and shadowed silhouettes of the business district for as far as I can see. It's strange to be sitting here in his arms without the frantic rush of knowing I need to get home, to make an excuse to my parents or Gordon for where I am, without a litany of domestic responsibilities piling up with each passing moment running through my head. I have nowhere to go, there's no one waiting on me, waiting for me.

"Penny for your thoughts," he says.

I realize I'm a world away—my mind running through what Addie and Drew are doing right now without me. Drew struggling through his homework, Addie taking her bath. I wonder what they had for dinner, whether Addie tried to hide whatever was green on her plate in her pockets. Will Gordon remember to give Drew his Lactaid with his milk? Will he read a story to Addie before she goes to sleep? Maybe Claudia will. Gordon works tonight. She's probably there. She's probably taken over right where I've left off. I wonder if they've even noticed I'm gone. It's been two days. Do they miss me?

"Jill?"

"Hmmm?"

"Thinking about the kids?"

I nod against his chest, then lift up to look at him.

"I'm going to lose them," I say, and the emotions choke in the back of my throat.

He kisses my forehead. "You're not going to lose them. You're getting a divorce. People get divorced all the time. At first it might be a little rough, but then it'll work itself out, and you and Gordon will figure out a way to deal with it."

There's such hope in his eyes. He sees a future, a time when he and I will be together and the kids will be a part of that, visiting us on the weekends or going back to Gordon on those days, a perfect twenty-first-century blended-family scenario.

A year ago, I told him that's what was going to happen.

"Why'd you go back?" he asks, the question soft but laced with accusation.

"You don't have kids," I say. "You can't understand. I knew then what I know now. If I left, I'd lose them. I thought I could control it. That if I went back and did better, Gordon wouldn't hurt me, and I'd be there to protect them."

"You're not going to lose them," he repeats.

His statement is a challenge, and I love him for it, but I also know he's wrong.

"I need to tell you something, but I also need you to just listen and not fly off the handle."

His caresses get less gentle, and his embrace more firm.

"Please, Jeffrey, promise me you'll just listen and let me figure this out."

Reluctantly he nods.

I rest my head back against his chest so I don't need to face him, then tell him about last night's arrest after he dropped me at Connor's after our date.

"He what?"

Jeffrey bolts upright, almost sending me to the ground from his lap.

"You weren't drunk. You didn't even finish your second glass of wine. I drove you home. That son of a bitch."

I put my fingers to his lips to try to quiet him.

"So you see," I say into his raving eyes, "it's not going to be okay, or simple, or easy. Gordon isn't going to come around and say, 'Gee, Jill, you're right. Let's play nice and share.' And he's going to win, and I'm going to lose them."

And he's going to kill me. I don't add this, because Jeffrey's already shaking with rage.

Jeffrey settles back into his seat, but his nose still flares with his breaths.

"He can't do this."

He already has.

33

I wake up full and empty. Jeffrey's scent lingers on my skin while Gordon's plot to eliminate me burrows in the core of my brain like some kind of weevil.

If I'm pregnant, I have nine months. If I'm not, I have until it's obvious I'm not. Everything else is irrelevant—work, money, what the world thinks.

I dress in jeans, sneakers, and a T-shirt, and pull one of Connor's Stanford sweatshirts over the top.

"Good morning," I say to Connor, who sits at the table eating a croissant. I reach for the box to help myself to the remaining one.

"Good might be a stretch," he answers, and hands me a folded over newspaper.

Featured in the *Orange County Register*'s blotter is my recent arrest for driving while intoxicated and child endangerment. *Jillian Kane, 40, of Laguna Beach was charged with driving under the influence of alcohol and endangering the life and health of her children...*

I drop the croissant back in the box, no longer hungry.

I'm on my way to Compton to meet Jeffrey at the new middle school. It's Saturday and the site will be empty other than the two of us—we wanted to be alone to visualize the future as the sun rises—a romantic notion that seems a little silly now, but that also makes my skin tingle like a schoolgirl.

As I drive, I listen to my messages. Two are from Tina about urgent matters that no longer hold any urgency for me, the third is from Jeffrey. The message was left an hour after we parted. It's brief and full of optimism, and as I listen to it, a clear stream of fear pools from my throat to my stomach.

"Hello, beautiful." His voice is giddy. "I miss you already. Just wanted you to know, things are going to be okay. After you left, I called Gordon..." My heart freezes. "...I told him he was being an ass. At first he was pretty harsh, but we hashed it out, and finally he came around..." Gordon never comes around, never, on anything. "He agreed he was just pissed off and that keeping the kids from you isn't right. He's going to back off, even said he'd talk to the Laguna police about dropping the DUI." My body shakes with my pulse. "I told you, babe, it's all going to work out. I can't wait to see you, and I know it's too soon, but I'm going to say it anyway. I love you. I love you so much."

I click the phone off and press the accelerator to the floor, praying my panic is paranoia and that Jeffrey's right and things are going to be okay. Half my drive is in the rearview mirror as I watch for Gordon. In front of me is the interchange for the 55. If I exit, I'll be heading toward Riverside, then Palm Springs, then Las Vegas. I could cash out my 401(k) and live for a year.

Addie and Drew, Addie and Drew, Addie and Drew. How is

it I've become such a coward, that my first thought is self-preservation before I think of them? I am an awful person, an awful mother. My heart pounds with fear and self-loathing. Please let me be wrong, let Jeffrey be right. *I told you, babe, it's all going to work out.*

My view shifts back to the mirror, trying to discern if the headlights behind me are Gordon's. In the frame of the mirror, I see the memory of Drew's forehead and eyes watching me as I drive, and my insincere words from two nights ago drum in my head. *I'll be back. I'm not going to leave you.*

The car in the mirror signals to exit, and as it passes, I see that it's a Honda, not a Porsche. I breathe and continue moving toward Jeffrey.

I walk across the dirt parking lot toward the new school's bones, which rise like an acropolis from the ruins around it. As the clouds close rank, the dawn darkens, causing the temperature to drop. I shove my hands deep into the pockets of my sweatshirt.

A pigeon or a crow flies lazily overhead with no particular destination, full from the night of feeding on the litter of Compton.

It's been only ten hours since I left Jeffrey's arms, yet it feels like a thousand years since we agreed to meet before dawn.

I take one last glance behind me to be sure Gordon hasn't followed, then unlock the padlock and walk through the eight-foot fence. I relock the gate and breathe, unconcerned now that I'm within the secure site.

Jeffrey's beaten briefcase, a brown satchel with brass snaps, sits on the contractor's desk inside the site trailer, and I allow myself another sigh of relief. He's here waiting for me.

The tattered skyline of Compton looms behind the site, graffiti on every surface beyond the school, but not usurping the razor-wired battle lines.

Across the playfield and fifty feet west, the new gymnasium rises half-finished, its concrete block walls climbing the steel skeleton against the bruised sky. Doors have been installed to protect the equipment and tools—bright rectangles of blue, red, and yellow set into the banded beige block. The red door is propped open by a brick, and as I move toward it, my heart shifts from fear to anticipation, the spot below my belly button flittering with expectation.

I smooth my hair before stepping over the threshold, then freeze in the shadows.

As though staged, Jeffrey's body slumps in a ray of light that filters over the wall from the east. His lifeless eyes stare vacantly between the girders to the glowing sky, his insides spilling out of the gaping hole in his chest, his left hand resting on the spot where it tried to hold them in.

I don't scream.

Movies have it wrong. Dead wrong. Letting out a bloodcurdling wail is the furthest reaction from the reality that is paralysis caused by disbelief—a denial of what I'm seeing blaring simultaneously with an acidic nausea that turns my stomach at the horror of it.

This isn't happening. That's not Jeffrey. It's a morbid joke. Not funny. Jeffrey, stop it, not funny, get up. Get up! Jeffrey, please get up. Oh, God, please don't let this be happening.

His eyes are open, still chocolate brown, but in a death throe that will blot out every other memory I have of those beautiful, kind eyes for eternity. His intestines are white and pink and burgundy, and the white shirt he wears and tan slacks are soaked with blood. Beneath him are the plans for the school. His shirt is ravaged where fragments of the shotgun buck splattered his chest.

Details. Each one imprinted permanently on my brain.

Every hair stands on end and my breath and pulse quicken until they throb and fill my head. My eyes forget how to blink. Then my lip begins to quiver, a small tremor spreading until my whole body shakes.

I step toward him; I want to help. I freeze only a foot closer than I was.

It's too late to help.

The horror roots me to my spot as time ticks, maybe a second, maybe a minute, until finally my thoughts break through the heinousness and the truth blazes like an explosion.

Shotgun deaths are brutal.

Gordon did this.

Gordon. Did. This.

Gordon.

My eyes whip around, then a bird squawks and I flee, my eyes scanning wildly.

I stumble as I run, tripping and skidding on the ground. My right knee and palms scraped and bloodied, I push back to my feet and continue racing to my car.

My tires shoot gravel as they skid from the parking lot and onto the streets of Compton. I drive away from where I came, away from where I think Gordon might be waiting. I grab my cell phone to call 911, then throw it to the seat beside me. I can't call the police. I can't tell them Gordon did this. They'll think I'm crazy. Gordon will not have made any mistakes. I'm certain Jeffrey's wallet has been taken to make it look like a robbery. Shotgun buck can't be traced. There's no evidence for anyone but me. I know too well how few of these crimes get solved. Gordon knew I'd know he did it, but no one else would.

I scan side to side in my mirrors expecting Gordon to appear, expecting a gun to be aimed at my windshield, waiting for the glass to explode.

I zig and zag through the labyrinth of filth that is downtown Compton until I'm sure I'm alone and surrounded only by the urban wasteland, then pull to the curb, my breaths coming in jerks and spurts.

Jeffrey's dead.

I can't get my head around it.

He's dead.

Gordon killed him, killed him because of me.

I did this.

Why did I involve him?

Things are not "okay."

Things did not "work out."

He's dead. Jeffrey. Gone.

My love, my friend, my future.

"Jillian, let's get married." A year ago he asked. What if I'd said yes, not gone back to Gordon?

I'm sorry. I'm so sorry.

Addie and Drew.

Focus.

Addie and Drew.

I can't seem to absorb it, remember it, then the horror flashes in my mind and I relive the shock of what happened and that it's real, and I can't breathe.

Think, I command, but it only makes my brain more muddled and my heart pound faster. My scraped hands quiver on the steering wheel, all panic and nothing else. The polish on my right index finger is chipped. I stare at the imperfection. A week ago, I was upset because I needed to cancel my manicure because Drew had a baseball game. I fixate on the marred polish, the fissure a lifeline to my sanity. I stare and stare until my thoughts begin to align.

Gordon doesn't know I'm here.

He followed Jeffrey, but unless Jeffrey told him I was meeting him, which is highly unlikely, Gordon doesn't know I'm here. I'm certain of this because I know Gordon so well. Gordon's meticulous—fastidious to a fault—and deliberate. He used a shotgun so I would know it was him, but me discovering the body wasn't part of the plan. It's too risky. It leads the investigation directly to him. Gordon's too smart for that.

I start the engine and drive back toward Laguna.

Jeffrey's dead. Gone. Permanently.

I know it, but the idea refuses to stay put. The horror in the gymnasium blinds me, but the implication beyond the savagery refuses to fix in my conscience.

Addie and Drew.

The thought keeps me from collapse and keeps me moving forward.

Gordon doesn't know I already know he killed Jeffrey. It's the smallest edge of knowledge, but it also might be the only advantage I'll get.

Today is Saturday. I look at my watch: 6:33. Gordon's shift ended at six. History tells me he'll return home and sleep until noon.

34

Claudia's Mercedes is parked in our driveway. I drive to the park half a block away and wait. From where I sit, I can see the house. The windows are dark, the neighborhood and my family asleep.

Jeffrey is dead.

I close my eyes, pinch my nose, and swallow back the grief.

Addie and Drew. I force myself into the moment, my brain buzzing with the focus it takes not to think of yesterday or tomorrow, to not mourn everything we shared and our future together that I dreamed of.

Addie and Drew.

Every other second, the carnage of this morning blazes in my brain—horror, ache, and fear accompanying the anathema...

...and guilt.

I did this.

Regret squeezes my heart, making it difficult to breathe, and tears fill my eyes.

Addie and Drew.

I force the emotions to the edge and stare at my house. I can't undo what I've done. I can only hope it's not too late to save what's left.

At eight thirty, Claudia's car leaves, and at nine, my mom's Buick replaces it. I feel the wind go out of me like I've been sucker punched. My mom is helping Gordon.

The light turns on in the living room, and for a long time I stare with hatred and hurt at my mom behind the glowing glass, unable to believe a mother can be that cruel.

A few more minutes and more lights turn on downstairs, and the neighborhood comes to life. Joggers and dog walkers pass, not noticing me behind the glare of my windshield as I continue to stare at my home.

My mom and my kids come out through the garage. Addie's on her bike, the training wheels intermittently making contact with the sidewalk; Drew rides his Razor. My mom walks behind them.

When they reach the park, my mom settles on a bench and opens a magazine. I'm parked along the curb beside the soccer field, where inevitably Drew and Addie will end up when they tire of the playground.

I get out of my car and climb the hill to the field to wait near the restrooms. It takes less than fifteen minutes before the kids bound onto the field close enough for me to call to them. I breathe deep to steel my emotions, paste a smile on my face, and holler out.

"Mommy." Addie runs into my arms, and I breathe in her sweetness. "Whewre have you been? Miss Claudia's been watching us when Daddy goes to work." She wrinkles her nose. "I leawrned how to do a cawrtwheel, want to see?"

"Maybe in a bit," I say as I stand.

Drew's still a yard away. He looks at the ground in front of his feet.

I take two steps toward him, kneel to his height, and pull him into a hug. His arms stay at his side. I left him and didn't come back like I said I would. I'm not forgiven.

I accept his grudge and stand. "How about we spend the day together?" I say, hoping my fake smile masks the panic racing through my veins.

"Wright now?" Addie asks excited.

Drew looks over his shoulder toward the hill that conceals my mom. I look with him and wonder how long I have until she comes to check on them.

"Right now. Let's go. It'll be an adventure." I take Addie's hand.

"What about Nana? Shouldn't we tell her?" Drew asks.

"I'll call her from the car."

He hesitates, some instinct telling him something isn't quite right, but when I call his bluff and march toward my car, his footsteps follow.

"Whewre awre we going?"

I have no idea.

I drive toward the freeway. When we get there, I'll need to decide north or south. I stay off the main roads, sticking to the side streets that wind through the suburbs—through endless tracts of pretty houses standing in homogenous harmony, each unique only in their details—and I wonder how many secrets those houses hide.

I choose north; it seems more optimistic.

The minutes stretch into miles and my panic settles into resolve. *I'm fine. The kids are fine. We're going to be fine.* It's a deluded mantra, but I repeat it over and over in my head in an attempt to convince myself.

The image of Jeffrey staring vacantly at the sky, his insides spilling from his chest, propels me forward.

There's no choice. We need to get away from Gordon. Addie and Drew don't know it, and there's a chance they'll never understand, but the man they love the most is also the greatest danger in their lives.

"Whewre awre we going?" Addie asks again. We've been driving two hours, and the promised adventure has turned out to be a bait and switch. "I need to go potty."

We're on a stretch of highway going through Los Angeles surrounded by industrial buildings and abandoned factories and warehouses.

"Can you hold it for a few minutes?" I ask.

Addie's red hair shakes in the rearview mirror. I exit at the next off-ramp and drive in circles trying to find any promising prospect for a public restroom.

Ten minutes later and miles from the freeway, we find a liquor store.

"Gotta go," Addie says.

I put the car in park and grab Addie as she fidgets and squirms to keep her bladder full.

"Stay here," I say to Drew as I sprint into the store.

We're a minute too late. Before I can ask for the restroom, Addie loses the battle, and pee leaks all over my jeans and onto the liquor store's floor.

The not-so-friendly-looking attendant glares. I ask for the restroom.

"Don't have one for the public," he says.

I turn to carry Addie out.

"You going to clean that?" he asks.

I set my crying daughter down and spend some of my valuable cash on a roll of paper towels and wipe up the mess. Then Addie and I return to the car.

When I open the door, Drew is crying, his bawling so intense, I can't understand his blubbering words.

When they become clear, I almost cry myself.

"I couldn't get out."

I realize then that the car was locked and the child safety locks in the back engaged. We were in the store for what must have seemed like forever to an eight-year-old, and he was locked in the car.

His face is red, and his hair soaked with sweat and tears.

"I'm sorry, baby, I'm so sorry." I pull him to me, holding him tight and rubbing his back. "Shhh. It's okay, you're okay."

Both kids are still sniffling and the car smells of pee when we pull back onto the road.

I'm a terrible mother. How am I going to do this? I can't do this. I'm not equipped.

Jeffrey's dead eyes stare at me in my brain. There's no choice. I have to do it. There's no turning back.

As we drive, the kids whimper, and my rage festers and grows. And I'm surprised when I realize the anger isn't for Gordon, but for Jeffrey, and the realization makes me hate myself even more. I hate him for being dead, for believing stupidly he could save me.

Last night, I believed we had a chance, that somehow, with him by my side, we'd figure it out, but now he's gone and I'm alone and the future I dreamed of with him is a terrifying black hole.

Why couldn't he leave it alone?

He lied, promised everything would be okay. Nothing's okay. Why'd he have to love me so much so soon?

It makes me want to scream and put my fist through the windshield, to take the shotgun that killed Jeffrey and blow a hole through Gordon, but when my rage turns again from Gordon to Jeffrey, I'm so ashamed that I want to die from the hatred I have for myself. And yet I can't stop the anger.

35

Our adventure has turned into a torturous journey that borders on child abuse. The kids stare blankly at the DVD player as it replays *Hercules* for the third time. They've given up on asking where we're going, how long until we get there, and complaining.

We need to stop, eat, and rest. My car bounces from the long highway into the parking lot of a motel in the middle of nowhere, somewhere between Redding and the Oregon border. The neon marquee and blinking vacancy sign buzz through the fading evening light.

I leave the kids in the car and the engine running as I walk into the lobby. The wind whips through the parking lot just above freezing, and I wonder if perhaps I should have chosen to drive south instead of into the cold.

The room costs sixty-eight dollars, leaving me twenty-three.

Tomorrow I need to figure out how to get enough cash to carry us through. My mom's out of the question, which makes my dad out of the question as well.

I clean Addie up in the bathroom and wash her underwear

and pants. She doesn't have a change of clothes, so I dry her bottoms with the hair dryer. It's nearly seven when I'm done, and all of us are miserable.

Tired of the car, we walk the half block to the diner that advertises breakfasts for $4.99.

The restaurant is empty except for the waitress at the counter hunched over a magazine.

The kids each order chicken fingers, and I order a bowl of soup. A paltry dollar will be left for a tip when we finish.

I'm so tired as I sit waiting for the kids to finish their meals that my eyes begin to close.

"Daddy, Daddy."

My eyes snap open, and my head shoots up.

Addie bounces beside me and points out the window. I follow the small finger as the taillights of a dark Cayenne drive half a block, then turn into our motel.

I throw money on the table, snatch Addie into a football carry, grab Drew's hand, and race from the diner. Addie's thirty pounds make my strides slow and quickly wind me as we run in the opposite direction of the motel.

Drew stumbles, and I screech for him to get up. His eyes are large as saucers as he scrambles to his feet, but he doesn't cry. My fear is contagious and leaves no room for emotions.

There's nothing but darkness and desert in front of us.

I'm panting now, my legs shaking like willow twigs. I slow, breathless, unsure where I'm running. Scared of what's in front of me, more terrified of what's behind.

Addie squirms to get down, and when I set her to the ground, she takes off back in the direction we came, back toward her father.

I hesitate, Drew by my side, and the awful thought occurs to me to let her run back to him, of how much quicker and easier it would be without her, how much more burdened Gordon would be with her. This all flashes quickly before I have time to censure the disgusting betrayal.

I'm not fast enough, but Drew catches her when she's a hundred yards past the diner and still a hundred more from the motel. She writhes in his arms, but he holds her until I catch up.

At that same moment, the silhouette of Gordon appears in the door of our room. He's in his uniform and looks very official. With my hand over Addie's mouth, I pull her from the road and into the shadows. Drew squats beside me, his eyes full of worry, and I wonder about the damage I'm doing to them.

The Cayenne passes us and drives into the diner's parking lot. I watch as Gordon opens the door and scans around him—looking at us, but past us—then disappears into the restaurant. When the door closes, I run. I don't bother to strap the kids into their seats, and Addie tries to climb out, but I lock the doors. She screams, but the sound is muffled by the hammering in my chest. I push the accelerator to the floor and turn at the first opportunity, onto a thin road that stretches into the desert toward the dark foothills, a small vein leading to nowhere. I turn off the lights and drive by the million stars and the sliver of moon that shine overhead.

The gas gauge hovers at empty, and when I'm certain I've only enough gas to get us back to our start point, I pull to the side of the road and tell the kids we're camping out for the night.

This is not a good plan. The desert holds no heat. I wrap the only blanket we have, the thin flannel Angels blanket I use at Drew's baseball games, around both of them and return to the front seat to shiver alone.

"Mommy, I'm cold," Addie says.

"I know, honey, but we need to stay here just for the night."

Drew says nothing, and my heart swells with his stoicism.

Addie's crying now, and it's revving up to be a tantrum.

"I'm cold," she says again, then launches into screaming as she kicks my seat, her shrieks ricocheting off the closed windows of the car.

I didn't use a credit card. I didn't give my real name, my cell phone is off. Yet he knew where we were.

"Mom?" Drew says behind me and through his sister's hysterics.

I turn.

"Where are we going?"

I put my fist to my mouth to keep my emotions inside. I need to hold it together; whatever I do, I can't lose it. I bite hard on my knuckle and squeeze my eyes, willing myself to be stronger than I am.

I have no idea where we're going or how we'll get there.

Gordon's a cop. He's resourceful, brilliant, ruthless. He has money, connections, time.

I'm just me—me with two kids, broke, and no plan. It's only been half a day, and he's already found us. No matter where we run, he'll find us. *Where the hell are we?*

I click the power on in the car to access my navigation system, *Searching for service.* And suddenly the monitor leaps to life as though it has claws. I grab the car manual and yank the fuse for the GPS system. How could I have been so stupid?

I turn the car around and drive back along the road we were on and toward our motel. The Cayenne is gone. I pull into the gas station and refuel. I buy everything the kids will eat from the minimart along with T-shirts and sweatshirts advertising Mount Shasta. I use my company credit card, and we get back on the road. Might as well add embezzlement to my list of crimes.

The warmth of the car and the exhaustion of the day lulls both kids to sleep within minutes, and I continue on, determined to make better choices this time.

At the next rest stop, I pull over and call home from the pay phone.

"Where the hell are you?" my mom asks.

"I need to talk to Dad."

"No."

"Mom, please, I need to talk to him."

"And I need a smaller ass. Jill, this time you've gone too far. Gordon's got half the force canvassing the state for his insane wife who took off with his kids. What the hell are you thinking? Gordon told me about the DUI. Christ, Jill, have you lost it completely, driving while drunk? And with the kids? And now, you just take them, as if that's going to solve anything."

I hang up. It would be easier to break through the Great Wall of China than through Grace Cancelleiri.

I return to the car and try to rest, but my thoughts won't allow for sleep. I'm doomed. Like a chess game already destined for checkmate, Gordon's three moves ahead of me and has set me up perfectly.

How easy it is to sabotage a life.

For a year, he's used my vanity and pride to my own demise. While I've covered up his abuse, his deceit, his lies, he took every opportunity to flaunt, exaggerate, and advertise every mistake of mine.

Like a magic trick, the illusion is seamless and unchallenged, and without another explanation, it's believed. Even my mom believes it. And when enough people believe the perception, it perpetuates itself—PTA meeting gossip, playdate whispers, Little League bleacher talk—until the deception becomes the reality.

In the mirror, I see Drew sleeping against the window. I stare at the slope of his cheek and the spiral of his ear.

Drew's teacher, if asked, would testify that Gordon's the greatest dad on earth while I would be maligned as the worst mother. I missed the conference, I send my son to school without lunch, I hung up on the room mom. Meanwhile, Gordon's chaperoned dozens of field trips, he helped build the Christmas set. He's handsome and charming and always holds the door open when the teacher walks through.

Drew's issues—his problems with bullying, his lack of effort and focus—these problems are attributed to me. And I do deserve the blame. He picks on girls, doesn't respect his teacher. Kids learn by example, and I've been a crappy role model.

My eyes skitter back and forth in my head in that strange state before sleep. *Live my life for a day, then let's see your opinion of me*, I defend.

But even in the subconscious, I'm ashamed, certain Mrs. Kramer would have done better, been stronger and more able, figured out a way to stop it from happening, left before it went this far.

Gordon capitalized on every mistake I made, and I helped him. Even now, I'm nailing my own coffin. It's only a matter of time until we're caught, and when we are, as always, I'll have made things worse.

I don't need a crystal ball to foretell the future. In a day, a week, certainly before long, I'll either be dead or in jail, and

Gordon will be the victim and the hero, and Addie and Drew will be his.

Ask a hundred people who know us, and other than Connor and my dad, the other ninety-eight will testify Gordon's the greatest thing since sliced bread and that I have serious issues. The setup was executed brilliantly, a masterstroke of cunning manipulation on a grand scale. And, as in *Hamlet*, the truth won't be revealed until the final act, and even then, it still won't be believed.

36

I'm hungry and so tired my bones hurt.

The freeway speeds toward me in the darkness, lights and signs flashing by in an endless stream. I've driven almost fourteen hours, and I don't know how much farther I can go.

A lit freeway sign glows in the distance, and my tired eyes widen as the lights clarify into words. The billboard advertises my car, "KIDNAPPED CHILDREN—SILVER LAND ROVER—LICENSE 2JVL227."

An Amber Alert has been issued.

Kidnapped children. I swallow hard, and my eyes flash to the rearview mirror. Square headlights shine half a mile back. My eyes flick from the mirror to the road, and at the first opportunity, I detour off the freeway and pull under the overpass.

When the car that was behind us passes overhead, I breathe and release the iron grip I had on the steering wheel.

How have I come to this place in my life? It's incomprehensible. I've always considered myself a good person, a law-abiding, conscientious citizen, a dedicated mother, a loving daughter. Now I'm a fugitive from the law, a wanted woman, a child-endangering felon, as well as a job-ditching, embezzling employee, and a sick-father-abandoning daughter.

In front of me, my headlights illuminate a sign, "Welcome to Yreka, The Golden City." Beneath the words are logos for the Kiwanis Club, the Lions Lodge, the Marines, and a dozen churches. We've arrived in quintessential America.

Freeways are no longer an option, so I forge forward into the unknown.

We turn onto a wide boulevard that leads to a downtown that, under different circumstances, I would admire for its well-preserved twentieth-century architecture—a definitive small western town of fine brick buildings, white wood trim, and colorful awnings over a patchwork of bars, stores, and restaurants. As it is, I quiver with nerves and pray the police aren't patrolling the streets looking for my fugitive car.

We pass half a dozen hotels, and I choose the Mountain View Inn, a shabby, low-lying motel that advertises clean rooms and cable TV. Its courtyard design provides covered carports between the rooms.

I walk into the dark lobby, a dingy box that offers no seat. On the counter are a dozen pamphlets advertising hiking, biking, and sightseeing activities in Yreka and a buzzer. I press the bell and two minutes tick by. Then the door opens, and a hunched woman with gray hair smooshed to one side of her face shuffles toward me. She wears baggy sweatpants and a *Betty Boop* T-shirt that reaches her knees.

She squints at me, and I'm certain all she sees is a blur. I've chosen our hotel well. It's unlikely this woman drives or will ever see the Amber Alert. I pay for a single night with Harris's money, uncertain of tomorrow, and return to the car.

I back into the carport, and, using a penknife from the glove compartment, remove the front license plate. I carry each kid to the room, lay them on the single king bed, then crawl between them.

Addie's body molds to mine, her back against my chest, and Drew rolls so our backs are touching—a child sandwich so warm and comforting that the troubles dissolve and I fall into an exhausted sleep.

37

It feels as though I've only just closed my eyes when pounding at the door startles me awake seven hours later.

I stare at the pale rectangle.

There's no other way in or out of the room. Drew pushes himself up to sit sleepily and rubs his eyes. Addie stirs, but doesn't wake.

I crawl to the edge so as not to climb over either of them, and the door pounds again.

"Jill."

The voice surprises me so much I almost fall off the bed, then I leap from it and throw open the door. "Mom?"

I scan past her for flashing lights or for Gordon, but behind her is only the dusty morning and the ugly silhouette of the motel.

"Are you going to let me in?"

I step aside, and she walks past me, her familiar scent of lavender and Noxzema trailing after her.

Drew hops from the bed and into her arms as she bends to one knee, and she kisses him a dozen times until he's squirming to escape.

She lets go and whirls to face me. "Better close that," she says, gesturing toward the door. "Don't want anyone to see us."

I push the door closed. "How'd...?"

Drew sidles back to my mom's side to huddle shyly against her hip, and my mom wraps a protective arm around his shoulder. "Drew called last night and read me the address from the notepad."

I glance at the notepad on the table beside the bed.

Vaguely I recall hearing Drew mumbling while I slept, but I dismissed it as a dream.

I kneel down and hold out my arms. Drew stumbles into them, and I hold him tight. "I'm sorry," I whisper into his ear. "This must be crazy scary for you."

His head nods against my cheek.

"You did the right thing. You can always call your nana if you're in trouble." I've told him this since he was a baby, and her phone number was the first one I had him memorize. As uncertain as I am about her devotion to me, I'm certain of it for my kids.

I stand. "Did you tell Gordon?"

Her face goes pale, and she looks as though she's been slapped. "You think that little of me?"

I shake my head at the ground. "I think you think that little of me."

The blush of anger replaces the pallor, and we're back in familiar territory.

"Jill, why didn't you tell us what was going on?"

"Why are you here?"

"I'm here to help."

"Why? Yesterday you were helping Gordon."

"Yesterday, I didn't know..." Abruptly she stops, her

mouth clamped to prevent the rest of the sentence from tumbling out.

"Didn't know what?" I demand.

She kneels down and faces Drew. "Drew, why don't you go take a nice warm bath?"

She's a better mother than I'll ever be. It didn't even occur to me to worry about Drew listening to our damaging conversation. Drew shuffles off and I glance at Addie, who still gently snores on the bed.

I turn away so my mom won't see me swallow my shame.

They have Gordon, and they have me—poor souls, they rolled craps in the parent lottery.

When I turn back, surprisingly my mom isn't looking at me with judgment, but with concern.

"I'm here to help," she repeats.

"Why? Yesterday you were reading me the riot act and demanding I come home. Now you're here to help? Why?"

"You're my daughter."

"Get out."

"What?"

"You heard me. Out." My finger points to the door.

Her chin shifts forward a centimeter. "Jill, stop being ridiculous. You can't do this alone."

My head shakes violently. "I'll take my chances. Why are you here?"

She looks away, her eyes on the carpet at my feet, and something in the slope of her shoulders and the shadow of disgrace on her face sends a chill down my spine. It takes more than a subtle scare to shake up my mother.

"What did he do?" I gasp. "Is Dad okay?"

"He's fine."

I scan her face and body for damage. "What did Gordon do to you?"

"Nothing."

"Mom?"

"He just scared us, that's all."

"How?"

"It's not important. We're fine."

"Mom?"

"Jill, drop it." Her tone leaves no room for debate, then her expression softens, and she looks at me with genuine regret on her face. "Why didn't you tell us?"

My eyes move to the wall and a seam of wallpaper that's begun to separate. "You wouldn't have believed me."

"I would have."

"You would have believed Gordon was abusing me?"

"I would have. If you had talked to me..."

My head snaps back. "If I had talked to you, you'd have told me I was insane."

Her head shakes back and forth, and she glubs several times, then she sets her lips into a tight line. She knows, as well as I do, she wouldn't have believed me.

"I've never seen that side of him," she says finally. "Then Connor called..."

My mom's still talking, but I'm no longer listening.

Connor. In all the craziness, I didn't think to call him, to tell him what happened, to tell him about Jeffrey and that I was okay and why I took the kids. I imagine him pacing his condo, waiting for me to come home, calling the police... *calling the police!!!*

He's going to tell them I was on my way to see Jeffrey at the Compton site. My fingerprints will be on the lock, my footprints in the gymnasium. Every *CSI* episode I've ever watched runs through my mind.

"Jill? You okay?"

"They're going to think I killed him."

"Killed who?"

But I can't explain, my brain fully occupied with Jeffrey's dead stare.

"The man who died in Compton?" my mom says. "Why would they think you killed him?"

My head snaps up. "You know about that?"

"Connor told me. He thought that's why you took off. You saw that man dead and snapped."

"Do the police know I was there?"

Her brow wrinkles in confusion.

"Did Connor call them?"

"I don't think so. Connor was concerned when Harris called and told him the client you'd gone to meet had been killed, so he called me. I told him you'd taken the kids, and that's when he explained what's been going on."

The oxygen returns to the room.

"And now, Jill, you're going to tell me the rest. Enough's enough."

Tell her the rest. What exactly does that mean? The rest back to my childhood, back to the beginning of my marriage, to the end of my marriage, to yesterday? For forty years, I've told my mother almost nothing, now she wants me to tell her the rest. Where do I begin? Do I want to begin? I don't. Like a kazillion times before, I don't want to tell her anything.

"Tell me, Mom, when Connor told you what's been going on, that Gordon was abusive, that he was trying to destroy me so he could take the kids, did you believe him?"

My mom leers at me. "Of course I believed him. Why wouldn't I believe him? I absolutely believed him." She's speaking so quickly and repeating herself so much even she doesn't believe the lie. Her chin falls to her chest and stays there shaking back and forth. "I just... He's always been... I thought the two of you were happy." Her face lifts, and there's so much regret etched in the lines that the words are lost in the sincerity of her remorse. "I'm sorry."

I bite my lip, the tears I've been holding back for a day now threatening to erupt.

"How could this be happening?" she says. "I don't understand."

I shake my head again, and my voice is so low that I barely hear it. "You can't understand, no one can understand, because none of it makes sense." My words gain momentum as I tell the horrible truth about my life, until the words tumble like an avalanche. My mom's eyes are wide with astonishment, and her face is pale, and she looks a lot like Addie does when she wakes from a bad dream.

I'm amazed how quickly the retelling of nine years is summarized, and after only a few minutes, I'm giving the CliffsNotes on Gordon trying to extend my life insurance so he can kill me and how I found Jeffrey dead, which drove me to taking the kids. "It sounds crazy, and it is crazy, but it's also the truth, and you can believe me or not, but whether you do or not, it won't change what I'm doing. If he catches me, he'll kill me, and if he kills me, nobody will be there to protect Addie and Drew."

"But Gordon's always been..."

"He's not!" I snap. "Whatever good thing you're about to say about him, don't. He's not a good man, a good husband, a good father. And if you can't just believe me, then you should go, because I have no proof. Jeffrey's death will be called a robbery that will never be solved, and everything else I'm telling you is just my word. So you either believe me or you don't."

My mom's brow furrows, and I can see she's trying hard to understand. "Just give me a minute to catch up. I just don't understand why he killed this Jeffrey man."

"Jeffrey was trying to help me."

The furrow unfurls and understanding crosses her face. "You were having an affair with him?"

I nod, and my mom nods along with me, and for a moment, I wonder why there's no condemnation.

But I know why—the reason glares between us—and hypocritically, I feel anger at her betrayal of my dad and I wonder how many times she strayed. But at the moment, there's no room for any more emotion, and I let it go.

"Jeffrey confronted Gordon, and Gordon killed him," I finish.

"You know this for sure."

"He killed him with a shotgun. It's difficult to explain, but it was meant as a message for me."

"Jill, isn't it possible it's a coincidence? The murder was in Compton."

My head hurts—it's pounding from exhaustion and stress and hunger—and I'm tired of trying to explain the inexplicable. "Mom, you don't need to be involved. I appreciate you coming here for the kids' sake..."

"And yours."

"But truthfully, you should go."

"Stop that."

"Stop what?"

"Pushing me away."

"It's just, on this one, I need you to just believe me."

"I'm here, aren't I?"

"Because Gordon scared you and Connor called you. You still don't believe me."

"Well, you haven't exactly given me much of a chance."

"You're my mother. You shouldn't need an invitation."

"Don't do that."

"What?"

"Turn this around. Since you were a baby, you and your father have been in your own little private club without any room for a third, so don't you dare tell me I should have shoved my way into your life. I'm here now."

And for a moment, time stops, and our history blares between us. And like a thousand other times, we're stuck—my mom trying to force her way into my life a day late and a dollar short—and me determined to prove I no longer need her, all the missed mother-and-daughter moments from my childhood creating an impenetrable barrier between us.

"Nana!"

My mom kneels to receive a catapulting Addie into her arms. I wipe the tears from my cheeks so Addie won't see them and stumble to the bathroom to check on Drew.

When I return, Addie and my mom are playing tic-tac-toe on the bed.

"Mom, you shouldn't be here," I say.

"Where should I be?" She puts an "X" in the wrong spot, and Addie quickly scrawls in her "O," declaring herself the winner with a whoop and holler.

"I could be in real trouble, and you could be in trouble if you help me. Plus, who's taking care of Dad?"

"Jan."

Aunt Jan is my mom's best friend, and she's much more nurturing than my mom could ever be. My dad's in good hands.

"Still, you need to go. If you help us, you're aiding and abetting, and that could be serious."

"Sounds exciting." She wrinkles her nose at Addie and smiles.

"Mom, this is serious."

My mom stands from the bed and smooths her linen slacks. "Jill, you're right, this is serious, and if it wasn't, I wouldn't be here. But it is, so I'm here to help." She opens her purse and holds out an envelope. "It's not a lot." She looks a bit embarrassed. "But at the moment, it's all we can afford."

"You're helping us continue running?"

She nods. "I don't necessarily believe Gordon killed anyone or is going to kill you, but I believe you believe it, and that's all that matters."

My dad's stroke devastated my parents financially. I haven't asked, but I know my mom no longer shops at the department stores she used to frequent, and unlike all the years I can remember, mostly they eat at home.

"Mom, I can't."

"You can and you will. It will hold you over until you figure out what you're going to do."

I nod and take the gift. "I don't know when I'll be able to repay you."

"Don't worry about that. Just get yourself somewhere safe and take care of these kids." She squeezes Addie's cheeks until her lips pucker like a fish.

"Now we'd better get this show on the road. When Gordon discovers I'm not home, he's going to get suspicious, and it wouldn't take Sherlock Holmes to figure out I wasn't flying to Medford, Oregon, for my health, and a phone call to the phone company will lead him here."

I nod, then tell her about the Amber Alert advertising my car.

She swallows at the word "kidnapping."

"We'll take my rental car and get you some new wheels," she says, sounding very Bonnie and Clyde.

The little white building in Altamont, Oregon, has a sign that says, "Benjamin's Buggies," and parked in front of it are a dozen beat-up cars with neon green signs advertising great deals. The least expensive car on the lot is an ugly white 1988 Chevy Corsica advertised for $1,600. My mom flirts with the comb-over salesman, sweet-talking the price down to $1,300, and I shell out the precious bills. Without counting, I know there are seven bills left. I have $700 to restart my life.

My mom hugs each of us extra hard, and when she pulls away, there are tears in her eyes, and I realize this might be the last time I ever see her.

"I'm sorry," I say.

She tilts her head. "This isn't your fault."

"About us."

She puts her fingers to my lips.

"A lot of the things happen that we never intend."

We both smile devastatingly sad grins, both of us wishing we had a redo or at least time to give it another try.

If only... the two saddest words in the world.

As I hold her for possibly the last time, I can't remember loving her so much.

38

We slept at the Altamont Motor Inn and got back on the road this morning.

I choose to stay on the 97 since it's been lucky for us so far. I drive toward the border, hoping to find a safe place for us to hide out until I can figure a way for us to cross into Canada.

Since we passed Bend, Oregon, three hours ago, there's been nothing but sagebrush and desert around us. Now in front of us is the Columbia River; we can either cross over it and continue north, or turn and travel along it.

The epicenter of this decision is Biggs Junction, population twenty-two, which comprises a truck stop and a dim motel with a blinking vacancy light. We get a room, then head to the truck stop for dinner.

At the table, I give Addie and Drew each a penny and tell them to flip it in the air. One head we turn left, two heads we turn right, no heads, we continue straight ahead. Tension fills the air as the coins determine our destiny.

Two heads, a positive sign. Tomorrow might be our lucky day.

39

Color leaks into the gray world as the sun lifts from the horizon, flooding the desert with gold, then painting in the colors like a paint-by-number scene—blue sky, olive scrub, a dash of purple, and a streak of rust. I drink a cup of instant coffee and watch the show through the dusty window as I wait for the kids to wake.

My mind wanders to places I don't want it to go.

Doubt. The mind's mechanism that allows for possibility and forgiveness.

I try to squelch it, to force the resolve I had yesterday onto the present, but part of me's already tired, wants to question my conviction, give up, go home, beg forgiveness. It bleeds like a cancer and feeds off my fear. Yesterday, I was so sure of myself. I had to get away, get the kids away, but today, my mind argues with itself, unable, unwilling, or simply not wanting to fully believe Gordon did what he did.

Like a leak—drip, drip, drip—maybe I'm wrong, maybe it's a coincidence, maybe this is a mistake, a grave mistake, the biggest mistake of my life.

I can't decide if it is fear of getting caught or fear of continuing on alone that scares me more, but cold feet are setting in simultaneously with doubt and this is no coincidence. If I don't pull it together, it's only a matter of time before I convince myself he didn't do it and that we need to go back.

A chill shudders through my bones as I recall Jeffrey lying dead, and my mind rewinds. I imagine Jeffrey in the gymnasium, probably whistling—he liked to whistle—perhaps scouting for the spot where we could make love, turning at the sound of footsteps, thinking I'd arrived, surprised when he saw Gordon, scared when he saw the shotgun. The blast.

I squeeze my eyes shut to clear away the apparition and return to the moment and to thinking about our future.

Drew wakes, and he half intentionally wakes his sister with his squiggling so he won't have to sit quietly waiting for her to get up on her own. I smile at the new buzz cut I gave him last night. His sandy curls have been trimmed to within a centimeter of his scalp, showing off his impish grin and the open handsomeness of his face.

My own hair has gone from tawny to deep brunette, and using a pair of sewing scissors, I shaped it into an abstract pixie cut that took a few years off my age and my dignity. Addie's red hair is a problem.

In the mirror, I don't recognize myself, and Drew looks like a different boy, but last night as I altered our looks, I couldn't bring myself to cut Addie's fiery locks. I settled for letting her pick out any hat she wanted at the truck stop. She chose a green one with a Mountain Dew logo on the front, a strip of yellow lightning on the bill, and the words "I love Dale Jr." embroidered on the side. It's man-size and covers most of her conspicuous hair and half her face.

She wears the hat with a pair of too large orange sweats, a dirty white T-shirt that advertises "Stonehenge, Maryville, Oregon," and purple flip-flops. I cringe at the idea of my daughter growing up thinking Stonehenge is a twenty-first-century tourist attraction in the middle of an RV campground, but it was the only shirt the truck stop had in her size.

"I'm hungwry," she says.

"We're going to the diner right now to have breakfast."

I finish stuffing the plastic laundry bag with our meager wardrobe and head out the door, holding it open for Addie and Drew to follow.

"I want waffles."

I nod. "Okay. The diner has waffles."

Drew walks through, but Addie holds her ground, her arms crossed in defiance across her chest, her colt legs wide. Her toes have spots of chipped purple sparkle polish on the big toes, and I wonder who painted them for her.

"Daddy's waffles."

I blink hard. "We can't have Daddy's waffles," I manage. "Daddy's still at home."

"Then I want to go home." And in her defiance are sadness and exhaustion, and I feel them, too, all the way from the roots of my newly dyed hair to the soles of my feet.

I walk back into the room, and Drew follows.

I kneel down and take hold of Addie's shoulders at arm's length. I give her all of me, my eyes so focused on her green ones I can see each gold speck. "We're not going home," I say.

Her eyes get wide, and her lip starts to quiver, and I pull her to me.

"I'm sorry, baby," I say. "I'm so so sorry." And I am.

∞

We travel along the Columbia River, and when the highway turns south, I veer onto the 82 in order to prevent us moving backward, and when we see the 12, Drew insists we take it because that's the number on his uniform.

An hour and a half later, we stop in the city of Yakima for a potty break and to pawn my wedding ring.

Rook Takes Pawn Shop is located on First Street on the east side of town. Its neighbors are a Laundromat and a used furniture store.

The bell jingles as we walk in. I've never actually been in a pawn shop, but it feels like I have. It's exactly what I expected, an accumulated mass of lost dreams and failure—hundreds of instruments of musicians who never caught their lucky break, crowded aisles of exercise equipment that never got used, heirloom engraved Rolexes generations old, and hundreds of wedding rings.

A stout woman greets us from behind the counter. Her hair is the color of black plums, and the lids of her eyes are painted shocking blue.

I set my ring on the counter. It's a two-carat oval with a platinum halo setting. It was a gift from Gordon for our fifth anniversary, an upgrade from the half-carat ring he'd proposed to me with.

The new ring was not only beautiful and expensive, it was perfectly chosen. Gordon knew me so well.

From a drawer behind the counter, the woman takes a jewelry loupe and holds the diamond to the light to examine it, her blue lid squinting against the lens.

She lowers the ring and the glass to the counter. "Three," she says, and my heart jumps with happiness. *Three thousand.* I'm sure Gordon paid twice that, but I thought I'd get less than half what she's offering.

"It's a good Z," she continues, "and the platinum setting's high-quality."

"Excuse me? A good Z?"

"Cubic zirconium. They did a good job with this one."

I look for the joke, but there is none—the woman's face is serious as stone.

I laugh anyway. I laugh so hard my stomach cramps.

"What's funny?" Addie says, walking over from the keyboards.

"My ring," I say, still laughing. "It's a fake."

"Like pwretend?"

I laugh harder. "Exactly, like pretend."

"I'm sorry," the lady says, stopping the humor. Like a war surgeon, she's used to delivering bad news and offering thin consolation.

"So when you said three," I ask, "you meant three hundred?"

40

It's our third day on the road, and at noon we arrive in Grand Coulee, Washington. A small town developed around the Grand Coulee Dam. We stop in front of the Tee Pee Diner, and Drew cracks up at the name.

"I don't want to dwrive anymowre," Addie demands.

Drew nods.

I can't help but nod along with them. My butt feels permanently molded to the seat.

"How about a picnic lunch along the water?"

We climb numbly from the car and stare at the wide river in front of us.

"Can we swim?" Addie asks.

I look at the running rapids and shake my head.

Addie looks so crestfallen it breaks my heart.

"Excuse me." I turn to a man sitting on a bench in front of the diner. "Is there a river near here where the kids can get their feet wet?"

He's got a great white beard and a round belly that hangs over his belt. He probably poses as Santa during the winter, but today he wears khaki shorts and a shirt that advertises Waylon Jennings. He scratches the beard in thought. "Elmer City," he says. "It's a few minutes up the road, but it's got some great creeks." He pronounces it cricks. "Flying Goat Kitchen is the place to eat, and they'll point you to the best watering holes. Good people there and good food."

"It means getting back in the car," I say, unsure, but both kids are already skipping back to the parking lot.

Flying Goat Kitchen is a two-story clapboard house that sags in the middle, causing the two dormer windows on the second story to slant like questioning eyes. The sign is so faded you have to squint to make out the soaring goat behind the letters.

The man or woman at the hostess desk sits motionless as a statue. I think, "Sitting Bull," as we approach. He/she is as wide as the desk, with ink-black, shoulder-length hair, folds of mahogany skin rolling beneath a fleshy face, and two slits for eyes set so deep I wonder how they see.

"Hello," I say, when he/she offers no greeting. "Table for three."

There's a grunt, and the head tilts just the slightest to let us know we're permitted to enter and choose our seat.

We move into the packed dining room, and every table is occupied. A few faces lift to look at us; most are white, a few are the color of our host. One scruffy, outback-looking man with whiskers at least a week old and a shirt that's older than me gestures us over. Tentatively, I approach.

"Kids can join me," he says, "and you can lunch with Fred."

A man sitting at the next table over, dressed in shirtsleeves and trousers, acknowledges me with a mouthful grin and pulls out the chair beside him.

I'm ready to turn heel and leave, but the kids have already assumed their spots on either side of the mountain man. Dining with them is a well-dressed woman in her sixties reading the *Seattle Times*. This gives me some measure of comfort as I move to sit at Fred's table.

I glance around for menus.

"Lunch today's roast chicken, fritters, and peas," Fred says.

Again, I'm ready to bolt and find the nearest Subway, but when I glance at Addie, the pickiest eater in the universe, she's popping one of her neighbor's corn fritters into her mouth and smiling. I reconsider and settle back to my seat.

"Not from around here?" Fred asks.

I shake my head. "Is this place always this busy?"

"Every day but God's day and Monday."

"Why not Monday?"

"Closed, and let me tell you, it's a shame. Starve on those days. Get used to Goat's cooking and it's like a drug; can't live without it."

"Always only one thing on the menu?"

"What Goat cooks is what you eat." Fred is probably forty. His hair is still dark, but thin on top. His body holds the remnants of an athlete, but his middle is soft.

A small woman, thin as a girl, brushes past carrying three plates; she plops one in front of each of my kids, then whirls and plops the third in front of me. Around me, people come and go, empty plates are snatched away, and full plates replace them. Fred continues to make pleasant conversation. He owns the general store in town, moved here when he got married a dozen years ago. He liked it, so he stayed. His wife didn't, so she left.

I crane my neck to see how Addie and Drew are doing, and they're just fine. The peas aren't being touched, but the fritters and chicken might as well be M&M'S. I dig into my own food, and my taste buds burst to life. If I hadn't chosen to be an architect, I'd have wanted to be a food critic.

Throughout my childhood, my dad and I traveled the country in search of lost treasure, adventure, genius (man's and God's), and good food. And I wish he were here to taste this. The chicken falls off the bone and tastes like it's been basted in syrup, the corn fritters are light as air, and the peas tossed with sweet onions and roasted almonds—the entire meal cooked to perfection.

"No dieting in this place," I say to Fred as I guiltily inhale another fritter.

"First three letters in diet's a warning, I always say." Fred chuckles, then stands. "Well, gotta go. It was nice chatting with you."

He lays a ten on the table where his plate was, tips an imaginary hat to me, and leaves.

A man dark as pine bark and as craggy takes his place. The man has a long black braid down his back and is dressed in a suede shirt with fringe along the seams and hem. He eats his food with focus and doesn't say a word.

I set my fork down, and the skinny girl whisks the plate away. I duly lay a ten in its place and sidle from my seat so the next waiting customer can have it. I put bills where my kids' plates were, and they stand and follow me through the crowd.

As we leave, Sitting Bull holds out three brown bags to us—no words, just an extended arm with the bags.

We step into the sun and open our prize—each bag contains two bite-size chocolate macaroons. Addie has my sweet tooth and pops hers into her mouth in quick succession. "These awre soooo good," she says through a mouthful of chocolate, then her mouth turns upside down when she realizes hers are all gone. I'm about to hand her my remaining one when Drew beats me to it. "Here, Ad," he says. "You can have mine. I'm full."

It's the nicest thing I've ever seen him do for his sister.

She takes them like he's handed her the moon, her face beaming.

"The man I was eating with says there's a river behind the restaurant. Should we go explore?"

We follow the worn dirt path that leads along the side of the Flying Goat. As we pass the back of the restaurant, a strange language lifts and falls through the open window of what I assume is the kitchen. Two voices, a man's and a woman's, argue and laugh—the woman's is old, probably Goat, the man's is young. Their banter, though I don't understand it, makes me smile.

The river is wide and lazy and sparkles with the early afternoon sun. We hike downstream until we find an inlet that's still with a flat rock beside it baking in the sun.

I sit on the edge as the kids wade in the shallow water. I take off my shoes and socks and wriggle my toes against the stone to soak up the heat, and for the first time in two days, I breathe. So much nothingness surrounds me that if I forget about my store-bought clothes and my modern-day problems, I can almost imagine I've stepped back in time. A pair of Canadian geese float by, the male bigger and more beautiful than his mate, the current carrying them effortlessly to another place.

Drew crouches on a boulder beside Addie to watch the pollywogs. Their heads—Addie's bright as a new copper penny, Drew's old gold—are bent so close they touch.

"Look."

I follow Addie's finger. A hawk soars for the sky, a trout at least ten inches long flapping in its beak.

"Wow," I say. "I bet there's tons of fish in this river. That's amazing. I bet people fish here all the time."

"I want to fish," Drew says.

And I nod. Why not? Here, in this moment, anything seems possible.

41

We walk to the general store a block away, and Fred sells us a pole, some bait, and a small notebook so I can sketch, then we return to the river to try our luck at fishing.

Drew casts his line just as Fred instructed, and I'm amazed how quickly he's caught on. School's been a complete wipeout for Drew, every report card for the past three years a testament to his lack of attention and motivation. But as Fred explained how to tie on the hook and how to cast and how to reel in the line, Drew was completely focused.

The string quivers as Drew slowly winds the spool, its rippling trail disappearing as quickly as it appeared, leaving no evidence of where it had been.

Addie loses interest in minutes, but Drew is mesmerized. He casts, reels, and casts again. His patience and determination are a mirror of my own, and for the first time, possibly ever, I recognize myself in the reflection.

He turns to give me the thin smile I love, and his contentment is contagious, his heart touching mine and we are united.

There have been times when we've been close, but the tumultuousness of my life has been so distracting that it seems I'm always more occupied with keeping my balance than doing anything more.

"In the wrong spot for that lure."

Drew and I turn to the voice, and I get nervous. Poorly executed blue tattoos cover sinewy forearms that protrude from a worn black shirt that advertises Johnnie Walker Black. The man walks toward us with a pronounced limp. His Wrangler jeans are low on his hips and don't have a belt. The elastic of plaid boxers peek from the top. He wears a baseball cap, the embroidered number 48 dark with age. He's probably in his early thirties, but his life's been harder than that.

"If it's trout you're after, need to move to where the water's running stronger." He gestures with his head downstream, half a smile screwing up his mouth and erasing my fear.

"Thank you," I say as I gather my notebook and shoes, and as I turn to pick up the bag of snacks I brought along, the water splashes behind me.

I whip around, but Addie's already floating past me, her arms flailing as she heads for the rapidly moving water downstream. I stumble across the rocks to catch her, but she's moving faster than I can run.

The cold snaps my body awake as I splash into it, and a moment later, the current catches me, and my efforts to get to Addie are overtaken by my efforts to stay afloat. I catch a glimpse of her in front of me and thrash to move in her direction, but I've never been a strong swimmer and my jeans and sweatshirt pull me down, my lungs screaming as they fill with too much water and not enough air. The shore is to my left, and Addie is drowning in front of me. My left hip slams into a rock, and for a moment, I forget to swim and sink below the current.

When I break back to the surface, Addie's gone. I scan the water frantically, then crash into another rock, my head dizzying with the impact. I roll to my back gasping for air, and panic takes over my body as I realize what's happening.

Water covers my face and fills my lungs. The river carries me forward, and I no longer fight it. The current's too fast, and I don't have the strength.

A yank on my hood snaps my momentum backward, and precious air rushes into my lungs as my head breaks above the water. Rocks and boulders bruise and scrape me, and then I'm facedown on the shore.

I cough and spit, then push to my knees and vomit into the bushes beside me, wishing I was still in the river and not in this moment.

"Mommy?"

My head snaps up.

Addie shivers in front of me, her face so white that her freckles seem to have multiplied.

"Oh, baby." I pull her to me, unsure the miracle is true, her body so cold I now know it isn't imagined.

Over her shoulder, our savior shifts uncomfortably from foot to foot. His jeans and T-shirt drip, and his hat is gone, revealing a thick head of mud-colored hair.

"You okay, ma'am?"

Awkwardly I unwrap Addie's shivering body from mine, and on trembling legs, stand. I stumble, and the man's hand shoots out to catch me by my elbow.

"One dip in the Nichi in a day's enough for me," he says with the same sideways smile he gave earlier.

I throw my arms around him, and he opens his wide, unsure how to handle my embrace.

"Thank you," I say against his cheek, fresh tears running down my face.

"Your little one's quite a *qmeye*."

"Excuse me?"

"Little fish, it's a Salish word."

It's then that I notice that although his hair is Caucasian, his skin is dark and his nose is wide. He's at least part Native American.

"Except fish have gills and know how to swim," I say.

Drew walks up beside us. "Can you show me where to fish?" he asks the man, as though we've all just returned from a relaxing swim in the river.

"Drew, I'm sure this man would like to go and get dry and that he's quite done with helping us."

"Come on, Drew," the man says, ignoring me. "I've been fishing this river since I was your sister's age. I'll show you where you can catch your ma and sister some dinner." He starts off downstream, and Addie and I trail behind still shivering from the fear and the cold. As we walk, the two geese from earlier fly low along the river back upstream.

The rock he leads us to holds the day's warmth, and Addie and I strip our dripping sweatshirts and lay spread-eagle to soak up the heat from the granite and the rays of the afternoon sun at the same time. We lay together, our fingers clasped, thin smiles of having survived something harrowing on our faces, until Addie drifts to sleep.

Above us, at the tip of the outcropping, Drew and the man fish. The man is quiet and patient and only speaks when necessary. Soon I stop listening to the river, the whip of the line as it's cast, the man's gentle teachings, and I, too, am lulled to stillness.

"I got one."

I bolt upright and so does Addie. And sure enough, a fish maybe six inches long flaps wildly on the end of Drew's line.

The man's crooked grin spreads wide on his face as he takes the small fish in his hand and gently pulls the hook from its gasping mouth. He lifts it toward the sky, whispers words I don't understand, then, bringing his arm down in an arc, releases the fish back into the river.

Drew's face melts from euphoria to crushing disappointment. "Why'd you do that?" he says.

The man looks at him earnestly. "Every animal has the right to grow up," he says quietly. "You'll catch another. One that's already lived."

The man's a stranger, yet he's familiar, and as I watch him beside Drew, I think of what it would have been like had I had a brother. I can almost hear my dad in the man's gentle voice.

The man rebaits the line, and Drew casts again. Moments later, he's rewarded with a fish twice the size of the first. This one, after the man holds it to the heavens, is set in the tall grass to die in the shade.

42

The sun fades along with the heat, and though our clothes are dry, cold has seeped into our bones. We gather our belongings, and the man uses a piece of line to tether up the catch—three trout and one smallmouth bass.

He extends them toward me.

"Thank you," I say, "but we can't keep them. We're just passing through."

He ignores me and turns to Drew. "Ever cleaned and cooked a trout?" he asks.

Drew shakes his head.

"Then follow me." And without further discussion, he sets off with the four fish, Drew traipsing after him. I'm caught between commanding Drew to come back or taking a leap of faith and following.

Today the world is different from what it was a week ago, and the decision—inconceivable only days earlier, an unfathomable breach of bourgeois decorum and common sense—is now not only logical, but certain, and I follow my son, who follows a young, tattooed Native American through the woods of Washington to cook the dinner they caught in the river.

ꝏ

We emerge where we started in the backyard of the Flying Goat Kitchen.

The man marches up the steps and opens the screen door that leads to the kitchen.

"Goat," he yells as he steps in and holds the door open for us to follow.

The kitchen is empty except for the enormous amount of clutter—mixers and stoves and ovens and pots and pans and racks and sacks and spoons and spatulas with barely a foot's space to move.

"Pipe down," squawks from somewhere beyond the milieu.

In response, the man lays the fish beside a sink, picks up two pot lids, and using them as cymbals, bangs them together making an insane racket. This causes Addie to squeal with delight and grab two cymbals of her own. Drew grabs a pot and a spoon and makes a drum.

A large onion flies through the pickup window that leads to the dining room and beans the man on the back of his head.

"Ouch."

"Now shut up."

The man, clanging away, marches like a drum leader through the kitchen and toward the onion launcher.

We parade after him into the dining room, and the man uses his pot lids as shields to ward off two more onion attacks before the person belonging to the voice notices us and halts her assault, her arm poised mid-motion from hurling a third onion.

"We've got company," the man says. "Goat, this is Qmeye and Cixcx," he says, calling the kids by their nicknames, Little Fish and Hawk. He pronounces the words Kmayay and Sissix. He hesitates as he contemplates me, tilting his head and screwing up his face. "...and Ntamqe." My name is pronounced Tomkay.

The woman could be sixty or a hundred and sixty. She's dark and tiny as a raisin, and her eyes are set so deep all I see is folds of skin. Her thick black hair, woven with gray, is braided and coiled on top of her head like a sleeping rattlesnake, and in her hand is a knife that glints orange with the setting light through the window. With it, she expertly carves the onion she previously had planned to throw at our escort.

"I'm not cooking," she says, not giving us another glance.

"Not asking you to, but I thought you might want to join us."

"I'm not cleaning."

"Not asking you to."

"What you making?"

"Trout and grits."

She grunts and grabs another onion, and we back up and return to the kitchen.

"Ntamqe," the man says, "do you cook?"

"Does cereal count?" I answer.

"You and Little Fish can cut the lemons and mince the garlic. You also need to grab some rosemary, thyme, and olive oil. There's a garden behind the house, and the pantry and the walk-in are in the back."

The man has already turned to the sink, and Drew remains at his side.

Addie and I head to the garden, which turns out to be a tangle of deliciousness, a large yard of everything from tomatoes to corn to pumpkins to blueberries. A greenhouse is in the corner. I pull two garlic bulbs from the earth and walk to the greenhouse.

Soil, water, and foliage fill the air to bursting, wet heat trapped in the glass and stewing the half barrels that are planted with herbs and potatoes and warm weather crops like lettuce and spinach and kale.

I find the rosemary without problem, but struggle to find thyme, unsure if the pretty green sprigs I pick are the herb I'm supposed to pull.

When we get back to the kitchen, Drew holds the knife.

I freeze at the sight, but breathe when I see how careful he's being and how attentive he is to the man.

"Behind the gill and straight through," the man coaches.

The knife must be very sharp because, in a single stroke, the head is sliced off clean.

The man takes over and slits the belly from tail to gill.

He sets the fish back on the cutting board. "Now you need to clean out the insides."

The Drew I know would refuse this chore, he'd wrinkle his nose and back away and cross his arms in protest and disgust. But the Drew at the sink doesn't hesitate. He pulls open the slitted belly of the fish and with his finger guts the organs and dumps them into the sink.

"Good, now score the bloodline."

Drew picks up the knife and makes several cuts deep in the fish. When the man nods, Drew sets down the knife and places the fish in a tub of water beside him. With a toothbrush, he scrubs the spine of the fish until the blood is washed from its body.

Addie and I approach with our offerings.

"Little Fish, you put the aluminum on the pans," the man says.

Addie sets to work lining the two pans that are beside the man with great care.

"Ntamqe, mix the thyme and rosemary with garlic, lemon, and olive oil. Keep the lemon wedges and sprigs for the carcass."

Like my children, I respond to his gentle directions, eager to do my job well.

I reach for a bowl above the sink and feel the man's eyes. Self-consciously I realize my shirt's pulled up, showing the skin below my bra. When I look at him, however, his eyes are not admiring my body, but instead stare at my exposed ribs. I quickly grab the bowl and lower my arm, but it's too late. His eyes have changed. The bruise is a week old, a faint jaundice blotch, but the shape is unmistakably that of a fist the same size as his own, and his reaction is the same as Jeffrey's and Connor's—an expression of pity and rage that sets my skin on fire and makes me want to cry and scream and apologize and run and slap him and hug him all at the same time.

He laughs. "You definitely don't cook, Ntamqe."

I follow his eyes to the cutting board beside me, and he walks to where I am and lifts a sprig of what I thought was thyme. He rubs it between his fingers and toothpaste fills the air.

"We almost ended up with peppermint trout," he says.

Embarrassed for both the moment before and the moment we are in, I rush from the kitchen and back into the garden, this time determined to get it right.

Half an hour later, we sit in the dining room at a table beside the window that Addie set for us. When Goat stands to join us, she's only half-straight. Her body is twisted and stooped, and as she hobbles toward us, I realize she's on the older side of my estimate, and I wonder about her relationship to the man. She's too old to be his mother; maybe she's his grandmother, or possibly even his great grandmother.

She takes a seat beside me, and a moment later, the room goes dark except for the flicker of a candle in the middle of the table. Ceremoniously, the man and Drew carry the plates to the table and set them in front of us; Drew and I are sharing the largest fish, and each of the others has a smaller whole trout to themselves. Addie wrinkles her nose at the headless fish in front of her, but my firm squeeze of her knee straightens the expression from her face.

Drew's proud as a peacock as he sits down, and he should be. The scent is magnificent, and the fish glisten with garlic and lemon and char. The man demonstrates the art of deboning, and even Addie gives it a try, though the man takes over when it looks like half the bones are being left behind.

The tails are set aside, and we dig in.

"This is magnificent," I say without the least bit of embellishment. It's the best fish I've had in my life—salty and garlicky and it melts on my tongue.

"Nothing like fresh river trout you caught yourself," the man says.

I slide my eyes to Addie's plate, concerned that fish not shaped like stars or sticks or dinosaurs and without a thick coating of bread crumbs, grease, and ketchup won't make it to her mouth, and am stunned to see her spooning the white meat in along with the grits. "I like the potatoes," she says between mouthfuls.

"It's grits, stupid," Drew says.

I'm about to reprimand him, but the man's laughter interrupts. "And you thought it was rice, so what's that make you, Einstein?"

Drew's face goes slightly pink.

Goat speaks for the first time. "Makes him smarter than you, Skutm. First time you saw grits, you thought they was white beans, insisted on it even when I told you different. Skutm."

I'm stunned at how perfect her English is—no accent or intonation—perfect, insulting, American English.

"Hag."

"Stma."

"Old Goat."

"That I am." And they both smile.

Addie's head goes back and forth following the insults. "What awre gwrits made of if theywre not potatoes?" she asks.

"What difference does it make so long as you like them?" the man says. "I like them and couldn't care a hill of beans where they come from."

Goat smiles. She has no teeth on the right side of her mouth and only a few on the left.

The meal is mostly quiet, and I'm surprised and happy the pair doesn't ask questions. They're content and peaceful as they eat. Outside the river runs, and inside, the sagging house creaks with the breeze. Goat and I share red wine from a jug that has no label, and I wonder where it came from. The man drinks a can of Coors, and the kids drink milk.

When we're done, Goat pushes to her feet and hobbles away without a word. I think she's leaving, but I'm wrong. A moment later she returns, and in her hand are three familiar brown bags—chocolate macaroons. Addie's face lights up.

"You'll stay in the room beside the kitchen. Paul will show you," she says. "Toilet sticks so hold it down when you flush."

I open my mouth to protest, but she's already turned and begun to shuffle toward a dark stairwell in the corner.

I turn instead to Paul. "We should be getting back on the road," I say.

Addie yawns.

He shakes his head. "If you're still heading in the direction you were heading when you got here, you're an hour from the nearest hotel, and if that one's full, it's three hours to the next one. Goat's right. Stay here tonight, and if in the morning you decide to move on, then you will."

43

The room has a single bed and a red futon wedged between it and the wall that you need to climb over to get to the bathroom. On the floor is a New England hook rug several generations old, and I marvel that something so beautiful and well crafted ended up where it did. In the bathroom, there's a tub and a sink with faucets that deliver cold and hot water. The bathroom's old and small, but clean.

I tuck the kids in on the futon, lie down on the bed, and fall into a fitful sleep.

The sound of the river.

Water running slow, then fast.

Addie thrashing away from me.

My lungs fill with water as I sink.

Gordon's arm around my throat.

Blackness.

Smashing glass.

Shards of porcelain.

Jeffrey kissing me.

A shotgun blast.

I wake with a start.

For a moment, I forget I'm not in Laguna Beach, not in my handcrafted ash bed surrounded by my priceless porcelain statues and collection of rare modern furniture.

I blink into focus my new life—the rough twin mattress, the flickering neon light of a beer sign blinking through the curtainless window, the sagging floor, and the Farmer's Almanac calendar from three years ago pinned to the wall beside the door.

When I wake again, the room is bright and full of noise. Goat's voice, Paul's voice, and the clanging and banging of pots and silverware and pans. The cacophony sounds through smells of gravy and grease and something cinnamon.

As I sit up my brain throbs so hard I expect to see it pulsing when I look in the small mirror that hangs beside the door. My head remains intact, but my eyes are etched with lines and shadowed with blue.

I reach for the door, but it opens before I touch it.

"Morning," Paul says. He carries a tray with a plate of eggs and biscuits and coffee. My mouth and stomach respond simultaneously. He sets it on the table beside the bed and hustles back out the door. Before it closes, I witness the fray past the threshold. The restaurant is full beyond the kitchen. The skinny server grabs several plates Goat throws in the window and hustles away. Steam and smoke sizzle, rise, and crackle everywhere.

The door closes, and ravenously, I eat like I've not eaten in a week.

Only when I'm done do I think about the whereabouts of Addie and Drew, and the tardiness of my maternal concern fills me with guilt.

I carry my tray into the kitchen, careful to avoid the spatula-wielding Goat, who works the grill, and the less frenzied Paul who works the pantry. Through the back door, Addie and Drew play with two children and a young woman who's the spitting image of the skinny server, but half the age.

Plates are backed up on the counter, and through the pickup window, I see the skinny server is caught up in starting a new pot of coffee. I glance at the tickets, deduce the logical numbering of the tables, and grab two plates and carry them to their respective spots.

I served at my dad's restaurants from the time I was twelve until I left for college, and like riding a bike, it comes back with only a slight wobbling in the beginning.

Without words, the skinny server, whose name is Sissy, and I move through the room filling waters and iced teas, delivering full plates and clearing empty ones. Breakfast ends at ten, and lunch starts at eleven. Today's lunch is chicken-fried steak, mashed potatoes, and collard greens, and there's hardly a scrap left on any plate I clear. The sweet departing gift given to the guests as they leave are cinnamon bonbons dipped in white chocolate.

Abruptly at two o'clock, the bell of the cuckoo clock that no longer has a cuckoo chimes twice, and though the restaurant is packed and customers still crowd the entrance waiting for seats, Sitting Bull rises and turns the closed sign in the window. "We're closed." Her voice is unmistakably feminine and surprisingly high.

It's another hour before the final customer leaves and an hour more before the side work and cleanup are done.

Sissy holds a handful of bills toward me.

I shake my head. "I just wanted to help."

"We share the tips," she says. "That's how it works." There's nothing friendly in her face—a chiseled carving of unsmiling cedar—and she almost sounds angry at my refusal. Yet I've worked beside her for hours, and I know she's kind. For a customer whose left hand was mangled, she cut his steak at the counter before setting it down. For another, she deftly removed a piece of toilet paper that clung to the woman's pant leg when she returned from the restroom.

The bills remain in her outstretched hand.

"It's my way of thanking everyone for helping me," I say.

"It gets split evenly," she answers as though I said nothing. "Two dollars per plate, one for you and one for me. Then we tip Isi for hostessing and because she makes the cookies, twenty dollars each."

I glance to the hostess desk where Isi, aka Sitting Bull, is tallying up the day's customers based on the number of bags of cookies she has left.

"I didn't even work the whole shift."

"I didn't give you money for what you didn't work."

Sissy is two inches shorter than me and thin as Gandhi. Her black hair is tied at the nape of her neck and hangs to her waist. There's a tribal band tattoo on her ring finger that serves as a wedding ring. She's about my age, and judging by the stiffness and exhaustion in her posture, I'm guessing her worries are as heavy.

I don't want her money, but to refuse seems to be more of an insult, so I take the extended bills with a thank-you.

"No thanks. You did the work, the money is yours." And she walks away.

I move toward the hostess desk to pay Isi. She sings softly to herself, and as I get closer, the words become clear, "...coming for to carry me home, swing low, sweet chariot..." When she notices me, she stops, but I wish she wouldn't. Her voice is beautiful, and the song transports me back to my childhood and the Sunday choral concerts at St. Catherine's. I look for a gold cross around her neck, some common ground, but her collar is adorned with turquoise beads that hold a mosaic amulet of a flower within a circle.

"Your voice is beautiful, and I love that song," I say.

"You know that song?"

"Every Christian knows that song."

"Why?"

"Because it's a song about the Bible."

And for the first time since I've met her, Isi smiles. It's only the slightest spread of her lips, but there's definite humor in the expression.

"It's not about the Bible," she says. "It's a Choctaw song."

Her large head shakes like I'm an imbecile, and she rises from her seat and stares at me.

It takes a second, but then I remember why I'm standing there. I count out twenty dollars from my tips. "Thank you."

She gives a slight nod, then raises her head to look past me. "One-oh-six today," she sings in her pretty voice.

I turn to see who she's talking to and Paul walks toward us, his crooked grin filling his face and part of my heart.

"See, Isi, I told you it would work out."

"You did," she chirps. "See you in the morning."

"So what do you think?" Paul asks. "Looking for work?"

Isi's voice trails after her. "...sometimes I'm up, and sometimes I'm down, coming for to carry me home..."

"She says that song's not about Elijah being taken to heaven."

"It's not. So what do you think—free room and board, built-in babysitting, and charming company while you work—namely me?"

"What's the song about then?"

"It's a slave song, written by a black man who went to live with the Choctaw after he escaped. He's singing about being sold as a young boy and missing his home and praying for his family to come and get him. It's incredibly sad."

"No, it's not. It's about the Bible."

Paul gives the same patronizing smile Isi gave me, and it riles me. "It even says, 'I looked over Jordan,'" I defend.

"The Choctaw live along the Red River in Oklahoma, but because he was talking to Jesus, he referred to it as Jordan."

The song plays forward in my mind: ...*but still my soul feels heavenly bound, coming for to carry me home...*

"It talks about going to heaven?"

Paul nods. "The man's struggling with whether he's a good man because of the bad things he's done to survive and whether he'll be forgiven."

I crinkle my brow, wondering about the explanation.

"Isi's uncle taught it to us when we were kids. He learned it working on the railroad."

"Somebody should tell the pope," I say, surprised how easily I accept an explanation different from the one I learned in Christian summer camp.

He smiles. "I don't think he'd listen. So what do you say? Want a job?"

I think of my dwindling funds and do the math. If the restaurant consistently does 106 covers, my pay, if I work a whole shift, would be eighty-six dollars. My prospects for employment, considering I'm a fugitive on the run from the law with two kidnapped kids, no social security number, and no references, are fairly limited.

"What are the terms?"

"Shift is from seven to four. You get room and board, child care, and there's no taxes. We're not real big on government around here."

I'm not real big on government right now, either, I think. *Eighty-six dollars for nine hours of work.* At Harris I made more than that in half an hour.

Addie bursts through the door like a marathon runner through the ribbon. "Drew caught a snake," she says.

Drew lopes in behind her holding a cardboard lettuce box. I peel back the lid to see a green garden snake slithering among a bed of romaine and cabbage. Both kids are red cheeked and dirty and the happiest I've ever seen them.

I look up at Paul. "You've got yourself a deal."

44

I walk to the backyard to see the kids, and my face catches in a mirror advertising Budweiser and I laugh. Saturday morning I woke up a highfalutin architect, orchestrating groundbreaking projects and negotiating multimillion-dollar deals. Now it's Wednesday, and I'm a fugitive from the law on the run with my two children, working as a waitress at a bootlegging backwoods grill and living in a room behind the kitchen.

Feeling rich with my newly earned tips, I offer to take the kids into town for a treat.

We march down the wide street that leads to the heart of the little town of Elmer City, small brick houses and spiraling pines watching us. In one window, a woman passes behind lace curtains followed by a boy a few years older than Drew. I imagine them moving to crowd around a coffee table surrounded by a husband and perhaps other children for a game of Scrabble or a late-night movie and popcorn.

There are cars in driveways and living rooms blue with television light. I smell a cigar, and it reminds me of my dad, and my chest tightens.

He doesn't know where I am. I never even said good-bye. I wonder if my mom will tell him the truth or spare him and make it better than it is.

In another window, a glass chandelier hangs above a dining room table that holds a bouquet of sunflowers in the center.

I'll never have that again—a house, a new car, furniture, a vase filled with sunflowers on a dining room table. Above the door, a sign reads, "Welcome—The Brown Family." Never again will I have my name. I can't fill out an application without lying. I'll never again be an architect or hold a job of any standing. Everything I've worked for and struggled for is gone.

And why? I was a good wife. I fought to make it work, overlooked Gordon's indiscretions, concealed his insanity, endured his abuse. And this is what I get?

As we walk, the satisfaction I felt from my new job, from protecting Addie and Drew for another day, transforms into despairing self-pity muddled with homicidal anger so strong that I'm certain if Gordon were in front of me and I had a gun, I would kill him.

He's robbed me of my name, my identity, my accomplishments, my family—and he's robbed Addie and Drew of their futures. How will they go to school, go to college?

I loved him, trusted him, believed him when he told me we wanted the same things. The first days of our marriage were the happiest of my life.

That was nine years ago.

The bell jingles as we walk into the general store and I paint on a smile. The kids run to the candy counter. Fred crouches in the bread aisle restocking the loaves.

"Evening," he says warmly. "You staying in town?"

"Goat hired me to work at the restaurant."

"God has a strange way of working," he says. "Shani had her baby last week, leaving Goat shorthanded, and along you come to take her place."

I want to believe there's some divine plan in everything that's happened, but I'm having a hard time keeping the faith.

"Looking for something in particular?" he asks.

"Do you have any books?"

He leads me to the back of the store. In the corner, beside the charcoal and the lighter fluid, is a crooked stand with a handful of cheap romances and two murder mysteries at least a year old. I sigh through my nose so Fred won't know my disappointment and remind myself to be grateful. This is my new life.

"You like to read?" Fred asks.

"It's the best way to know we are not alone."

His head tilts, and his grin frowns.

"C. S. Lewis said that."

"I thought Lewis's first name was Meriwether."

"It was," I say, switching gears from *Narnia* to Lewis and Clark and giving up on literary chatter.

This is my new life, devoid of literary reference and worldliness and intellectual discussion and debate. Devoid of any hope for it to be more than it is—no identity, no future, no house, no furniture, no pretty chandelier.

At the counter, Addie and Drew argue about whether to each buy their own treat or whether they should share two treats. I told them two pieces were all we were buying.

I browse the slim selection of novels.

Glass shatters, and my heart fires in my chest as my eyes dart around like a mad woman's until I realize it was only a jar of jelly.

Gordon's not here, I remind myself. *He doesn't know we're here.*

We're safe. I repeat the words over and over until my heart stops pounding.

A woman enters the store. She wears a denim skirt that barely conceals her panties, a purple tube top, and a pair of heels two sizes too large.

"Evening, Clem," Fred says.

She smiles a lipstick grimace around teeth that lilt to the left, buys a pack of cigarettes, and leaves.

Through the storefront, I watch the girl smoke and smile at a lone car that drives down the street. From this distance, she looks vaguely like Claudia.

If I had two calls I could make, the first would be to my dad to try to explain, the second would be to the woman who thinks she's in love with my husband and is about to make the biggest mistake of her life. I'd warn her, though I know she wouldn't listen.

Women are stupid when it comes to love. We want to believe the fairy tale, though every episode of *Oprah*, *Dr. Phil*, and *The Simpsons* disproves it.

I was warned, but I didn't listen. All the warning did was make me hate the person who delivered it and love Gordon more.

A month before I married Gordon, I met Gordon's dad. It was the first and only time I would meet him.

He was dying, and he told me not to marry his son.

Too many cigarettes and too hard a life had put him in the hospital at the age of fifty-eight. Gordon and his dad hadn't seen each other since Gordon had joined the Marines ten years earlier.

They looked alike, though Gordon was young and strong and his father was decrepit and dying.

The scene was surprisingly tender. Gordon hugged his father, who didn't have the strength to hug him back, and when he pulled away, both men's eyes were wet. Gordon introduced me as his fiancée, and his father nodded but offered nothing else—not approval or disapproval or congratulations or good wishes. Beyond the introduction, the men didn't talk, and I remember liking that, thinking words would have trivialized the moment. An hour later, I found out the truth.

Gordon left to speak with the doctor, and I remained in the room.

"Don't," Gordon's dad rasped, startling me from my day-dreams.

"Don't what?" I scooted my chair closer.

His parched lips parted less than a shadow. "Don't marry him."

The effort caused a convulsion of coughing and phlegm that made me want to leap back, while his betrayal made me want to attack.

Had he not been dying, nothing would have stopped me from wanting to kill him for his treachery against his son, but his eyes were closed and he didn't appear to be breathing, so instead, I took his hand and did what as a Catholic I'd been taught to do. "I forgive you," I said.

His hand gripped mine with more force than I thought was possible, and I tried to snatch it back, but he held tight, and his eyes bulged. "He's not who you think he is," he rasped. Then his hand released, and I ran from the room and away from the coughing and the sickness.

Hours later, as I waited in the lobby for Gordon to sign away his father's body, my anger was overcome with a profound sadness. Had Gordon met my mom under the same circum-stances—with limited tomorrows and no belief in heaven or hell—it's possible she'd have said the same thing about me, that she'd have told Gordon he was making a mistake.

The debate at the candy counter has escalated to shouting, and I move toward it, but Fred gets there first.

"Guess what, kids?" he says. "There's a special today. Two candies for the price of one, so you can each pick two."

I roll my eyes at him and mouth the words "thank you," as the kids grab the two pieces they each wanted.

He offers a sweet smile. He has a nice face, not especially handsome, but still young and touched with hope.

I may not have a name, an identity, a future, a glass chandelier, or a bouquet of sunflowers, but in the last twenty-four hours, I've been introduced to some of the kindest people I've ever met.

I pay for the candy and for a book titled *Witness Seduction*, and I wonder how long it will be until I go insane, desperate for a conversation of substance, a colloquy about something other than the weather, tomorrow's menu, or where the best place is to fish.

We walk back toward the Flying Goat, and I want to scream at the people behind the pretty brick houses, to warn them. *It can all be taken from you. Everything you think is yours, everything you think you're entitled to because you earned it, worked for it, all of it can be destroyed. Look carefully at the person you think you love, be wary of your husband or your wife, because, if they choose, they can destroy you.*

My crime was loving Gordon and trusting in the love he vowed back.

I wish life had an undo, that I could turn back time, and this time do it differently, this time listen to the warning. Addie offers me an orange JuJu Fruit from her box because she knows the orange ones are my favorite, and she smiles Gordon's smile, and my heart fills with regret over my thoughts. I just wished she didn't exist.

Addie's choice of JuJu Fruits also makes me want to cry. I wonder if she remembers it was Nana who loved them with her first.

We walk home to the serenade of crickets and mosquitoes, the night song of the forest.

On the bridge that crosses the river and leads to the restaurant, Paul leans against the rail with a beer balanced beside him and a fishing pole held lazily over the edge.

I stop, and the kids run down the bank to try to find the frogs who are croaking in the muddy grass below.

"Evening," I say.

He toasts me with his Coors, then lifts his line and drops it in a different spot, letting it sink a little farther.

"Fishing for something in particular?" I ask.

"Actually, nothing at all. That way, if I catch something, it's a bonus."

I smile at his lack of expectation.

I wish I could be as content. I stare at his veined forearms with their arbitrary etchings—a rose, a snake, a skull. I could never have a tattoo—the decision is too permanent: What if trends changed or simply my taste? To ink something indelible on my skin, I'd have to be absolutely sure I wanted the image forever, and I could never be that certain of anything. Yet Paul doodled on his body without a second thought, with a capriciousness that matches his lack of expectation.

I envy him.

"Mommy, look, the bugs glow."

Addie points to the lightning bugs flashing in the blackness beside the trees.

"Fireflies," I say. "Papa used to tell me that they fly to heaven, touch a star, and fly back to earth bringing the star's fire with them."

Addie and Drew both look at the sparkling heavens, and all of us think of Papa. I wonder how long it will be before they forget him, until he's reduced to a legend in the stories I tell.

I glance again at the riddled ink on Paul's arms and think perhaps my tattoos are simply less obvious, that I'm as marked as he is by my young, impulsive choices—a rushed romance followed by quick nuptials. I was thirty-one and ready for the next stage of my life to begin, afraid if I waited or hesitated, Gordon would choose someone else.

Three months later I was pregnant. My choices don't brand my skin, but instead, scar my life.

"Okay?" Paul asks beside me.

"Just something in my eye."

With the heels of my hands, I press on my sockets. I can't erase the mistakes I've made, but if I press hard enough, maybe for a moment, I can forget them. And as my eyes blur, the past shifts to the present, and I begin to imagine the mistakes I'm making now or that I'm going to make that will doom us in the future—a fingerprint taken for a library card, a broken taillight that causes a ticket, a tourist at the Flying Goat who recognizes me.

I can't change my past, and I can't outrun it. Gordon will never stop pursuing us, and we will always be hunted, nameless, scared. And as certain as I am of my love for my children, I'm certain he will find us.

"Want to give it a try?" Paul holds out the rod. I take it from him and drop it into the blackness below and let out the line.

I'm amazed we've made it this far. No money, no plan.

I feel a pull on the line, and excitement lifts the hair on my neck as I reel in whatever it is I've caught.

Paul smiles beside me.

The hook comes up empty, and I'm filled with disappointment. Too much expectation; whatever I thought I had is gone.

"Next time," Paul says.

And having faith in his words, I drop the line again, hoping this time I'll be lucky.

45

It's a warm day, the warmest it's been since we came to Elmer City over a month ago. I sit reading the paper on the front porch. I wear a pair of shorts I bought at the Salvation Army store in Omak, where I went to buy bathing suits and a few more clothes for me and the kids. Across the butt of the shorts are the letters "UCLA," which is why I bought them. Gordon's a fanatical USC fan. It's the first time I've worn shorts in six years, the first time the back of my legs and my thighs don't bear the marks of Gordon's abuse. If you look close, a faint yellow patch peeks from below the short line, but it's very light and only the memory of the pain reminds me what it is.

The unfriendly man with the long braid who sat next to me at lunch our first day at the Flying Goat walks toward me. His name is Boris, and he's the only lawman in Elmer City, a part-time sheriff who, when not dealing with the minor infractions of the small town, runs the post office. He's also a grandnephew of Goat and the brother of Isi. Every day he eats his breakfast and his lunch at the restaurant, and like his sister, he doesn't have much to say.

But today is different.

It's two hours after the restaurant closed. Paul and Drew are fishing, and Addie's in the kitchen helping Goat. Every afternoon, Addie spends hours with Goat prepping for the next day. Today's lunch, a tri tip sandwich with caramelized onions, was served with double fries and Addie's special sauce, a barbeque ketchup concoction she created that was delicious.

"Afternoon," Boris says, causing me to lift my head. Unlike his sister, Boris's voice is a deep baritone that ruminates from his thick body as though his vocal cords are in his stomach rather than his throat.

"Afternoon, Boris."

"Do you have a minute?" His wide, dark face is serious, and my stomach turns cold. Of the members in Goat's family, Boris is the only one I'm not fond of. His eyes follow me too long, and the taunts and insults he slings at his relatives, while similar to those of Paul and Goat, are delivered with too much veracity.

He sits beside me on the steps, removes his straw cowboy hat, and hangs it on his knee.

"Do you know the story of Goat?" he asks.

I shake my head and set down my paper. Over the past month, I've learned that Goat and her family take the long way around to get to a point.

"Goat is the last Chelan who still speaks Salish fluently, and although she's not our chief, because we do not have women chiefs, she's the most significant elder in our tribe."

Through the battered screen door, I glance at the tribe's proclaimed potentate as she stoops over a bucket, peeling potatoes for tomorrow's breakfast. This is the other thing about Boris I do not like. Unlike Goat and Paul, Boris feels obligated to display his Chelan heritage like a badge of honor, a purple heart.

He boasts ad nauseam about it, as though it's an open wound we all need to apologize for.

His long, black braid, which looks ridiculous on his middle-aged face, and his clothes—cheap suede and leather jackets with orange and cream beads stitched at the cuffs and collar—scream, "Look at me, I'm Native American and proud of it." Today he wears an imitation suede shirt bedazzled with zigzags on the cuffs and collar.

His eyes roam over my legs, and I pull them closer.

"When Goat was a young girl," he begins, "a cattleman driving his herd north found a nugget of gold in the river. It was the time of the Great Depression, and when rumor spread of his discovery, thousands of desperate people came here to find their fortune." His laugh is deep and mean. "What most of them found was what the Chelan have found for two hundred years, barren land and bitter disappointment.

"What they brought with them were diseases and mouths to feed. Many Chelan, fearing starvation and sickness, left. And those that stayed did whatever it took to survive. Goat was thirteen when the rush first happened. Her two older brothers joined the railroad, and a few months later, typhoid took her parents, leaving Goat and her two younger sisters alone and starving. So Goat did what she had to to protect her sisters; she went to live among the men."

My eyes grow wide, and I swallow hard. I can't imagine the hunched woman peeling potatoes as a desperate girl of thirteen prostituting herself in a camp of miners.

A small light flickers in Boris's eyes as he enjoys my astonishment. "Goat moved from site to site and came to be appreciated, not only for her body, but for her knowledge of the river and her ability to cook.

"The rush never amounted to much gold, and after a few years, the wagons and the men and the campsites moved on, and the only things they left behind were a couple dozen half-breeds, this house, and the small town of Elmer City."

He almost spits the word "half-breed," and my hair prickles in defense of Paul.

"Goat was living in this house with a man and his wife when it ended. The woman was the one who taught her to cook white man food. Nobody knows what happened to them, except one day they were gone and Goat wasn't."

"She killed them?"

Boris shrugs. "No one's ever asked, and Goat's never said. She just kept on doing what she'd been doing, cooking and cleaning. Only now, she sold the food and used the money to raise her sisters and to help anyone else in the tribe who fell on hard times."

"So the house isn't hers?"

Boris shrugs again. "It's hers as far as anyone around here's concerned."

"But who owns it?"

"Not registered far as I know. No record anywhere about the house, the restaurant, or Goat. No taxes, no health inspector, nobody asking questions about where the people who built it went. Been that way for seventy years." His eyebrows rise, and my hair prickles. "Can you imagine what would happen if that changed, Jillian?"

At the mention of my birth name, ice fills my stomach and my mouth opens to speak, but I can't figure out what to say.

He removes a folded sheet of paper from his breast pocket and extends it toward me.

I open it and stare.

I no longer look like the woman in the picture on the page.

It isn't just the hair. The woman in the photo looks like a mannequin modeling for the professional woman's department at Nordstrom or Bloomingdale's—glossy hair draped to her shoulders, airbrushed skin with a thick layer of well-applied makeup, and a fixed smile. The collared silk shirt she wears was bought from Anne Fontaine on Rodeo Drive. The sleeves hide bruises, the frozen expression hides everything else.

The woman sitting on the porch staring at the picture of herself is a barefoot waitress, a hardworking single mom wearing a cotton tank that flaunts tan, unbruised arms, and shorts she bought at the thrift store for two dollars.

No one would recognize me. I don't even recognize myself. If I pass a mirror or a storefront, my reflection still jolts me with a split-second reaction of *Who the heck is that?*

And the photo of Drew could be any boy of eight with light brown hair. He's still wearing his hair buzzed, and there's nothing else in the photo that defines him.

The problem is that Addie looks exactly like Addie, her carrot top curls swirling around her smiling freckled face. And she's one of a kind.

The title reads, "KIDNAPPING, Information Wanted."

My hand shakes as I read our descriptions and last known location. It describes us driving in a white Chevy Corsica and the license plate number. It knows we were in Biggs Junction a month ago and that we traveled east. The date on the header is from a day ago.

"You're turning us in?" I ask.

His mouth gets thin, and he looks past his knees to the worn floorboards and the busy ants scurrying between the cracks.

"I'm not the only one who's going to figure this out," he says. "This bulletin went to every jurisdiction in Washington. And what I don't want is the attention that's going to come when you're discovered, outsiders asking questions. That's not good for the restaurant, Goat, or Paul."

"Paul?"

"Let's just say it's best if Paul and the authorities avoid each other for a while."

I swallow hard and shake my head.

Boris puts his hand on my knee. It's fleshy and damp. I want to remove it, but I don't dare.

"I know that's not what you want, either," he says.

Through the screen door, Goat rinses the peeled potatoes in an ice bath.

"I'm sorry," I say, the words strangled with emotion.

Boris pats my thigh and stands. "I'm not looking for an apology," he says. "I'm looking for you to leave."

46

A summer sunset in Washington is a remarkable sight, a spectacular light show that fills the world and reduces everything beneath it. It's the kind of sunset that stills the soul, makes the wind pause, and causes time to slow. The prismatic, neon display is as brilliant as Fourth of July fireworks and is accompanied by the song of geese and fowl settling down for the day, and river frogs and crickets waking for the night.

Paul sits on the steps, one leg propped on the porch, his Coors resting on his knee. Isi sways on the porch swing, her body filling both seats and her weight creating a rhythmic creak. Goat snoozes on the rattan bench, her snores keeping time with the swing.

The stack of Uno cards are centered between Paul, me, Addie, and Drew, each of us holding our hand close. This has become our routine, a few moments to wind down before we head off to our beds. Each night, we play cards or Yahtzee, talk about the day, the customers, the fishing, plot out what bait or fishing hole the boys are going to try next.

Tonight I'm unusually quiet, my conversation with Boris making the night heavy.

"Everything all right?" Paul asks when the kids have gone into the house to get ready for bed.

I turn so my feet are on the step below me, resting my elbows on my knees and my forehead on my steepled fingers. "I need a favor," I say.

"Shoot."

"Tomorrow we need to leave, and I'm hoping you can help us."

Paul stills to such quietness even his breath seems to stop.

I continue, "We need to drive across the border, and we can't drive my car. Sissy gave me a passport that might pass for me and one for Jon Jon that looks enough like Drew. If you drive, and we hide Addie, we might make it."

I thought all this out in the hours between Boris leaving and our nightly games beginning. They're looking for a woman in a white car with two kids. I'm hoping since Paul's the real thing, they won't look too closely at who else is in the car.

My heart pounds with the thought of everything that can go wrong—Paul in trouble, the kids returned to Gordon, me arrested at the border—but I can't fathom another solution no matter how many times I turn it in my head.

We can't stay one more day. If something happens to Goat or Paul or Sissy or Isi because of me, I couldn't forgive myself. I want to do it without Paul, but I can't see how.

I've saved almost every penny I've made in the last month. It's amazing how frugal I've become. Me, a woman who used to spend a hundred dollars to trim her hair when it had barely grown an inch, now clips coupons to buy toilet paper and only shops on double coupon days.

The kids have become fellow Spartans. Drew catches his own worms for bait so he doesn't have to spend the meager dollar allowance I give him each week, and Addie's saving her money to buy a bike. She's had three lemonade stands outside Fred's store. The sign hung on the table reads, "Little Fish Lemonaid, 50¢." Fred helped her make the poster, and I didn't have the heart to point out the misspelling; seems most of the customers don't notice anyway.

The money I've saved combined with the money from my parents and the sale of my ring is enough for a fresh start. And with Sissy's passport, I can get a new identity, a job, and eventually apply for citizenship. The kids can go to school.

Paul looks at me hard, and not for the first time, I wonder about the crude tattoos and the limp. A dozen years ago, I worked on a prison expansion, and as part of the research for the project, we toured the grounds. The tattoos of the inmates were similar to Paul's and so was the hardness in the faces of the men.

"Where's this coming from? This morning you were fine."

"It doesn't matter."

"Boris?"

"What difference does it make?"

"It makes a difference because we decided you and the kids should stay."

My head snaps up. "We?"

He nods.

"You know?" I feel so betrayed and humiliated and angry and stupid all at the same time that I'm not sure how to react. These people are brilliant liars. I consider myself an expert in the art of deceit, and I've been fooled by them completely. "And Goat? And Isi? And Sissy? They all know?"

He says nothing.

"And you discussed it and discussed me and discussed my future and you didn't think to include me in the conversation?" Indignation has trumped all the other emotions.

"We needed to decide what to do."

"About my life?"

"About our lives."

Like a slap, the reminder of the jeopardy I've put everyone in deflates my anger, reducing it to guilt, gratitude, and regret. I lay my head on my knees to try to process the fact that for a month I've endangered everyone around me and that they've known it, but I didn't.

"Ntamqe..." he says softly.

I raise my head. "My name's not Ntamqe. What the hell does Ntamqe mean anyway?"

He turns so he's beside me, our shoulders touching. "Ntamqe is bear."

I slide my eyes toward him. "As in the big, dumb, hairy mammal?"

He shakes his head. "You're so white. You take everything so literally."

"And you're so damn red. Why don't you just say what you mean?"

"Because most things aren't that simple."

So you make them more complicated by saying everything in circles and riddles? I think, but I keep the thought to myself. Like a duck trying to be a swan, I'll never understand the complexities of the Chalen.

"Ntamqe isn't about the animal, but about the spirit. The bear is a powerful guardian who is peaceful unless provoked. Threaten her children and she unleashes a fury of courage and strength. Ntamqe means spirit of the mother."

And I'm struck speechless. This man who's known me only a month—this strange man, half Indian, half white, who stumbled into our lives—this wonderful man sees me as the mother I've always wanted to be.

"Thank you."

"For the name?"

I shake my head, but answer, "Yes, for the name."

"So I can still use it?"

I nudge my shoulder into his in a friendly gesture. "Yes. You can still use it until tomorrow when we leave."

He shakes his head, and my mouth opens to explain, but a hand on my head stops my words.

I crane my neck to see Goat standing over me. Her leather fingers rest on my hair. I'd forgotten she was still on the porch, asleep on the rattan bench. "Tomorrow's not the time," she says. "You'll leave after you have the baby."

Paul rears back at the same time I do, putting a two-foot gap between us. We both wear identical expressions of shock and bewilderment, his at the news, mine at the fact that Goat was able to tell. For the past week, my jeans have been too tight, but I refused to acknowledge what I knew, blamed it instead on Goat's cooking. I want to ask how she could possibly know when I wasn't even certain myself, but she's already shuffling away from me, heading into the house for the night. She mumbles something in Salish just before she gets there, and Paul answers back.

"What did she say?"

"She says Boris is an idiot."

I raise my eyebrows.

"Actually what she said was worse than that, but that's the general gist."

"He's just worried."

"If he'd stop worrying and running around like a *likok*, everything will be fine."

I wish I could share Paul's optimism, but Paul doesn't know Gordon. If it were only the law after me, I might agree that the Flying Goat is safe, but Gordon's smarter and more tenacious than any policeman or detective or agency, and he will do anything within the law or outside of it to find us.

"You're pregnant?" Paul asks, interrupting my fear.

"I think I might be," I say more to my hands wringing in my lap than to him.

"Wow, and I thought my life was complicated."

And that's when I start to cry. It's too much. The multiple revelations of the day overwhelm me—a statewide manhunt is in hot pursuit; each day I'm here, I endanger Goat and Paul and the family; and I'm pregnant with Jeffrey's baby. It's too much.

My sobs come in great gasps, and Paul's arm is around me, and I'm mortified with myself and sorry for Paul trapped beside me with my incoherent blubbering.

Finally when I get a breath, I wail, "I can't do it. I can't have this baby. I can't. How can I?"

"Shhh," he says, and kisses the top of my head and rubs my shoulder. "You'll figure it out. It'll all be okay, you'll see."

"How? How can this possibly be okay? I can't even take care of the two kids I have."

"Little Fish and Hawk are fine."

"Fine? They don't have a father, they don't go to school, they don't even have a last name. What kind of a future do they have?" Then I bite my lip, and my forehead crashes to my lap in another blazing blast of regret. Paul's father left when he was a baby, and he dropped out of school when he was younger than Drew. "I'm sorry."

He shrugs. "Once you become a man, your future is not the fault of your childhood."

I turn my head on my lap to look at him. He smiles peacefully without an ounce of pain. Perhaps it's the Chalen in him, but in a dozen lifetimes, I won't understand the world as well as he does.

I'm a decade older, and yet I still blame so much of my life on my past. My dad's been my champion, my crutch—and for the past year, the reason I chained myself to my marriage. My whole life I've isolated myself from my mom, pretending I'm better than I am because of pride and vanity. I blame my childhood and my parents, not entirely, but in part, for the state of my life. But Paul's right; at some point it's time to grow up. Do I want my kids to be tethered to me for eternity, to use me or this moment as an excuse for their mistakes even when they're my age?

But I also don't want to be deserving of their blame. "I can't have this baby," I repeat.

Paul nods, and for a long while, the running water of the river and the wind are the only sounds.

"How far along are you?"

It feels like a year since Jeffrey and I made love, so much has happened, but it's only been slightly more than a month. "Not too far."

"Then tomorrow you'll see a friend of mine."

"I don't have insurance. I don't even have a license."

"This man won't ask for that."

I try to see Paul's face, but the night hides his expression.

"Good night, Ntamqe," Paul says as he stands. "Sleep well."

47

I'm parked in my fugitive car in front of a clapboard building with worn yellow paint, a river rock chimney, and no sign. It's on a road that leads out of Elmer City and toward the back country of the reservation where there are a few homes, a dump, and an old iron mine.

I sit in my car as the minutes tick toward my appointment, then past it. Paul asked if I wanted him to come along, and I shook my head. I'll call him when I'm done, and he'll come with Sissy to drive me and my car home.

My jeans are tight, the waistband digging into my thickened stomach. I finger the small gold cross given to me by my dad at my first communion and that I've not taken off since.

All day I've done nothing but cry and hide from Addie and Drew so they wouldn't see me crying.

I can't do this. I can't have this baby. It's not fair to Addie and Drew, the two kids I already have and who I already can't take care of. How will I manage with a newborn?

I can't do this.

I repeat my reasoning as the sun falls in front of me.

A man, perhaps fifty, tall, with long legs and a short waist, steps into the doorway and looks at me through my windshield. He wears a white coat, probably the doctor. Paul explained the man's license was revoked years ago because he was a drunk and killed a woman on the operating table while he was wasted. He stopped drinking, and as repentance, has practiced backwoods medicine ever since—cash accepted, no questions asked.

Jeffrey and Gordon spin in my mind. I feel Jeffrey making love to me and Gordon choking me. I see Jeffrey dead in the gymnasium and Gordon finding us.

I'm the only car in the parking lot. The doctor looks at the glare of my windshield and tilts his head in query, waiting for me to make my decision.

I start the engine and turn the car around. As I drive back to the Flying Goat, I unbutton my jeans, relieving the pressure.

"I'm sorry," I say aloud, smoothing the shirt over the bulge of my abdomen, the guilt so heavy I'm certain the child inside me feels it.

This baby may destroy us and bringing it into the world when I can't protect it isn't right, but if Gordon catches us, which I think he will, this baby may be my only chance to survive.

48

It's been two weeks since my decision and morning sickness has set in with the bad weather, and we're all miserable. Addie hasn't been feeling well for a few days, and Drew's going crazy being cooped up inside with the rain.

We need supplies. I need children's Motrin for Addie, prenatal vitamins for myself, and Drew needs new shoes—supplies that can't be found at Fred's general store.

It's Sunday, and except for us, the Flying Goat is empty. On the days the restaurant is closed, Goat returns to her family's house on the reservation where her two sisters live and Paul goes into Spokane where he has several girls he sees.

I'd like to leave Addie home since she's not feeling well, but there's no one to leave her with, so I lay her in the backseat and put a blanket over her and I allow Drew to ride in the front with me.

Omak is the nearest town, and it's an hour's drive from Elmer City. It's not a big town, but it does have a few fast-food restaurants, a gas station, and a few large stores.

We fill the car with gas, lunch at McDonald's, then drive

to Walmart. I carry Addie into the store, her head resting on my shoulder, her thumb in her mouth. Drew pushes the wagon. We shop quickly and are in line to check out when I notice two young men behind the customer service counter looking at us. One holds a sheet of paper and they both look down at it, look at us, then repeat the sequence. The one not holding the paper lifts a telephone to his ear. I forget about the supplies being rung up and grab Drew by the wrist. I run directly toward the counter and grab the paper from the other boy's hand. "REWARD." There's a photo of each of us and below is Gordon's cell number. The prize is $50,000.

I'm out of reach of the boy with the phone. He's backed up against the items that need to be restocked and is saying the words "Walmart in Omak."

I sprint for the door, Addie bouncing in my arms, Drew on my heels. We skid from the parking lot, and when we reach the junction for the highway, I turn away from the Flying Goat.

"Mommy, I don't feel good," Addie says.

"Hang in there, baby."

But she can't. The stench of vomit fills the car. I put my shirt to my mouth to prevent my own retching and pull behind an abandoned jerky stand. Using napkins from our McDonald's lunch, I do my best to clean up the mess.

Addie's skin is burning up.

Sirens race past us heading in the direction we just came. I sink to the gravel, holding my sick daughter, and pray.

It takes two hours to drive back to Elmer City going the long way, and it's almost eight by the time we reach the house.

I carry Addie to our room, grind up an Advil, and stir it into some milk. She only drinks a mouthful. I lay her on my bed, make Drew a sandwich, then return to lie down beside her. Light from the porch lamp filters through the dusty window, and I watch Addie's eyes flutter behind her thin, closed lids. Her pink lips are open, and she takes quick, shallow breaths. Rain begins to pour, and the old house creaks.

I bury my face into my pillow so I won't wake her with my sobs.

My mind imagines Gordon racing like a NASCAR driver on meth to get to Omak, clenching his teeth and the steering wheel. Then those same tight hands wrap around my neck.

Gordon's out there—so close I can feel him.

Drew stumbles into the room and climbs onto the futon beside the bed. "Mom?"

"I'm here."

"Okay. Good night."

"Good night, sweet boy."

His frightened tears are quiet, silenced by his young boy pride and muddled with the rain until they blend into a single sound.

The crack of thunder startles me, and I sit up, my heart pounding.

Lightning flashes, and through the rain-streaked window, a shadow moves along the side of the house.

I creep through the room, stumbling on the futon and stubbing my toe on the doorjamb. In the kitchen, I pull a *Fatal Attraction* knife from the cutlery block, crouch behind the hostess desk, and stare at the front door.

Nothing but dark, rainy silence.

The thunder rumbles, a distant drumroll, and the porch light flickers.

The door pounds, and my heart pounds with it. I consider yelling for Drew to wake up, shouting for him to grab his sister and run out the back door.

Then there's another flash, and the silhouette behind the door is revealed. The shadow is short and thin with a wide brim hat, and my heart relaxes. I set down the knife, walk to the door, and unlock the deadbolt.

"Hi, Fred, come on in."

Fred holds a soaked brown bag and drips from head to toe.

He wipes his feet on the doormat, hangs his raincoat and hat on the hook beside the door, and follows me inside.

"Thought you might be needing some supplies," he says, holding out the bag. "Storm's getting worse, and power's gonna be spotty tonight."

I peer inside the bag to see two flashlights and a dozen candles.

Fred's dressed as he always is in a short-sleeve dress shirt and tan Docker pants.

Small-town hospitality, each day it amazes me—kind words, kind thoughts, simple respect and compassion. "Thank you."

"You okay?"

It's then I realize I've started to cry.

His hug after the first minute is awkward, and I pull away. "Would you like some coffee?"

He nods, and I turn on the coffee machine.

Fred's easy to talk to. He was raised in Spokane by a minister and a seamstress and still has a sister and brother who live there. As the coffee brews, he talks a little about his childhood and the wife that left him. "'Slow is one thing,' she told me, 'dead's another.' Last year, she married a plumber and moved to the valley."

He keeps the conversation on himself and doesn't ask questions about me or the kids, and I wonder if he, too, already knows the truth.

I pour the coffee, and Fred searches the cabinets until he finds a bottle of whiskey and holds it up in invitation.

I nod, and he pours a dash into each of our mugs.

The coffee, alcohol, and company soothe my ragged nerves, and I begin to relax.

The conversation turns to Paul.

"Used to steal from me," Fred says with a smile. "When I first opened my store, every day he'd come in, say hello, cheerful as can be, then he'd lift a six-pack of beer, a bottle of vodka, or a bag of chips. Wasn't a bad kid, just dealt a tough hand. Got sent away for a knife fight when he was nineteen, then again for destroying public property when he was twenty-two. Came out the second time with the tattoos, the limp, and only half the attitude that got him sent to prison in the first place. Goat took him in, and he's been doing real good since."

After another cup of coffee and a little more whiskey, my eyes get so heavy they begin to close. Fred stands and carries our mugs to the sink. I walk beside him to put the whiskey back in the cupboard, then grab a dish towel to dry the cups so they can be put away. Fred holds the last one between us a second too long, and his body leans in, barely crossing the invisible line where friendship ends, and like a cat's whiskers, I feel it immediately and move the few inches it takes to make us nothing but friends again.

In the past month, there have been a few customers who have flirted, but I'm immune to that kind of attention. Something deep inside me is broken, a switch turned off, and I don't know if I'm permanently ruined as Goat seems to be, but I'm certainly not ready to care for a man again.

The pregnancy, his seemingly sincere, incessant apologies, his pleas for forgiveness, and his promises to never hurt me again convinced me to return. And all through my term and for a short while after, he kept his word.

I stretch my legs to the corners of the small bed. It's always these rare moments of quiet that are hardest. Alone with my thoughts, the past haunts me.

There's so much about my life I miss—my dad, my mom, Jeffrey. I long for oysters and crab cakes, a dramatic literary novel by Anne Tyler or a dark thriller by Stephen King. I miss my Krups coffeemaker and the special blend of almond-roasted coffee I ordered from San Francisco. I think about my mom's rosebushes and the lemon tree my dad and I planted in my backyard when Gordon and I bought our house. It never gave me a single lemon, but it provided my dad and me lots of laughs.

Drew and Addie are thriving, but a part of me is shriveling.

Two days ago, Addie spotted a "big deewr," and she raced to get me so I could see it. I set down the newspaper, and hand in hand, we walked to the backyard where she had seen it. I didn't shush her because I was on the phone, or say "just a minute" because I needed to return a dozen e-mails that had popped into my box in the previous ten seconds. I didn't say I couldn't because there was laundry or dishes or because I was just too tired. I simply went with her when she asked, and I was glad I did. The big deer she spotted was actually a moose, its giant fuzzy antlers so large that I wondered how he balanced them on his head. It stood, legs spread wide, pulling radishes from Goat's garden.

That is until Goat hobbled from the back door with a mop in her hand and, screaming Salish, chased it away. It galloped off, and Addie and I laughed and laughed until our stomachs hurt.

When I told Paul the story, I said the antlers were so large they reminded me of a *Beach Blanket Babylon* hat and he stared at me blankly, and again, I was reminded of how much I've left behind.

I'll never again own a Kate Spade purse or a Noguchi end table. I miss my shoes and my clothes, the artwork Gordon and I shopped for together, then debated over where it should hang.

When I'm working, the restaurant filled with people and chatter, I forget about what I've lost, but in moments of stillness, it floods me with such grief that it takes over every part of me.

The ceiling above me has water spots, and with the nausea, the stains spin into shapes—the one that before I thought looked like a rabbit today looks like a gun. I stop the spiraling thoughts before they lead me back to Compton.

Drew slams into the room. "Mom, Addie threw up."

I'm exhausted, and it feels like my body weighs three hundred pounds, but I drag myself from my bed.

Addie lies on the small daybed in Paul's room. Her thumb is in her mouth, and she holds a Barbie with no clothes in her other hand. Vomit drips down her cheek and the front of the mattress, pooling on the floor. I cover my mouth and nose with my shirt to keep from retching, but the stench is overwhelming, and I lunge for the bathroom down the hall, barely making it to the toilet in time to throw up myself.

When I return less than a minute later, Addie's crying and so is Drew. Between yesterday's narrow escape and today's events, they know we are doomed, that I'm not equipped to save them.

"It's okay, baby," I say as I bundle Addie into my arms and carry her downstairs to our bathroom and start the tub. Her skin burns through her shirt and shorts.

I stare at the rain running down the window like clear veins. Lightning flashes and thunder claps and I jump, half expecting to see Gordon filling the frame. At every sudden sound, I'm certain he's found us. Like a dinosaur stuck in a bog of mud, I await my certain fate, only unsure of its impending form—a drowning flash flood, starvation, or a merciful strike of lightning.

The baby inside me is like a ticking time bomb. My hand moves to my swollen belly, and the warmth beneath my shirt shifts my grief imperceptibly to tenderness. I look at Addie, her smooth, white skin surrounded by warm water and bubbles. *This is your big sister*, I tell the baby.

From beyond the door of the bathroom, the door to our room opens, and I freeze, turn off the spigot, and strain my ears toward the intrusion.

"Hi, Paul," Drew says, and I relax.

"Hey, Hawk, your mom here?"

"In there; Addie's sick."

"Yeah, I saw that in my room."

He steps into the bathroom. His hair is mussed, his chin unshaven. He looks like he always does when he returns from the city, like he didn't waste a moment of it on sleep. His jeans sit so low on his hips they look in danger of falling down, the elastic of his boxers sticking out above.

"Sorry about your room," I say. "I haven't had a chance to clean it."

"Is she okay?" He steps toward us and kneels beside the tub. Addie looks listlessly at him through half-open eyes. "Hey, Little Fish, how you doing?" His concern fills my heart.

Addie shakes her head.

Cackling Salish interrupts from behind us, and Paul stands to make room for Goat.

Goat bends over the tub, moves Addie's face by her chin so she can look in her eyes, touches her forehead with the back of her hand, then stands and barks something else at Paul in her native tongue.

She walks away, taking Drew by the hand as she goes.

I look at Paul. "Goat's going to give Drew some lunch. We need to get Addie dressed so we can take her to the doctor."

"The doctor who is your friend?"

Paul shakes his head. "We need to drive to Spokane. Addie's very sick. She needs to go to the hospital."

I bite my lip so I won't cry, so Addie won't see me fall apart. Paul looks like the emotions are getting the better of him as well. He turns away, wiping his nose on his sleeve as he reaches for a towel. We both know it's over. The jig is up.

"I'm going to get changed," he says. "I'll meet you out front."

I wrap the towel around Addie, dress her, then, from behind the bureau, pry off the envelope I taped there six weeks ago that holds my license and our insurance cards.

50

We drive faster than I thought Paul's antique truck could go and arrive at the emergency room in under an hour and a half.

The admitting nurse takes one look at Addie's limp form slumped over Paul's shoulder, and mercifully, without asking questions, directs us through the double doors and into a curtained room containing a bed surrounded by machines.

The doctor, a man slight as a jockey with a trim dark mustache and goatee, arrives within a minute. He ushers Paul and Drew from the room and directs me to stand in a corner. He uses a stethoscope to listen to Addie's heart and a light to look in her eyes. He rattles off Addie's vitals to a gray-haired nurse twice his size, and she records them onto a chart.

"How long's she been sick?" he asks as his fingers prod Addie's listless body.

"A couple weeks. I thought it was the flu and that she was getting better because it would come and go. But yesterday and today it got much worse."

The nurse says nothing and keeps writing, but I feel her condemnation. She wants to know why I waited so long to bring her to a doctor.

"Mommy." The voice is small and weak but powerful enough to stop time.

The entire room quiets, and everyone turns to the bed.

I move to Addie's side. "Hi, sweetie," I whisper, and kiss her damp forehead. "It's okay. Don't be scared. You're in the hospital where they can take good care of you and make you all better."

She nods, and her thumb goes into her mouth and her eyes flutter closed.

The doctor's hands linger on her stomach, above her pelvis. He focuses on the ceiling as he prods deeper on the left side.

"She needs an ultrasound and start an IV of fluids," he says to the nurse, and walks away.

The nurse follows him from the room and returns ten minutes later with a bag of liquid attached to a rolling stand. She inserts a needle in Addie's arm, and Addie barely moves, and I'm filled with horror at her lethargy.

"I need you to fill out these forms," the nurse says.

I sit on the edge of the bed and stare at the blanks.

"Would it be okay if I go to the restroom?"

"Down the hall and through the waiting room."

I stumble through the curtain and out the double doors. Paul stands, and Drew looks at me, and I mumble something about still not knowing anything and continue down the hall that leads to the restrooms and the exit out of the hospital.

I rub the swollen bulge of my stomach and clutch my purse, which holds the identity of my past, as well as Sissy's passport, which could be the identity of my future. I glance back at Drew.

The exit sign glows red, and the arrow points to the late afternoon.

I take another step toward it, then the sliding panes open and Goat walks through the door, followed by her sisters and Isi and Boris and Fred and Sissy and Sissy's three kids.

I abruptly change course, turn into the women's room, and lock myself in a stall.

51

I'm in the medical director's office, and the director sits across from me, his hands folded over his pressed white coat.

He says the word, but it doesn't register; there are too many circuits misfiring.

He says it again. "Tumor."

His lips pucker around the first syllable before settling into a grim line after the second.

There are other words that fly around that one: "cancer, surgery, nephrectomy, one kidney, long-term prognosis."

"She's four," I answer.

He nods. The office is cluttered with files and papers and computers and anatomical skeletons, and it's very warm. "The pediatric surgeon's driving in now. He should be here in about an hour. In the morning, when Addie wakes from the surgery, we'll transport her to the children's hospital by ambulance, and after a biopsy, we'll know more."

"You're doing the surgery tonight?"

"Mrs. Kane, I know this is a lot to process, but we don't know what we're dealing with, and every minute could be of the essence. We'll take out the tumor, then we'll know more."

I put my face in my hands, the heels of my palms pressed into my eye sockets.

"Is there someone we can call for you?" he asks. "Your husband perhaps?"

I shake my head. I'm sure he's already on his way.

I stumble from his office and back toward Addie's hospital room.

To get there, I need to go through the waiting room. A dozen people stand when I enter. Fred holds Drew's hand, and Drew breaks away and runs to my side. I hold him close as we pass by the Flying Goat crew. Goat touches my sleeve, and her sisters bow their heads. Paul steps in my path, and I fall into his arms.

He whispers a prayer into my ear; the words I don't understand, but the meaning seeps into my heart.

When I get to the room, Addie's sleeping, her shallow breaths keeping rhythm with the bleeping machines that surround her. I glare at her round tummy beneath the sheet and the malignancy beneath her skin. *The size of a grapefruit*, that's what the doctor said.

How could I not have known? Why didn't I take her to the doctor sooner?

We sit for an hour, then a nurse comes to prep her for surgery.

I'm signing the last release form when I hear a commotion down the hall.

Drew shrinks back in his chair at the sound of his father's voice, and I leap to my feet. I recognize Paul's voice as the one Gordon's arguing with, and I run toward the waiting room.

"Who the fuck are you?" Gordon barks.

Through the square glass panes of the swinging doors, Paul blocks Gordon's advance. Paul's a head shorter and weighs a quarter less than what Gordon does, but his gaze is leveled on my husband's.

"I'm a friend," Paul says.

"You fucking my wife?"

Paul winces; Gordon looks crazed. He looks a decade older than he did six weeks ago. His face is unshaven and etched with lines that weren't there before. His shirt is wrinkled, his eyes bloodshot with lack of sleep, and his mouth is a thin slash pinched tight with rage.

Shoulders straighten and chests expand, then one by one, the other Elmer City citizens rise to their feet and move to stand behind Paul, creating a human gauntlet. Even Boris stands in defiance.

Gordon wears his windbreaker, the shoulders splattered with dark spots of rain. Beneath it is his Glock, so tight against his ribs it doesn't even make a bulge. He reaches for the zipper, and I burst through the doors.

Everyone turns as I push through the crowd to step between Paul and Gordon and to cower in front of my husband. "Addie's sick," I say. "They're taking her to surgery. You need to come now so you can see her before they put her to sleep."

I pretend not to notice his hands in fists at his side.

As Gordon walks beside me, Paul says something so quiet only Gordon can hear it, and Gordon's head snaps back to look at him. Paul doesn't flinch. Like two lions competing for a pride, the challenge has been declared, and if they meet again, only one will remain.

The nurse mercifully waited for me to return before she put the mask on Addie.

Gordon actually freezes at the sight of her in the bed, her skin pale as the sheets, her eyes drooping and sad.

"Hi, baby," he says as he walks to her, his voice breaking.

"Daddy?"

He nods and lifts her hand that doesn't have an IV in it to his lips, and even through all my fear, and all my hate, my heart feels for his love of his little girl.

I move to the other side of the bed where Drew stands back from the scene, and I put a protective arm around his shoulder.

"We need to go now," the nurse says.

Addie rotates her head to look at me, and I step forward still holding firmly on to Drew.

"It's okay, baby," I whisper. "You're going to go to sleep now, and when you wake up, you'll feel much better."

"What's wrwong with me?"

Gordon looks at me for the answer as well.

I let go of Drew so I can sit on the bed beside her, and I put my hand on her tummy. "It's actually kind of silly," I say, forcing a reassuring smile onto my face. "There's a ball in your belly."

"Like the one in your belly?" she asks, and I feel Gordon's eyes shift from my story to the bulge of my waist.

I shake my head. "Mine's a baby and it's supposed to be there, but yours is a ball that's making you sick, so the doctors need to take it out so it won't keep growing."

She nods, and I kiss her dry, hot cheek, then stand so the nurse can put the mask on her face. Her green eyes get wide, then slowly close, but they never stop looking at me.

Gordon, Drew, and I walk her to the doors that lead to the inner sanctum of the hospital, then we're asked to return to the waiting room where we'll be kept posted on the surgery.

With tension thick as sludge and Drew between us, we walk like a worried family to await the news of our loved one.

Paul and Goat and the family are gone when we arrive, and in their place are two men in identical dark suits. With a deep breath, I bravely step toward them to face my future.

The two men stand. They're both well over six feet and both are black, and I wonder if the FBI recruits ex–NBA players the same way the post office recruits Vietnam vets.

Both men shake hands with Gordon.

"Mrs. Kane?" the shorter one says.

I nod.

"And this must be Drew?"

I nod again and put my hands on Drew's shoulders, pulling him back against my hip.

"A lot of folks have been looking for you," the man says, bending slightly at the waist and extending his hand. "It's nice to meet you."

Drew weakly gives the man a handshake.

The man straightens. "How's your daughter?"

My stoicism abandons me, and I feel a griefquake threatening. "Don't arrest me till I know?" I plead. "Please, let me just wait until she's out of surgery and until she's woken up. Let me at least say good-bye."

Drew stiffens at my breakdown, and I try to pull myself together for his sake, if not for my own. "Please," I say with only a small tremor, "I just need to know she's okay."

Both men look at Gordon. I can't bring myself to look with them.

Drew is pulled from my grasp.

"Arrest her," Gordon says. "Arrest her before I kill her. It's her fault Addie's here in the first place."

And with his arm around Drew's shoulder, he leads him away. I watch as they walk out the doors that lead to the cafeteria. Drew cranes his neck, his eyes over his shoulder, until he can't see me anymore.

52

We walk into the cold night, the two men flanking me like suited columns. The rain has stopped for the moment, but the world is wet. My hands are cuffed loosely behind me. It's regulation, the shorter man explained apologetically. Both men are very polite.

A shadow walks toward us, and the men on either side of me stiffen.

"I'm a friend," Paul says when he's ten feet away. "Do you mind if I say good-bye?"

"Hands where we can see them," the taller one says, sizing up Paul and not liking what he sees.

Paul raises his arms, and the man walks toward him and runs his hands up and down his body, and I want to scream, *He's not the one you should be frisking. He's not the one who's a sadistic animal. The one you should be patting down is the one you just handed my children over to.*

"You've got one minute," the man says, taking a step back.

Paul nods and steps toward me. "How's Little Fish?" he asks.

I shake my head, and tears run down my cheek. He wipes

them away with his finger, then leans in close, so near I feel his unshaved skin against my ear. His left hand rests on my swollen stomach. "You're better than him," he whispers. Then, for a pause, we stand unmoving, the moment that will begin the rest of our moments without each other between us, the icy Spokane mist around us. When he pulls away, his warm lips graze my cheek.

"I'm glad I knew you, Ntamqe." And I watch as he limps into the wet night.

∞

The federal holding facility is in Seattle.

From there, I'll say good-bye to my escorts and be extradited to Orange County to await trial. The two agents are courteous, even kind. They exchange discouraged looks and talk in a cryptic language that makes me believe they're not fans of Gordon.

I was uncuffed as soon as we were out of the hospital parking lot, and the taller one gave me a bottle of water and a protein bar.

When we're an hour into the drive, the shorter one asks, "Is there someone you'd like to call?" He holds out a cell phone.

My hand trembles as I dial.

"Jill," my mom cries with joy, then her voice cracks into fear. "Are you okay? Are the kids okay?"

And I start to cry. I can't bring myself to tell her all that's happened—to recite the misery and to drown her normal life in the aberrance of mine.

"Jill, please," she pleads, "you're scaring me."

I nod. She should be scared. Her perfect daughter, magna cum laude from Berkeley, her daughter who was an accomplished architect, who had a gorgeous husband, two beautiful kids, a designer home. Her daughter, who she bragged about to all her friends. Her daughter is now pregnant with her dead lover's child and on her way to jail to await trial for kidnapping. Her four-year-old granddaughter is having a tumor removed from her stomach, and her grandson is in the custody of her maniacal, sadistic son-in-law.

When the hysterics continue and my mom's squawking escalates through the earpiece to fill the car, the tall man reaches over the backrest and takes the phone from my shaking hand.

"Good evening, ma'am," he says smoothly.

More squawking, then silence as he grimly explains what he can about the situation. His voice is low and compassionate and breaks when he discusses Addie, and I wonder if he has a daughter.

"Your daughter will be arraigned in Seattle, and if you post bail, she'll be released there and you can avoid her being transported by bus to Orange County."

53

I've been numb and nearly mute since my mom picked me up from LAX. My parents took a loan from Jan to bail me out, and one of the conditions of my release is that I not contact or come within a hundred yards of my kids until my trial. If I violate the condition, I'll be arrested, the bond will be forfeited, and I'll remain incarcerated until my trial.

For most of the drive, I gaze dazedly out the window. My mom talked with Addie's surgeon. The tumor was removed successfully and had not attached to any organs other than her left kidney. This is good news. The tumor and her kidney are gone, and the rest of her is tumor-free. In a day or two, when she's strong enough, she'll be moved to the children's hospital in Spokane, where she will recover, and then she will return to Orange County to begin chemotherapy.

The surgeon wouldn't speculate on the type of cancer or the prognosis, and I didn't want him to. I couldn't handle the information he'd already delivered, couldn't handle that my baby had woken up in the hospital without me, or that she was in pain and would be subjected to more pain, and I wouldn't be there to hold her or help her through it. Like the cancer, I'd been abruptly, savagely cut from her life.

As my mom drives, my memory replays the journey we took seven weeks earlier backward until we reach the place where it began. We drive through the town of Laguna Beach, and I wonder if the people here were starting to forget about me—if when they saw my parents, they remembered only to say how sad it was, believing the scandal was a thing of the past and that now it was over.

It's a little after two, and Main Beach is crowded with tourists and beachgoers—the boardwalk bustling with kids eating ice cream, skateboarders showing off, couples strolling hand in hand through the craft boutique. Pretty people blissfully enjoying the gorgeous summer day.

Everything is familiar, and in the crowd are faces I recognize.

That everyone who lives here knows about my crimes and my arrest, that it's most certainly been headline news, creates temporary heart stoppage, and jail is starting to become the more attractive option. At least there, nobody knows me. In the same way the name Charles Manson conjures *Helter Skelter* and the bludgeoning of Sharon Tate, in the microcosm of Laguna Beach, population 23,000, my name will be synonymous with child abduction and insanity.

My parents live in the north part of town, in a turn-of-the-century Normandy Revival cottage with a wavy Cotswold roof. The home is featured annually in the home tour and is affectionately known as the Hansel and Gretel house. My mom's fat roses are in full bloom and spill over the short front lawn, and my dad stands crooked in the open, arched door.

At the sight of his bent body and slanted, encouraging smile, the chill in my bones thaws a little, and I'm transported back to a time when my dad could fix anything, or at least that's what I believed.

"Welcome home," he says and, with his good arm, hugs my shoulder and gives me a kiss on my temple.

I expected him to look weaker than when I left, but he doesn't. His smile almost reaches both sides of his face, and he's put on a few of the pounds he lost after the stroke.

Déjà vu haunts the moment. A year ago when I stumbled up these steps, my dad answered my knock dressed in the same flannel pajamas he'd worn when I lived with him twenty years earlier. Martha jumped and yipped around me. I wanted him to hug me. Instead, he took one look at the marks on my throat and turned, his face a mask of fury. He yanked on the loafers he kept beside the door, and when he reached for his jacket, he fell.

For a moment, nothing, then pandemonium.

My dad convulsed at my feet, his eyes frozen open, his mouth suspended in a silent scream. I collapsed beside him, screaming for my mom to wake up. Then Gordon leaped through the door like a superhero.

My mom shrieked into the phone that her husband was dead while Gordon knelt beside me breathing life into my father.

Then the world went black.

When I regained consciousness, a paramedic was beside me checking my pulse. Through the door, I watched as my dad was wheeled to an ambulance on a stretcher, my mom following.

The sirens faded as the ambulance drove away, and in the halo of the porch lamp, the fire chief held Martha in his arms as he congratulated Gordon on his heroism.

Thanks to Gordon, my dad was alive.

Gordon had followed me when I fled from the house.

"Where's Martha?" I ask, suddenly aware I'm not being herded and barked at by a ten-pound rat dog.

My mom frowns. "She was hit by a car. Ran out and got hit." She says it quickly and repeats it, so I know she's lying, but I let it go.

"Oh, Mom, I'm sorry."

She hurries by me and into the house.

I want to run, flee from this moment, spare my dad any more pain, not tempt fate again, but his arm's around me and he's already turned and is guiding me through the door. He still limps, and his right side lags behind his left, but he's graduated from a walker to a cane, and I wonder if he's better off without me. My dad, Jeffrey, Addie—I destroy everyone who's close.

I slide off my shoes beside the entrance, next to my dad's loafers, my mom's sneakers, and a pair of gardening shoes my mom wears when she works on her bushes. My mom doesn't believe you should wear shoes in the house.

My parents' living room is like their marriage—a struggle. Like Archie and Edith from *All in the Family*, each has contributions to the décor. The French silk, fussy couch is my mom's, the La-Z-Boy leather recliner with massage and built-in cup holders is definitely my dad's.

Exhausted, I stumble up the familiar stairs toward my childhood room.

In the hallway, beside the banister, is a new addition. On the narrow book table that throughout my childhood always held a bouquet of my mom's roses is the twelfth diorama of our collection, five jubilant, white-bellied men and women parading toward a celebration—my birthday present. I run my hand over the smooth porcelain and almost smile, then almost cry, as I continue down the hall.

The room is exactly as it looked in my high school days. As a junior, I'd gone through a retro sixties stage. The orange walls are plastered with album covers from The Doors, Led Zeppelin, and Pink Floyd; my bedspread is a medley of neon circles; and my curtains are sheets of purple glass beads I strung myself.

On the mirror, above my track trophies, are pictures of boys I knew and of girlfriends I thought would be in my life forever. My room is part of the house, but not really. It's more of a shrine to the past, faded with age, and covered with a layer of dust.

54

The beads rattle as they're pulled back from the window, and the sun blasts into the room like a flare of lightning when the shade snaps up.

I pull the pillow over my head, and a second later, it's yanked away and thrown from my reach.

"Up," my mom barks.

I fling my arm over my puffy eyes, and she grabs it by the wrist and pulls, spinning me sideways so I'm half off the bed. I scramble to my feet so I won't land on my head, then slide against the mattress to sit on the carpet and put my forehead on my knees.

"Enough. It's noon. Up and at 'em. You've got things to do."

I shake my head. *No kids, no job, no house to clean, no clothes to wash—no clothes.* She's wrong. For the first time in my life, I have absolutely nothing to do.

"In the kitchen in five minutes." And she marches away, her sweats swishing against her thighs.

I crawl to my childhood bureau—it's teal blue and plastered with bumper stickers: "I let the dogs out"; "Peace, Love, Fashion"; "Don't have a cow, man," featuring Bart Simpson; "Ross Perot for President."

The drawer sticks from disuse, but then pulls open to reveal the wardrobe of my youth. I find a pair of gym shorts, "Property of Laguna Beach High School," and a T-shirt that advertises the New Kids on the Block Magic Summer Tour.

The wall of the stairwell that leads to the kitchen is the obligatory portrait homage of our family. Oval framed, sepia-toned photos of ancestors I never met, but who bear a resemblance; grade school portraits with mottled gray backgrounds; and military portraits, most of relatives who died too young. I stop at a silver framed photo toward the left, but prominently displayed in the middle of the montage. In the photo, I'm glancing over my shoulder at Gordon, whose black tuxedoed arms are wrapped around my gorgeous, strapless Vera Wang wedding gown. I'm laughing and he's smiling, and my mind strains to remember some sense of what it was that had made us so happy.

My mom sits at the table paging through *Redbook* and drinking her coffee as though the world is right as peaches.

I plop down across from her with a cup of decaf.

"Connor called," she says. "He needs to talk to you about your DUI. He got you a continuance so you wouldn't be in contempt of court."

I drop my forehead to the table and roll it back and forth. There should be some sort of mercy law that says that if you're arrested for a humongous crime like kidnapping, you get a pass on your minor crimes like having a glass of wine before you pick up your kids from your mom's house.

"Sit up."

I lift my body to a slouch.

"Enough," my mom barks. "Snap out of it and get it together.

Addie and Drew need you, and that baby needs you. Now get off your tuchis, take control of the situation, and get your life back on course." She glances at my bulging belly. "Before it's too late."

I stare at her blankly, and my head falls back to the cool oak of the table. For the life of me, I can't figure out what it is she wants me to do. My kids are gone, I have no money, no job, no hope for a future. I'm facing one felony charge and two misdemeanor charges and looking at possible time in prison. Addie and Drew need me, this baby needs me—I agree—but what the hell am I supposed to do about it?

I borrow my mom's car and drive two and a half miles to my old home. Gordon's still in Spokane with the kids, because Addie won't be well enough to travel for a few more days. Mostly I drive there out of habit. I have nowhere else to go, and I can't stand to be around my mom's nagging for one more minute.

I stare in shock at the stucco and glass masterpiece that was once my greatest pride aside from my kids. The lawn is brown, the shades drawn, and planted in the middle of the thirsty grass is a real estate sign with the words "Short Sale" across the top and the word "Sold" across the smiling face of a man named Jim Stanaland.

"Jillian?"

I turn to see Michelle, long-legged, tan, and beautiful—upsettingly unchanged from a lifetime ago—jogging toward me.

She stops, leaving a yard of sidewalk between us. Her focus moves from my face to my stomach and her pretty hazel eyes grow, then she forces them to normal and returns her gaze to my face. "You're back," she says. "It's good to see you. I barely recognized you."

I'm surprised she did. I'm a pathetic sight—my chopped, poorly dyed hair, unwashed for three days, my teenage clothes squeezed over my pregnant body, my makeup-less face unable to hide my humility and shame.

"He found you," she says, and I'm shocked by the candidness and the sympathetic tone.

I nod.

"I'm sorry," she says, and I believe she is. She turns to look at our house. "It's been empty for a month."

"Claudia didn't move in?" I ask.

Michelle shakes her head. "I heard Gordon moved in with her, though he hasn't been around much. Was home for a few days about a week ago, but then he left again. I only know because Bob's sister has the same housekeeper as Claudia."

Silence hangs between us.

"He has the kids?" she asks.

"Except for this one." I smooth my stomach. "Addie got sick. It's how he found us. She has..." My throat tightens around the word. "Cancer." It's the first time I've said it out loud, and with the utterance, my bones melt, and Michelle is catching me and lowering me to the curb. She sits beside me.

"She's going to be okay," I say, hoping to ease the panicked worry in Michelle's eyes and to reassure myself. "The doctor said he got it all, but she doesn't have a kidney. You can live without a kidney, that's what he said."

"God gave us an extra," Michelle comforts, her arm around my shoulder, her hand holding me tight enough that I can feel her heart beating through her tank top, pounding for Addie and for me.

"I haven't seen her since I took her to the hospital."

"But she's okay?"

I nod. "Gordon wouldn't let me stay, had me arrested right then at the hospital. I'm out on bail. Which means, you, Michelle, are talking to a bona fide accused felon—a kidnapping, child-endangering criminal..."

I'm laughing and crying at the same time, and rambling like a lunatic. Like a New Orleans flood levee, the torrent of the confession is too strong, and in an incoherent exorcism of blurts and spurts, I confess everything I've done and haven't done, all the mistakes I made and all the diabolical ways I tried to fix them that led me to this horrible place, where I'm sitting on the curb in front of my house that's no longer mine, spilling my guts to a woman I barely know.

"...so you should run, Michelle. Run as fast and far as you can, because I'm like the plague, everyone who comes in contact with me gets destroyed."

Michelle ignores my deranged rant and her arm continues to hug me, and she rocks me back and forth and tells me it's okay. "You don't look all that dangerous to me," she says.

I try to disengage, to push her away, but her arm holds tight.

"I'll take my chances."

"You don't even know me."

She shrugs. "I have good instincts."

I stop struggling, and finally, she releases me, and we sit in silence looking toward the park, where seven weeks ago I told Addie and Drew we were going on an adventure.

Michelle chuckles. I look over at her, and she's shaking her head and still laughing through her nose.

I can't imagine what's funny.

"I actually didn't understand most of what you just told me," she says, "and yet, somehow, I feel like I understand you perfectly."

And I have to smile as well. "Crazy understands Crazy?"

"More like, At Your Wit's End understands At Your Wit's End."

I feel a little less foolish. I stare at the hill that Addie and Drew loved to roll down until they were so dizzy they were drunk with silliness when they stood up.

"I should have taken her to the doctor sooner," I mumble to the hill. "I just thought it was the flu."

"Did it seem like the flu?"

"When it happened? Yeah, it did." And this time when I tell her the story, it's coherent. I tell it in reverse, starting with rushing Addie to the hospital after she threw up in Paul's room. I tell her about Paul and Goat and fishing in the river. I tell her about our late-night Uno games and about Addie almost drowning. I tell her how we ended up where we did and how Gordon almost found us our first night on the run.

Then I hesitate. Jeffrey dead in the gymnasium fills my memory, then in hyperspeed, my mind replays every episode of abuse, Gordon's guns, his hands on my throat, his threats. I remember each moment in high definition, as if I more than lived it—I see it, I feel it—the bruises still hurt, I feel his fists, his kicks. I hear every threat, remember every moment of fear. Each horror of the last nine years flashes through my mind with impossible clarity—but as near as it is, I can't reach it or bring it forward to speak of it out loud.

"He hurt you," Michelle says beside me, bringing me out of my frozen stupor. It's not a question, but a proclamation.

My head nods an inch, and my eyes slide to Michelle, whose own eyes now stare at the glowing horizon. And suddenly, I'm not alone. Michelle understands. Michelle more than understands, Michelle's been there.

I stare at her. It doesn't make sense. Bob, her husband, has the spine of an octopus and the impetus of a sloth. I can't imagine him even saying a harsh word and definitely can't imagine him hurting Michelle. Even I could take Bob in a fight, and Michelle's a much stronger woman than me.

She answers my unspoken skepticism. "My father," she says in a voice so quiet I'm unsure she spoke, then she stands and offers a hand to help me to my feet.

She releases her grip, but I hold tight. "How'd you get away?" I ask.

She shrugs. "He died. Got caught on the anchor of his boat when he was spear fishing and drowned."

And I don't know what's funny about that, but something is because we both laugh.

"I've got to go," she says. "Bob's going to think I fell off a cliff."

Panic fills my face.

"Don't worry," she says. "What you told me won't go any further than this curb."

"How will you explain to Bob why you've been gone so long?" We've been talking at least an hour.

"I'll tell him it's none of his business, if he asks, which he won't. Or, if I really want to toy with him, I'll tell him I was contemplating my life. That'll freak him out."

I manage a small, grateful smile.

"Keep them on their toes," she says as she turns to trot back toward her house. She looks over her shoulder as she starts her jog. "That's the secret," she yells. "They may be stronger, but we're smarter. Let them think they're in charge, when really you're the one steering the boat."

55

Still unready to return to my mom's pestering and my dad's worry, I drive aimlessly along the coast until the sun gives up its fight and darkness obscures the waves and the view.

An hour later, I'm in front of Sherman McGregor's mansion. I'm relieved it doesn't appear to be shrouded in mourning. The downstairs' lights blaze, and an upstairs' window is open. It's been seven weeks since I left. I'm glad I'm not too late, that I still have the chance to say good-bye.

Yes, I want to see Sherman out of compassion, but my motives are also selfish. Sherman's possibly the only person in my life who doesn't know what I've done. I want a break from the madness, a moment to pretend I am who I used to be—a respected member of society, a married, churchgoing, law-abiding, God-fearing citizen with two beautiful children, a husband, and an enviable life.

My knock is answered by the same nurse I met before I left, and she's definitely surprised to see me.

"Thought you gave up on him like everyone else," she says. Her name tag reads, "Greta Thompson, R.N." She's a substantial woman, her butt high and her large breasts hanging low, making it appear as though she has no waist.

"I've been out of town."

"Well, he'll be glad you're here. Never asks about his no-good sons, but he asks about you." There's a slight southern drawl to her words and more than an ounce of feeling for Sherman, and it makes me like her very much.

I follow her up the stairs to Sherman's room and stifle a gasp at the skeleton lying in the massive four-poster bed. He's less than half the man he was before I left. His lids droop over his bulging eyes, and the skin on his arms and face is so loose it appears to be melting. I take his thin, veined hand in mine. It's warm, and the fingers curl around my palm as his eyes flutter open.

"Hey," I say brightly, masking my pity.

He smiles, then coughs, then groans, then resumes his thin smile. "Thought you ditched me," he says.

"I needed to go out of town. There was a family emergency, and it took longer than I planned to get things sorted out."

"All's good now?"

I nod, then change the subject. "Did you finish Hemingway?"

His eyes shake more than his head. "Greta reads like my grandson. She tries, but Ernest needs to be read right."

I move to the bookshelf across the room, find *Death in the Afternoon*, and open to where we left off. Fifteen minutes later, Sherman's asleep. I stay watching him for another half hour, hoping he can feel my presence, hoping he knows he's not alone.

56

Connor happily agreed to meet me at Las Brisas Cantina after work for a drink.

He looks wonderful. His blond hair has a summer glint it didn't have when I left, and his skin glows bronze.

After our kiss-kiss on each other's cheeks, Connor's skin smoother than mine, we're shown to an outside table that overlooks Heisler Park and the waves. Connor orders a margarita and some chips, and I order a virgin piña colada.

"You look amazing," he says, and I laugh. "I don't mean the clothes, those are a crime of fashion..." I'm wearing a pair of my mom's Lycra workout sweats that barely expand enough to reach around my growing center and a batik tunic with wood beads at the neckline that I bought at an African bazaar when I was sixteen. "...but your skin looks fabulous and I love the hair, very Liza Minnelli. Though it looks like you put on a few pounds in the middle."

"What a mess, huh?" I say.

"Gordon's?"

I look at him and he shakes his head.

"Wow, Jinks, I like drama, but only the melodrama variety, the kind I concoct myself. This is like a poorly scripted episode of *Melrose Place*. You'd even give Lindsay Lohan a run for her money on screwing up your life."

"He killed Jeffrey," I defend.

Connor's nod is noncommittal. "It was investigated as a mugging."

"Was?"

"It's cold now."

I close my eyes at the injustice and say a silent prayer for Jeffrey and one for myself, begging forgiveness for my cowardice. More guilt compounded onto the already behemoth load I carry for what happened to Jeffrey.

"Jinks?" he says. I refocus my eyes. "Have you considered that maybe that's what it was, a robbery gone bad? Wrong place, wrong time?"

My head shakes back and forth too adamantly.

I can't be wrong. The ramifications of doing what I did without being justified are too great—stealing Addie and Drew from their father, uprooting them, putting them in danger, not taking Addie to the doctor in time.

When I first saw Jeffrey dead, I was so certain, but time and distance distort things, or perhaps clarify things, and it's hard to maintain the same conviction.

"Okay, well, as your lawyer, I'm telling you to keep your suspicions to yourself. You've got enough to deal with without implicating yourself in Jeffrey's death."

My eyes widen.

"Settle down. I know you didn't shoot him. I'm just saying, you need to stay out of it so no one else thinks you did."

I nod. I'm almost surprised I'm not being investigated as a suspect, that shooting Jeffrey isn't being added to my list of crimes: drunk driving, child endangerment, kidnapping...murder. I'm ashamed I'm not brave enough to tell what I know to the police, but I know Connor's right, going to the police will only implicate me. If Gordon did this, he's too smart to be caught. If there were any evidence, Gordon would already have been investigated, but as always, he's gotten away with it and no one even suspects him of being anything but what he portrays himself to be, a doting father with a crazy wife who tried to steal his kids from him. He's brilliant and ruthless—a consummate psychopath.

"How's Ad?" Connor asks, changing subjects and bringing me from one horror to another.

"She's okay for now. She's recovering from the surgery and it will be a few days before she's strong enough to fly home."

Connor takes my hand. "Hang in there. I can't imagine how hard this is for you, but you need to hang in there."

I nod. "I'm not allowed to see them." My voice is so plaintive it almost sounds like a howl. "I don't know how I'm going to keep myself away. It's one thing to obey the court order when they're in another state a thousand miles away, but how am I possibly going to stay away when they're in the same town?"

"I'm working on it," he says. "But, Jinks, look at me." I lift my head to meet his eyes. "You need to be good. I know it's hard, but this is important—you need to play by the rules."

"Addie's sick."

"I know, and this is awful, but your only chance to turn this around is to be smart this time."

Unsaid is how stupid I've been so far.

I nod. "Okay. So how do I do that?"

"It's not going to be easy, but we're going to declaw the lion one claw at a time."

I furrow my brow. "You've been talking to my dad?"

It's Connor's turn to look confused. "No. What's your dad have to do with this? I'm referring to an Aesop's fable."

I laugh. Typical of my dad to plagiarize someone else's work, then take full credit for it.

"You've heard it before?"

"Not Aesop's version."

"Well, the gist is, there's a lion who falls in love with a smokin' hot maiden and he wants to marry her, but the father doesn't want to give his princess to the lion. But, of course, if the father says no to the lion, the lion's going to have them as an appetizer. So the father comes up with this plan. He tells the lion he's worried that the lion's going to hurt his daughter because of his sharp teeth and claws, but if the lion gets his teeth and claws removed, he'll consider the lion's proposal..."

I interrupt. "So the lion has his teeth and claws removed, and then the father's no longer afraid, and he tells the lion to get lost."

"Exactly. He tricks the lion into defeating himself."

"Well, you tell me how to trick Gordon into declawing himself, and I'll get right on that."

"One claw at a time."

"Stop speaking in metaphors."

"Jinks, when the court's deciding who gets custody, they're looking at what's best for the kids. If you can prove you took the kids because you were justifiably concerned for their safety, and if you can put your life back together and show you can provide a stable home for them and prove Gordon can't, you win."

"That's an awful lot of ifs."

"One claw at a time."

I roll my eyes.

"Okay. Let's start with what Gordon's got going for him, his claws and teeth if you will—he's got a stellar reputation as a good guy and a good dad."

I nod.

"He's got his job as a cop, which gives him power, resources..."

"...and the right to carry a gun and shoot people."

"Let's keep on task here, Jinks. We're only talking about what the court's going to care about in determining custody. He's got his job as a cop, which gives him an income and the ability to support himself and the kids."

"Which I don't."

"Actually, you do. Harris wants you back."

"He what?"

"He wants you back. Told me to tell you to call him."

"Are you crazy? Is he crazy? I abandoned the job, totally left him hanging. I'm an accused kidnapper. I embezzled money."

"Yeah, but you're also damn good at what you do, and the company's having a rough time."

I shake my head, but a little flame in me ignites. Until two months ago, my job defined me. I was damn good at what I did. It would be nice to be good at something again, and even more important, to have an income so I can prove I'm able to provide for Addie and Drew.

"So make sure you call him. Now, back to what we were talking about. Gordon's claws. He's got his reputation, he's got his job, what else?"

I close my eyes and think. "He's got Claudia."

"His side dish?"

"More like my replacement. Gordon moved in with her. Poor thing."

"And she offers...?"

"Money, and lots of it."

"That's not good."

"Nope."

"What else?"

"Meanness, cunning, intelligence, strength, obsessiveness, perseverance, evilness, lack of morals and conscience..."

Connor holds up his hand. "We all have those things," he says. "Back any of us into a corner and we're all capable of diabolical behavior."

I shake my head. "You're wrong; you and I are not like Gordon. You could never be like him. Never. Not in your worst nightmare. You can't even smoosh a spider who spent the night feasting on your flesh."

"Because the spider's not going to kill me and he's not a bad spider, he's just a spider doing what spiders do. He doesn't deserve to die for that. But if a murderer came into my condo and threatened Pete, you'd better believe if I had a giant fly swatter, I'd squash him without a second thought."

"But could you go out and hunt down the murderer before it happened? Take your giant fly swatter and lure him into a trap so you could squash him because you think he's going to do something bad to Pete?"

"Absolutely."

"I think you're wrong. My mind doesn't work like Gordon's. He has no conscience. I could never be like him."

"You need to hope I'm right. Because if this gets ugly, Jinks, you're going to need to grow some claws and teeth of your own."

Perhaps it's because Connor is a man and I'm a woman, or perhaps it's because I believe in God and the Bible and Connor doesn't, but I refuse to accept his notion that, at our core,

Gordon and I are the same, that circumstances can alter us from lambs into lions, from good into evil. I have more faith that our souls are better ordained and that our consciences dictate our actions no matter what the circumstance or consequence. If I prevail, which I don't think I will, it will be because we are an evolution beyond where it's just about claws and teeth.

"So basically, Gordon's got money because of this woman Claudia, his job, and his reputation. Strip those away and you win?"

"Strip those away and he'll kill me."

"He can't know you're the one doing it."

"Oh, okay. And I thought this was going to be difficult. No problem. All I need to do is destroy the livelihood and reputation of my extremely intelligent, highly perceptive, uber-paranoid husband, who believes I'm the devil incarnate, without him knowing I'm the one doing it. Got it. Simple."

"I aim to please. But, Jinks, really, it actually is that simple. Destroy his foundation—money, job, reputation—and he'll crumble. Put some of that wasted IQ to work on the problem, and I'm sure you'll find a way."

We both fall quiet, and I stare at the ocean. Three dolphins—two large, one small—lazily swim south. Tourists below us on the beach jump and point at the novelty.

Money, job, reputation—do we really exist on criteria so tenuous? Take away any one of the three, and the foundation becomes unstable. Destroy a reputation and you lose the job and the money. Lose the job and the same thing happens. The only one that doesn't destroy you entirely is money, though with Gordon it may be his Achilles' heel.

For Gordon, money and things define him. It's like a drug.

No matter how much he has, it's not enough. He chases it, needs it, and as I think about it, I know it's his spot of weakness.

"You look like you're starting to understand."

"I understand the principle, just not how it's going to help me."

"It's time to turn the tables. We need to repair the damage Gordon's done to you and cause some damage of our own."

My head collapses to the table and rests on top of my hands.

"It might not be obvious how you're going to do that right now, but you'll see—now that you're looking for it—you're going to find a way. That's how it always works. Before you were just reacting to the shit Gordon was doing, but this time, you have your own agenda, and you're gonna be driving the boat."

I feel like Connor, Michelle, and my mom are all in a conspiracy, all of them deciding I'm some sort of captain who can chart my own destiny, when all I feel like is a woman overboard, hoping someone will throw me a life vest before I drown.

57

They arrived last night, and it's only noon and already I'm a wreck. I had coffee with Connor this morning and this afternoon I'll see Sherman, but at the moment, I'm at home with my parents, and there's nothing for me to do but think about Addie and Drew being so close and that I'm not allowed to see them. I feel like a caged animal.

Addie's at the Children's Hospital in Orange for her first chemotherapy treatment. It will make her very sick. Her hair will fall out. She'll be scared and will feel betrayed. The doctors are doing this to her, and her parents are letting them. They'll explain that they have to because otherwise she could die, so she'll realize she's mortal, something no four-year-old should realize.

She'll be only forty minutes away while all this is happening, and I won't be there for her. I won't be able to talk to her, console her, hold her.

"Stop pacing; you're gonna wear a hole in the carpet," my mom says.

Where's Drew?

I assume Gordon's staying with Addie, so who's staying with Drew? *Claudia?*

I pace faster.

"Jill, why don't you and your father go for a drive? It will do you good to get out of the house."

My parents both agreed it wasn't a good idea for me to be left alone when the kids got back into town, that the temptation to break the court order would be too great. They're right. The moment they let me out of their sight, I'm bolting straight to Addie and Drew.

"Come on," my dad says, pushing to his feet and grabbing his cane. "Let's get some dessert." Then, with his back to my mom, he winks, and I realize he's a conspirator not a jailer, and I practically leap into my shoes.

When we're safely on our way, he says, "No court order against me as far as I know."

I drive to Children's Hospital within an inch of reckless and let him out at the curb. He has a bag draped over his non-cane-bearing arm. In it is a pair of Dora the Explorer pajamas, a night-light, a stuffed elephant, because Addie collects elephants, and a tape recorder with my love on it.

I stare at the stucco and glass wall for the entire time my dad is gone and wonder which room is hers. Ten minutes later, my dad hobbles from the entrance still carrying the bag. I drive to pick him up at the curb.

"How is she?" I ask when he climbs into the car.

His jaw clenches and unclenches, and I think this was a very bad idea. Stress will kill him, and whatever just happened was very stressful.

"Bastard" is all he says.

"It's okay, Pops. It's okay. We just need to be patient. We'll figure out a way. It's just going to take a little bit of time."

"God damn bastard."

58

I drop my dad off at home, and as I've done every day since I've returned, I drive to Anaheim to see Sherman. As I drive, my mind fills with Addie and Drew.

I count red and blue cars out of habit. I think about Addie clambering into bed beside me, the way her body shapes itself to mine, how she clings to me. She smells of strawberries and Johnson's baby shampoo, and Drew smells like earth and Johnson's baby shampoo. I hope they never stop using that shampoo, though I know they will.

I think of them every day and always, and as I drive, I wonder how I ever made this commute and forgot about them long enough to do my job.

On Monday, Harris and I will meet to discuss my return, and I'm looking forward to going back, but I also know something in me has changed.

Since high school, I've been barreling through life a thousand miles a minute, determined not just to succeed, but excel—competing in an imaginary competition with the world. At school, then at work, even with my kids—I needed to be the best, they needed to be the best, my husband needed to be the best—or at least, we needed to appear that way.

For almost two months, my ambition has been derailed, my priorities wildly shifted, and my competitive, overachieving, type-A personality thrown into a vacuum with nobody to compete with. I was living in the backwoods of Spokane where a Kate Spade purse is considered inane because it's completely impractical, and an Ivy League education means nothing, but if you can divine a deer migration during the hunting season, you're deigned a genius. And like a fire without oxygen, the flame was extinguished.

I look at the traffic stretched out for miles in front of me. There must be an accident. And I actually smile at the suit mongers beside me with their shoulders hiked up to their ears, their hands gripping the steering wheels so tight their knuckles glow, their pulses pumping in their temples as they try to will the progression to go faster so they can get to wherever it is they're so urgent to get to.

I used to be one of them.

Monday, I will accept Harris's offer to return to work. I need an income if I want any chance at all of getting custody, but I could never be the way I was—frenetic and stressed over every little detail. I will never be who I was before. Something in me is changed.

59

I settle into my seat beside Sherman and open to the page we left off, but his head shakes, or rather his eyes inside his head move side to side. "Not today," he says in a strangled whisper, and in his weakness, I see the sands of time running through the hourglass. I pinch my nose to hold back the emotions, and though he's still here, I already miss him.

His voice is barely audible above the gentle sounds of the day—a bird beside the window, a passing car, Greta doing laundry down the hall. "The chest below the bed," he rasps. "Get it for me."

I kneel to the thick Persian rug, my knees sinking in an inch, lift the Damask bed skirt, and pull out the intricately carved box that's tucked deep beneath the frame. It's the size of a thick briefcase, and judging by the carvings, I'd guess the piece is from the early eighteenth-century Qing dynasty. Each face is carved with a relief of monkeys playing between grapevines. I smooth my hand over the craftsmanship in appreciation of the artist who lived two thousand years ago.

The motif is common from that period, and I recognize it

from the trip I took to China with my dad when I was a teenager. The grapes symbolize one's wish to have many children as grapes bear much fruit, while the monkey represents one's hope to gain a high-ranking position. The chest was probably a wedding gift from a parent to a son.

I pull it toward me. It's very heavy. The wood's like stone, and the chest weighs almost as much as Addie, which is about thirty pounds. When I lift it into the light, I gasp. It's the unmistakable deep purple color of zitan, a wood so rare and valuable only the imperial household was allowed to use it.

I struggle awkwardly to my chair, wondering how a piece so beautiful and valuable could be kept hidden beneath a bed.

I lift the lid, and inside is a framed photo, a gun, and a box of bullets.

A shiver shudders my spine.

I look at Sherman and I feel his pain, but I can't shoot him. I believe in euthanasia, we all have the right to call it quits when we decide we're done, but I can't be the one to do it.

"Jillian, the photo, put it on the table so I can see it," he wheezes.

I lift the silver frame from the box.

The woman in the photo is attractive, but was never beautiful. Her face is wide, and her teeth are too large. She squats on a lawn in front of a modest house with a baby cradled in one arm. Her other arm extends toward a toddler who takes a teetering step away from her and toward a man bent at the waist ready to catch him in outstretched arms. Sherman's young smile is as large as the woman's, and there's so much hope and promise in that moment that if I didn't know how the story ends, it would make me smile. As it is, it makes me want to cry.

I shift the clutter of pills and needles and the blood pressure cuff to make room, then prop the photo on its easel and angle it so it's in Sherman's view.

"Thank you," he mumbles.

I take his hand and together we stare at the past and imagine how different things could have been.

∞

The shadows grow long, and Sherman sleeps.

The box is still on my lap, the lid open. The gun stares at me, and I stare back.

Gordon has pointed a gun similar to this at me many times. It's a favorite game of his. He comes home stealthily from work like a night prowler, stands at the foot of our bed with it aimed at my head, and waits for me to wake up.

"Bang," he says, then he laughs.

I don't like guns. Even looking at this one lying beside its bullets with its safety on scares me. It shouldn't be so easy to end a life.

The door to the bedroom opens, and I turn to see Greta.

"You okay?" she asks.

I close the lid, and the sound causes Sherman to stir. His eyes drift to the photo on the table, then to me and the chest.

"Keep it," he says. "I want you to have it."

I shake my head.

"Please. I don't want it anymore."

"Sherman, I can't. It's too valuable."

"It's worth nothing." He coughs and his face changes shades, and I put my hand on his to calm him.

"Okay," I say softly.

He nods, and his eyes close. "It was a gift for her." I need to lean very close to hear him, my ear almost to his lips. "But I ruined it and she left before I could give it to her."

"It's okay, Sherman. We all make mistakes."

A tear squeezes from his eye.

"I just want to pretend I did it right."

I don't know if he means he shouldn't have screwed up, or he should have given her the box, or he should have used the gun.

"I always was a coward. Thank you, Jillian. I'll rest better knowing it's gone." And he stills to an exhausted sleep.

With the hoodoo in my hand, I stand and brush a kiss against his forehead.

Across the room, Greta fusses with the curtains, her busyness a poor disguise for the heaviness of the moment. We both know the time has come to say good-bye.

60

I return home to two pleasant surprises, my dad's spaghetti and hope.

"Jill, guess who I ran into at the market today?" my mom says, a smile playing over her face. "That nice mom of Drew's friend, the chubby little boy. She's always at the baseball games. I think her name's Michelle."

My dad's at the stove making his famous marinara, and my mom's slathering butter onto a French roll to make garlic bread. She pauses mid-stroke to set down the knife and open a can of tomato paste that my dad then picks up as though some telepathy told her he needed it at that moment.

Since I've returned home, I marvel at their relationship. They still quibble and squabble and insult, but they also have an amazing synergy. Like cogs in a wheel, they move around each other and with each other like they are one.

"And?" I ask, my mom having forgotten she was telling me about Michelle. I pick up an onion from the counter and begin to slice it.

"Oh, that's right. Michelle. What a beautiful girl. She has wonderful legs..."

"Mom?"

"Right. So Michelle says hello, then she tells me that Gordon asked her if she could watch Drew for him tomorrow and that she agreed, and that she's planning on taking the boys to the Discovery Center. She said she was going to get there at around ten, in case you..." My mom looks up at me and tries to give me a wink, but instead it's a lopsided blink. "...Maybe wanted to go to the Discovery Center that day also by coincidence."

My hand stops slicing, and there are tears in my eyes, and it's not from the onion.

Tomorrow I'm going to see Drew.

61

It's five minutes past ten. I sit in my car, my eyes straining toward the entrance gate of the Discovery Center's parking lot, praying the next car will be them. I've been here forty-five minutes.

The exhibit today is magnets, and dozens of early birds are already inside. I'm jealous of each mom who walks through the door—some look exhausted, others look like they'd rather be anywhere than where they are—and I'm so envious that the world is tinted red.

Finally, Michelle's white Sienna pulls into the driveway. I watch her park, then anxiously wait for the exodus. Max and Drew run ahead of Michelle and immediately begin to leapfrog over the concrete sphere balustrades. For a moment, I'm paralyzed to move and just stare at my son, his long limbs, his goofy smile, the awkward way he has of hitching up his pants that he insists on buying two sizes too large.

When Michelle reaches them, I step from my car. Michelle looks around, and when she sees me, she waves and smiles, then says something to Drew that makes him turn.

His face lights up, and he runs at me and I kneel to hug him, but he stops short of my outstretched arms, his eyes skittering side to side. He's in front of his friend, and a hug is uncool.

"Hey, buddy."

"Hi, Mom." His smile is so wide I think his cheeks must hurt.

"Mind if I hang out with you today?"

He grabs my hand and yanks me toward the door, but I pull him back before we take a step. "You can't tell Dad," I say.

He shakes his head. "I don't talk to Dad."

My face tilts.

"He won't call me the right name. He still thinks I'm Drew, and my name is Hawk."

I give a small grin of victory. "Well, then, Hawk, even if he does call you by your name, you still can't tell him. It's important. I'm working on fixing things, and until I do, he can't know I'm breaking the rules to see you."

"Okay. Can we go now?"

And I let him pull me the rest of the way, no longer the least bit jealous of anyone.

Beneath the Plexiglas top of the table, the iron shavings shift as you move the magnets either from above or below. Michelle makes a neat pattern of little mounds while I create an ocean scene. The boys stand at a gigantic magnetic wall with metal cylinders and ramps tacked catawampus all over it. The object is to connect the pieces so a marble can roll from piece to piece across the wall.

"How you holding up?" Michelle asks.

"Not great, but I suppose as good as can be expected, considering."

Michelle's gorgeous as always. She wears a kelly green, sleeveless blouse that ties at the neck, white linen slacks, and beige sandals. She's entirely unaware of it, but she's a woman who turns heads—men in admiration and women in envy.

I feel dumpy in my Target maternity blouse and elastic-waist shorts. My ankles and feet have swollen to elephant proportions, so the only shoes I can manage are flip-flops.

Michelle's smart and funny, and I regret not becoming friends with her sooner. She's Stanford educated with a degree in literature and had originally thought she wanted to be a teacher.

"...but turns out I don't really like kids other than my own." She laughs. "I'm also basically too narcissistic and lazy to work. I like my tennis, my yoga, my novels—I like the idea of having a career, just not the part of actually having to work."

It's been a long time since I've had a girlfriend, and at first, I'm awkward and a little shy. Since Gordon and I started dating, he's wanted me to himself, and I allowed him to isolate me.

"Look," Michelle says.

I follow her glance to where the boys are. A group surrounds them, and I stand to see over everyone's heads. Drew steps onto a chair, and Max hands him a marble. On the magnetic wall in front of him is an amazing track of switchbacks ingeniously designed to catch, drop, and turn the marble until it reaches the opposite corner. If the design is too steep, the marble will miss, and if it's too shallow, its momentum will stop. There must be a hundred pieces tacked together to reach the end. Michelle and I have been talking for almost an hour.

It's the moment of truth.

Max says, "On your mark, get set, go," and Drew drops the marble into the first channel.

Clickety clack it rolls smoothly through the first row, teetering at the last cylinder for a breath-stopping second before dropping cleanly onto the channel below.

It takes almost a minute for the marble to make its journey, and there are several moments of suspense followed by universal relief as the marble makes it past an obstacle. It reaches the end and plunks into a bucket, and the audience breaks into applause. Max takes a dramatic bow, then raises Drew's arm like a prizefighter who just won the heavyweight title. Drew smiles shyly, and my heart bursts with pride.

The boys move on to another adventure, and Michelle and I retake our seats. "That was amazing. Drew's a special kid, very bright."

"Not at school."

"Yeah. I volunteered in the classroom last year. School doesn't suit him real well. It's too bad because he's so smart."

And with the segue, I tell her about Washington and how well Drew did while we were there, how he thrived and what a different boy he was.

"You should send him to Anneliese's."

"The private school?"

Michelle nods. "They take more of a holistic approach to education. To teach chemistry, they bake a cake. To learn about photosynthesis, they grow a garden. The founder doesn't believe in traditional testing. It's not for everyone, but sounds like it might be perfect for Drew."

And it does. But I'm not the one who will decide where Drew goes to school. I won't even have any input. I stare at my son, who now pulls himself up on a chair using a pulley system. He stares at the mechanism, and I know he's figuring it out, but if I gave him a written test on it, he'd write his name and leave the rest blank.

After lunch, the boys return to more adventure, and Michelle and I stay in the cafeteria.

"Thank you," I say. "It's been really tough not being able to see them."

"I can't imagine. I don't know what I'd do if I were in your shoes. It would be hard to contain myself."

There's something more in her eyes.

"What?" I ask.

She tears a napkin into small pieces; paper confetti sprinkles the table in front of her. "I sometimes wonder," she says, "what would have happened if my father hadn't died. I was fifteen when it happened, and I was just at that point when I felt like I could do something about it. And sometimes I wonder if I would have."

I swallow hard. We're entering dangerous territory.

"Every night, I used to dream how I would kill him. Mostly I imagined that I would somehow get a gun and shoot him. Other times I thought I'd poison him or stab him while he was sleeping. Then he died, and it was no longer up to me. But I still wonder if eventually, I would have. It's like that William Blake poem."

"'Tyger, Tyger'?" It's the only William Blake poem I've heard of.

"Yeah. It's one of my favorites, and maybe it's because the meaning's so close to what I struggled with back then."

I try to recall the poem but can only come up with the first line, *Tyger! Tyger! Burning bright; In the forests of the night.*

"'What immortal hand or eye, dare frame thy fearful symmetry?'" Michelle recites. "I think God makes us good and evil, and that's what I struggle with. If my dad had lived, I think I would have killed him."

I shake my head. "You interpreted it wrong. The poem questions how a single God could have created both the lamb and the tiger. It's about God creating good, and Satan creating evil."

She laughs. I love her laugh; it's a sweet, high giggle that almost rings. "Nope. I'm sticking with my interpretation because you, girl, need to become the tiger."

62

Since the kids returned home, I can't keep still, and there's not enough to keep my mind from obsessing on what I can't have and on spinning in circles trying to solve the riddle of how to declaw Gordon so I can get them back. So I've decided to plant a garden.

I miss the Flying Goat and working with Sissy and Isi pulling weeds, harvesting the fresh vegetables, and planting for the next season. Tuesdays and Thursdays were our days to work in the garden. Sometimes Goat joined us, mostly just to bark orders, but it was always my favorite time when she was there.

My parents have a large yard. The house was built in an era when quarter-acre parcels were standard, and my mom, excited I was showing gumption for anything and thrilled to have my dad occupied, eagerly agreed to the plan.

My dad's overseeing the project. He has a sheath of printouts an inch thick that he gathered from the Internet on garden design, fertilizer, drainage, and plants.

He sits in a lawn chair beneath the giant magnolia sipping iced tea and snapping orders like a warden overseeing a chain gang, while I wield my pick and shovel and answer, "Yes, Boss." "This where you want it, Boss?" "I'll get right on that, Boss."

It's stifling hot; the thermometer on the porch hovers at ninety-four. We've been at it for a couple of hours, and I've removed all the grass from the ten-by-ten area we've staked as "Goat's Garden West."

"Now we need to shovel out a foot of the dirt," my dad says. "Start digging."

"Yes, Boss."

I grab the pickax and start to loosen the soil. My plan is to start in the upper corner and work my way out in rows. The ground is hard, and my progress is slow. It takes half an hour to reach the end of the first row. At the last foot of the patch, I slam the pick into the dirt and it sinks to the handle, causing me to stumble. I pull the ax from the ground, and there's a chunk of white dangling from the tip. I look closer and recognize it as bone.

I look back at my dad to tell him, but he's asleep in his chair, his cheater glasses falling sideways off his face, his mouth gaping open.

I grab the shovel and dig in the spot where the ground is soft. It takes two shovelfuls to reveal what's beneath.

"Jill, what are you doing?"

I turn quickly. "Nothing, Pops," I say as I throw a smile on my face and dirt back over the discovery.

"It's Boss, remember."

"Nothing, Boss. Just taking a break. I think we should call it a day."

"Okay. I'm going to take a nap."

My dad limps into the house, and I follow.

The door to my parents' room closes behind my dad, and I continue on to find my mom. She's in the garage doing laundry.

"Tell me what happened," I demand.

"What happened to what?" she asks brightly as she folds a shirt that at one time was white, but now is gray.

"What happened to Martha? I just found her in the garden. That was no car accident."

She blinks hard three times, her face loses its color, and her hands stop folding the shirt she holds. "Does your father know?"

I shake my head. "Gordon did that?"

Her mouth is tight, and she inhales deeply to hold in the emotions, her head nodding up and down, her eyes on the ground.

My whole body trembles with rage, but my tone softens. "Why didn't you tell me?"

"You had enough to worry about."

"When?"

"The day you took the kids, he came to the house. It was very late. Somehow he knew you'd called me, and he thought I knew where you were and that I was helping you. After he left, I let Martha out, and when I went to get her..."

Her voice trails off and I want to comfort her, but I can't because I'm already too far away, marching toward the car and the box Sherman gave me. I barely hear her voice as I screech from the driveway.

63

Gordon's Cayenne is in the hospital's long-term parking lot. I park beside it, pull out the gun, and am surprised at its simplicity. The clip pops out, the bullets pop in. Release the safety, squeeze the trigger.

Aim low, because a gun has a tendency to rise when you shoot—Gordon told me that. I think about where I need to aim. I'll aim at his balls and hopefully hit them, but if not, I'll hit his gut or his heart.

I drape my sweatshirt over my arm to conceal the weapon and walk through the sliding glass doors of the hospital. I look at the menu beside the elevators. Children's Oncology is on the fifth floor. Time ticks as I watch the three elevators' glowing lights descend. The one on the right wins, and I step in and press five. A woman steps in beside me and presses two; her belly is much larger than mine. A hand stops the doors before they close, and the man attached to it says, "Thanks," and, "Sorry," as he steps in and presses the number three. The gun is heavy, and my hand trembles. The pregnant woman waddles out onto a floor decorated with colorful handprints and balloons. It takes forever for the doors to close again.

The man beside me rocks heel to toe. He's about thirty. He wears a simple gold wedding band and a load of worry. The floor he steps onto is unadorned except for the navy letters ICU painted neatly on the wall.

The door closes again, and I'm alone for the remainder of the ride.

I step onto the fifth floor. "Can I help you?" a pink-scrubbed nurse sitting behind a pair of locked glass doors asks through an intercom.

"I'm here to visit Addie Kane."

"And you are?"

"A friend."

"Your name?"

"Michelle Garner." I hope Michelle will understand. She punches the name into the computer, and the door buzzes. I push it open with my left hand.

"Room five-oh-eight," the woman says with a smile as I walk past.

Even numbers are on the left.

In 502, a Hispanic family, maybe six of them, laugh and eat food from Tupperware containers.

On the door of 504, a finger-painted star says, "Liza's Room," but the bed is empty.

In 506, a boy about twelve sits in bed watching television. He's bald, and his eyes are bruised.

Addie's door is decorated with a drawing of an elephant, and the "e" on her name is backward. We had been working on that, but sometimes she still forgets. The lights are off, but I see her through the window sleeping in the bed.

Addie.

Her skin is almost as white as the sheet, and the bed is so big around her that she looks like a doll waiting for a little girl to come and claim her. Her hands rest on top of the neatly tucked-in blankets, and a pulse monitor is taped to one finger. An IV drips into the neck of her hospital gown. Gordon isn't there.

I step close and watch her small shallow breaths—they're thin and steady—and every few, she double gulps, then licks her lips. Her hair has been cut short, and she must be losing it because patches are thin and bristles sprinkle the pillow around her head.

"Oh, baby," I whisper, "I'm so sorry." My voice is only to myself because I don't want to wake her.

Tears trickle from the corners of my eyes.

My baby.

Footsteps behind me cause me to turn.

"Her father's in the chapel," the pink nurse says, "if you wanted to say hello. Addie's going to be asleep for a while."

I nod.

"Ground floor next to the cafeteria."

I don't pivot and storm from the room as I intended. The rhythm of Addie's breath has captured me. I stay rooted where I am, studying how her nose twitches and her lashes flutter.

The gun dangles loose in my hand, a ridiculous, dangerous notion of irrational impulsive thinking that weighs down my arm and makes me feel very stupid. I am not him. I can't be him. I won't be him. I close my eyes. *No more mistakes.*

Addie is mine. I am hers. I am all she has.

I'm going to fix things, baby.

The promise is silent, but the conviction in my heart is deafening.

I ride the elevator to the ground floor, glance down the hall that leads to the chapel, then continue through the lobby and into the glaring sun. The time has come to fix things.

64

The beach is teeming with sun worshippers and families soaking up the last days of summer on a perfect afternoon.

I sit on the boardwalk and lift my face to the sun, feeling the heat on my skin and the light behind my lids. I inhale the scent of summer, and it fills my nostrils—pizza from Cucina Alessa on the corner, salt and seaweed, exhaust from the Coast Highway, and suntan oil.

I exhale, open my eyes, and squint at the waves. A swell rolls from the south, and the sea looks lazy and dangerous.

I'm not a murderer, I'm not Gordon. It's both liberating and terrifying—I'm not evil, I'm not him, I'm at his mercy. Overwhelming relief, petrifying fear, and I wonder if again, I will come to regret this moment. I need to fix things, Addie and Drew need me to fix things, and today might have been my chance. I would have destroyed myself in the process, but it might have been worth it. Declaw the lion—it sounds so simple—but I'm not as wily as Aesop or his crafty farmer; either would have shot the lion had they had a gun. How many chances will I get to save them? Or was today the only one?

Seagulls wheel overhead. I watch them spin in circles, effortlessly suspended in the breeze, until my eyes blur and all I see is Addie in the hospital bed. Life isn't fair. It's full of injustice and tragedy and unforgivable mistakes that beg for forgiveness.

I turn the revelation in my mind until the clouds take on the pink of the setting sun and the air chills, causing me to shiver, then I pick myself up and drive back home.

My mom and dad sit at the table. My dad holds my mom's hand; in her other hand is a tissue. When they see me, my mom jumps to her feet and my dad breathes. Until I had children of my own, I couldn't understand those expressions—the way they looked when I was five minutes late from a date, how angry my dad would get if I didn't call to tell him I was going out with friends after school—now I feel horribly guilty for the worry I caused them.

"Sorry."

"You okay?" my mom asks.

I nod, then my head reverses direction, and in an instant, she's beside me and I'm in her arms.

"Come, sit," she says, and guides me to the table.

"I'll get coffee," my dad says, and limps toward the ancient GE percolator.

The quiet lingers between us, the only sound my dad pouring the coffee and adding cream and one cube of sugar. I've since graduated to taking my coffee black, but I've never told my dad that. He holds out a steaming cup to me. My mom releases my hand, and I take the mug. My dad brushes my hair with a kiss. "Good night, ladies," he says, and both of us watch him go.

I sip the warm coffee, focusing on the taste and the smell, wishing it could transport me back to a time when I sat at this table drinking out of this same cup and my greatest worry was whether Gary Branch, a boy with a Mustang and really great sideburns, would ask me to the prom.

My mom's voice brings me back. "I'm sorry I didn't tell you about Martha. I don't know why it's always been so hard between us."

And for perhaps the first time, I see my mom as she is, a woman like me, not at all sure of herself, just trying to do the best she can, bumbling her way through life like the rest of us. Stuck with an only child who's bucked her every step of the way, a daughter who always chose her father over her and never let her in. And I wish I could rewind time, have the chance to do things over.

"It's still that way," she finishes, "always arm's length, a line in the sand between us."

I want to deny it, to say, "Don't be ridiculous. We're good. I love you," but I don't. I won't trivialize what we've lost with placation. We shared my dad and existed in the same bubble, but not in each other's lives. And though the past two months have brought us closer, history can't be undone, and I won't pretend we're something we're not.

"I saw Addie," I say instead.

My mom accepts the truth with only the smallest twitch of her right eye, then her attention turns entirely to worry for Addie. "How is she?"

I shake my head and swallow to hold back my tears.

My mom takes my hands. "She's a fighter. She's got your spirit. She'll pull through this."

I nod.

"And Gordon?"

"I snuck into her room while he was in the chapel." I leave out the rest.

My mom crosses herself in thanks.

I'm not as grateful, and I wonder if, in thirty-five years, Addie and I will be having a conversation similar to this one, as estranged as my mother and me, a lifetime of regret between us, because today I failed.

65

Michelle's watching Drew again for Gordon. She's taking the boys to Little Corona in Newport, a remote beach where I can join them and we won't be spotted. So I'm waiting on the corner, tucked out of sight, for Gordon to drop Drew off. It's a sweltering day, well over ninety, and even with the windows down, my skin sticks to the seat with sweat.

The car that pulls up, a white Mercedes SUV, is not Gordon's.

Drew slinks from the passenger side, and Claudia steps from the driver's seat. She reaches into the trunk to retrieve a beach bag, then follows Drew to the front door.

I watch as she crosses the lawn and climbs the steps to the porch. Something's different about her, but I can't put my finger on it. Her gold hair still drapes to her shoulders. She's still fit and toned. She still walks with more swagger than necessary. And she still has the annoying habit of flicking her hair back every five seconds. But something's changed.

Michelle answers the door, and Drew launches away from Claudia and into Michelle's home without a good-bye. Michelle and Claudia have a brief exchange, then Claudia turns to leave.

Michelle stays in the doorway, the heather gray beach dress she wears revealing her athletic legs.

My eyes shoot to Claudia as she climbs back into her car and I realize what's changed. There's not enough skin.

Claudia's notorious for the short shorts and tank tops she wears that reveal J. Lo legs and Angela Bassett arms. Today, on the hottest day of the year, she wears jeans and a long-sleeve polo. And I'm probably the only other person in the world who knows why.

The Mercedes drives away, and I run to the front door.

"Michelle, I can't stay," I say, barely allowing her to say hello.

Drew runs up behind her. "Hi, Mom."

"Hey, buddy." I kneel to his height and give him a high five. A smile fills his face.

"You're coming to the beach with us, right?"

I shake my head, and his smile gets smaller.

I take his hands in mine and hold his eyes. "I can't," I say. "I wish I could, but from here on out, you and I are going to follow the rules because I need to figure out how to make this whole crazy mess right, and to do that, I need to be smart and you need to be strong, and that means I can't take the chance of messing up."

"I don't want to live with Claudia."

I nod. "I know, and I don't want you to live with her, either, and I'm not sure exactly how I'm going to fix things, but I have an idea. So, if it's okay with you, I'm going to pass on going to the beach today, and instead, I'm going to see what I can do about making things better."

His small jaw pushes out a centimeter and quivers. I pull him into my arms, and he must have forgotten about Max because his thin arms are around me.

"You need to hang in there," I whisper into his ear. "Like the way Paul taught you to be patient and smart. Can you do that?"

He nods against my hair.

"Don't make your dad and Claudia mad, just do what they say so I know you're safe."

"I don't like her."

"I know. But for now, you need to pretend."

He pulls away and sniffles once. "You gonna be able to fix things?"

"I'm gonna try."

Claudia lives in the gated community of Three Arch Bay. I drive to the gates and wait, and an hour later, when Claudia's Mercedes pulls onto the Coast Highway, I follow.

We end up at Fashion Island in Newport Beach, an outdoor mall where I'm sure Claudia spends a lot of her time and her father's money.

"Claudia," I say, causing her to turn with a fake smile, obviously thinking she's running into a friend. The smile drops when she sees me and her eyes get big, then they run me up and down and she sneers at my less-than-glamorous appearance. Today, for my beach outing, I'm wearing a Dodgers T-shirt I borrowed from my dad over a pair of elastic-banded nylon shorts.

She turns and continues to hurry on her way.

I hustle in front of her. "Please, Claudia, just hear me out."

She whirls, her eyes skittering around as she yelps, "I have nothing to say to you."

She's either grown a conscience and feels guilty or she's so humiliated by the truth of the situation, that Gordon beats her, that she can't look me in the eye. Or perhaps it's a combination of both.

Again my emotions are torn—I resent her at the same time I feel sorry for her. Claudia and I were never friends, but we grew up in the same small town and have known each other our whole lives. Our boys are the same age, and though I don't like her, I've watched compassionately from the sidelines as she charted a tragic course of destruction for herself, first getting involved with a serial rotation of surfer boys, then getting pregnant by one of them who wanted to live off her money while he continued playing the field and surfing the circuit.

Searching for love—or actually, *searching for romance*—should be her tagline. I've watched for the last twenty years as she's been sorely, brutally used and her heart bruised, the dozen times she thought she found it, and now she's with Gordon.

Shame. Desperation. Not wanting to acknowledge she chose wrong again. I get it. Oh, how I get it.

"He hits you," I say bluntly.

Her head shoots up and scans rapidly around her, certain Gordon's watching her. I get it. He knows, he always knows.

"Leave me alone," she cries, running past me. "He chose me, not you. He loves me."

Pride, obstinacy, vanity, arrogance. I let her go. A wounded bird, desperate to be loved. *Scared, yes. Lazy, maybe. Weak, definitely.* Oh, how I get it.

I get it, but that doesn't mean I'm not going to use it. I watch as she race-walks into the mall probably to buy more long-sleeve blouses or heavier foundation, her pale hands swishing against her pants. Her skin is like Addie's; she probably bruises like a peach.

Time to declaw the lion.

Nellie Gail Ranch is nestled into the foothills of Laguna Niguel. It's a wealthy, gated community of horse ranches and mansions. Claudia's father, Frank Rousseau, and my father have known each other over thirty years. While my dad eked out a living from his restaurants, Mr. Rousseau made a fortune selling him and thousands of other restaurateurs salad dressings and soups. My dad called ahead to let him know I was coming.

I pull up to the sprawling ranch house nestled behind mature eucalyptus and a sprawling, manicured lawn and park in the horseshoe driveway.

The door opens before I reach the steps.

"Hello, Jillian."

"Mr. Rousseau, thank you for seeing me."

Tight and petite like his daughter, he has a small chin, a large nose, dark blue eyes, and his face wears a smile and a layer of distrust.

"Would you like to come in?" he asks.

I shake my head. "This will only take a minute."

He's relieved.

"Mr. Rousseau, you've known my father a long time, and through him, you know me. I'd like you to consider that when I tell you what I'm about to tell you."

I rehearsed this in the car, my nerves jacked up high. I have one shot, a single chance to turn the tides and get my kids back.

Claudia is Gordon's Achilles' heel, she just doesn't know it. She's stalwartly loyal. It's tragically romantic, and I know I can't change that; I won't even try. But I don't need her consent, I just need her pale, bruised skin.

Claudia loves Gordon, and Mr. Rousseau loves his daughter.

Claudia is searching for love to save her, and hopefully it will. I'm counting on it to save us all.

It's time to cash in all my chips, ante up all the goodwill I've socked away in the solitary hope of convincing Mr. Rousseau I'm telling the truth, something he's not going to want to believe.

I wait as he turns my words. For as long as he's known my father, he's heard my dad bragging about me. While Claudia was getting into trouble with boys and ditching school, I was charging forward in my career and walking the straight and narrow.

When his focus returns, I take a breath, and with great courage, tell him what I've been hiding from the world. "Gordon's an abusive man, and he's hurting Claudia."

His poker face flinches, his eyes blink, his right cheek twitches.

"Get out," he seethes through clenched teeth.

I don't move. "Please, Mr. Rousseau..."

"Leave. Now." He closes the distance between us in a stride, and I back-pedal, stumbling toward my car.

Before I reach it, I yell over my shoulder, "Check her arms and legs." I stutter, "If I'm wrong, I owe you an apology..."

He interrupts, "You owe me an apology now. Accusing a man of abuse is a hell of a way to try and get your kids back. No woman worth a dime would stay with a man who hurts her, and as you said, Jillian, I've known you a long time, and you certainly believe you're worth more than two nickels. Christ, you and your dad think you're the fucking Queen of Sheba. And now, for the first time, Claudia's got something you want, and you can't handle it. Claudia said you were crazy."

My hand's on the car door handle, but I don't open it. Instead, I whirl around and stomp back toward him. He glowers at me from the top step, his arms folded triumphantly.

"I may be crazy, and if I am, it's because Gordon made me that way. And you're right, I'd do anything to get my kids back, and I'd do anything to protect them, including lying." I'm the one seething now, the words spitting like daggers. "So maybe I'm crazy and maybe I'm lying and maybe I'm just a spoiled bitch trying to get my way. The question is, Mr. Rousseau, are you willing to stake your daughter's life on that?"

66

It took only four hours for all hell to break loose.

"Hello, Frank," my dad says into the phone. He grunts a few times, nods, then hangs up, his face red with rage. If he were a cartoon character, steam would be blowing from his ears and nostrils.

"Is Claudia okay?" I ask.

He ignores me. "Grace, you need to pick Drew up. He's at the police station."

"The police station," I croak.

"Gordon was arrested. He's in jail."

My heart pounds and sings and panics all at once. There's a small sense of victory that's completely overwhelmed by the feeling that I've just bashed a bat into a beehive.

"Should I bring him here?" my mom asks as she gathers her purse.

My dad shakes his head. "Gordon's going to be released..."

"What?" I scream.

My dad holds up his hand. "Claudia is refusing to press charges. They only took him in because he was threatening

Frank. He'll be out in a couple of hours. Take Drew to the mall or something, then you'll need to give him back. Gordon still has custody. Nothing's changed."

My mom returned an hour ago without Drew, and she was so defeated that I couldn't bear to ask her what happened.

I'm too upset to sit still, so I'm in the garden that's still nothing more than a torn-up patch of lawn. Unsuccessfully, I'm trying to distract my concerns about Addie and Drew by engaging in a useless struggle against the roots of the magnolia tree that refuses to relent the small patch of yard I've declared as mine.

"Jill, someone's at the door for you," my dad says from the porch.

I wipe my hands on my jeans and walk around the house to the front.

Gregg Lackey, the officer who arrested me for my DUI, stands on the porch; his black-and-white is parked at the curb.

"Mrs. Kane."

"Jillian," I correct.

"Jillian."

He folds his arms across his chest, then unfolds them, then refolds them, like he's unsure what to do with his appendages. Finally, he lets them hang by his side. "I'm sorry," he says. "I'm so sorry. I didn't know...I had no idea. The way Claudia explained it, I thought you were trying to set Gordon up so you'd get custody..." His eyes focus on a spot past me, then rise to meet mine and he repeats, "I'm sorry."

My head nods just slightly, but I say nothing.

"I talked to my captain. The DUI's going to be dropped."

"As in gone?" I ask. "Taken off my record?"

He nods. "And Uncle Frank's on a rampage. Gordon picked on the wrong girl..." He stops abruptly, and his eyes slide away again as he realizes he just implied that I was the right girl. I let him stew in his discomfort. "Sorry," he mumbles. "I didn't mean...Anyway, what I meant to say is it looks like Gordon's going to be suspended from his job."

"Is Claudia okay?" I ask.

His nose pinches tight as he says, "She will be. Uncle Frank's sending her to stay in Hawaii with her mom to get her away from Gordon, give her some distance. She's messed up right now, still wants to go back to him." He shakes his head. "I don't get it. He beat her black and blue, and Claudia's still insisting she loves the bastard."

My face shows compassion, while inside I cheer. I hate myself for rejoicing that the bruises are bad, but I can't help the hope that rises knowing Claudia's beaten body might be exactly what I need to get Addie and Drew back.

I wait for his emotions to settle, and as much as I was determined not to like him and to hold a grudge, I find myself forgiving him. He obviously loves his cousin very much.

When the moment's passed, his eyes find mine again. "I really didn't know," he says. "I thought I was doing the right thing. So many dads get the raw end of the deal." His stare reveals a hurt that has nothing to do with me.

"You have children?" I ask.

"A son. I haven't seen him in two years."

"I'm sorry."

"Not an excuse for what I did, though it's probably the reason."

"We've all done things we regret."

He toes the ground, and an awkward silence stands between us. It's because he's the right age and I'm the right age, and he's a man and I'm a woman, and all emotionally charged moments between X and Y lead to this strange tension. I wait for it to pass. I don't know if I'll ever care for a man again, but I'm certain of my inability now, and as the moment fades, I marvel that despite the apocalyptic condition of my life, the energy still exists.

He reaches into his pocket and pulls out a business card. "If there's anything I can do to help, to make it up to you."

I take the card with a thin smile.

"Gordon's done as a cop," he says. "I know that doesn't make up for things, but whether Claudia charges him or not, my uncle's gonna make sure everyone knows what he did."

I shrug. Somehow it all seems so far removed from Addie and Drew.

He steps away, then hesitates. He wants to do more, wants to make things right, undo what he did wrong. But it's never that simple.

I watch him go until the taillights disappear.

I should be celebrating. This is what I wanted, what Connor told me needed to be done. I've shaken the foundation—stripped Gordon of Claudia, his job, his reputation. I should feel victorious. Instead, all I feel is terrified.

Back a bear into a corner and you end up with an angry bear.

67

Despite exhaustion, I can't sleep. My pregnancy's moved from the sick stage to the uncomfortable stage, and heartburn, hiccups, and swollen ankles, combined with incredible stress over the latest turn of events, make sleep impossible.

I pass the mirror in the hallway and catch a glimpse of what I might look like in another twenty years. Dark circles ring my eyes, and worry lines scar my face.

It's seven in the morning, and my parents are asleep, so when the phone rings, I grab it on its first chime.

"Jill?"

"Gordon?"

"We need to talk."

"How's Addie?"

"When can you meet?"

"Is Drew there? Can I talk to him?"

"This afternoon. Meet me at the food court on Sand Canyon at one."

The phone clicks, and my heart races.

∞

I walk with measured steps toward the tables with the yellow-and-brown-striped umbrellas. Gordon sits beneath the one farthest to the left. He looks relaxed, his posture slumped back in the seat, his left arm resting on the table.

He wears his Oakley Flak Jacket sunglasses, a newly trimmed buzz cut, and his signature windbreaker that conceals his gun.

I'm scared all the way to my marrow, and all that keeps me moving forward is the thin hope that staying on course might lead me back to Addie and Drew.

In front of him is a tray with a Baja Fresh burrito and a lemonade. I take my seat across from him.

"Aren't you going to eat? You know you're eating for two." He smiles magnanimously at me like he's my friend, and I realize with a shudder how truly sociopathic he is.

"Where are the kids?"

"You need to eat." He stands and returns ten minutes later with a gyro from Daphne's and sets the tray in front of me.

"Gordon, where are Addie and Drew?"

"Eat."

I push the tray aside, and his eyes pulse.

"Fine, Jill. Be a bitch."

"Where are they?"

He sighs through his nose, his eyes twitching, and finally, he says, "Addie's at the hospital, and Drew's at baseball camp."

I breathe. "What do you want?"

"I want you to eat."

"I'm not hungry."

The pause sits between us, and as Gordon contemplates my newfound defiance, I wonder how I ever thought I loved this man. So much hate fills me, I'm certain, at this moment, my soul is black. Intellectually, I understand he's handsome—well proportioned, strong—but I abhor him, and I hate that Addie shares his smile and that Drew has his eyes. I don't want them to have any part of him.

Finally, he leans forward, interrupting my hatred, and says, "You need to get your job back. Addie's still sick, so I can't go back to work, so you need to start working again." Unsaid is the fact that he was suspended from his job because he beat the crap out of Claudia.

"You want me to support you?" I say, incredulous.

"To support the family."

I can only stare blankly in response.

"It's the way it is. We have two kids...I mean, three kids. So, like it or not, we're in this together."

"Together? As in you and I?" I point back and forth between us. If it wasn't so completely insane, I'd laugh, but because he's looking at me with such sincerity, there's absolutely nothing funny whatsoever about this conversation.

"For the kids' sake and the baby's sake, yes. Somehow we need to make this work."

Silence lingers, until finally, I break it. "I'm not going to support you."

I stand, and he stands with me. Then he smiles, his teeth white as a Crest commercial. His arm slides around my waist, and his lips press over my ear, his words vibrating against my skin. "You'll never see them again. I'll take them and...You. Will. *Never*. See. Them. Again."

He sits back down, unwraps his burrito, and begins to eat.

My breath knots in the back of my throat, and every inch of my skin breaks out in a cold sweat.

I stare at the horizon beyond the parking lot until my eyes blur, but I don't take a step. He's telling the truth. All he has left is the kids. Nothing holds him here—his job, his reputation, his money. I destroyed these. Once Addie is better, he will leave, and they'll be gone.

I want to tell him hell will freeze over before I give him a dime, that I'm not afraid; instead, I sit back down and meet his icy gaze.

"Eat," he says.

Dutifully I unwrap my gyro and choke down a bite.

When I've swallowed, I speak. "I'll talk to Harris, but he's not going to hire me back if I'm facing trial for kidnapping and am possibly going to be sent to prison."

This morning I met with Harris, and he practically begged me to come back, could have cared less about where I was or what I'd done, his only concern how soon I could return. He even offered me a raise. I negotiated for more vacation time and working flex hours from home in lieu of the money so I can work my job around the kids' schedules, assuming I get the kids back.

But Gordon doesn't know this, and money is definitely the one advantage I've always had over him, and I plan on using it. I could care less about money. Flying Goat changed me. I can live happily on eighty-six dollars a day. I can't live without my kids. And in order to get the kids back, I need him to drop the charges against me.

"I'll talk to the DA about dropping the charges."

I nod and take another bite, chewing slowly. "Then I'll talk to Harris."

"Jill, at some point, you're going to forgive me."

My head shakes.

He stiffens almost imperceptibly, then slumps back to perfect amity and sighs a sound of mild disappointment. "You know you will. You always do."

I look across at him looking so certain. Is it possible he really believes this is like the other times?

"You killed a man."

His brow furrows. "I what?"

"You killed Jeffrey."

"You think I killed someone? Who's Jeffrey?"

I'm surprised how calm my voice is and how perplexed Gordon is, and for a flicker, I wonder if I could be wrong, if I could have jumped to the wrong conclusion—if it's possible Jeffrey was just in the wrong place at the wrong time and the weapon just happened to be a shotgun.

"What are you talking about?" he asks.

"Jeffrey, my client, my friend. You killed him."

He flinches, but only slightly, then reveals the truth. "Jill, I have no idea what you're talking about." My name pierces like a bullet and erases all doubt. He's lying. He killed him.

"Jill, I know you've been under a lot of stress, but I didn't kill anyone. That idiot called me, and we had a conversation and I told him to butt out, but that was it."

I stare blankly.

"You honestly think I killed him?"

I nod.

"Jill, that's insane. I was pissed off, but I'm not a murderer."

After a full minute with no response, he continues. "I'm concerned about the baby." He looks at my stomach. "We need to put this all behind us and do what's best for the kids."

My eyes squint as I try to process his words.

"You need to come home," he clarifies.

68

I've been working for two weeks, and without the burden of having to rush home to a husband, a house, and kids, I'm finding the job remarkably easier. I stay until the work is done, answer e-mails sitting on my bed at night, and even have time to take long walks and work in the garden.

Each day, Connor and I review our strategy for challenging Gordon for custody. Connor is not a divorce attorney, but this is hardly a standard divorce, and he's the only one I trust to handle this. He's brilliant, and though I've not actually seen him in action, his reputation as a ruthless litigator was what got him the job with Harris.

Our strategy is the same as it was when he spoke to me at Las Brisas: destroy Gordon and redeem me—not an easy task.

True to Gregg's word, the DUI charges have been dropped. Now all we are waiting on is for the kidnapping charges to be dismissed. Gordon spoke to the DA the day after we met for lunch.

Each day is impossibly long as I wait for the slow wheels of bureaucracy to spin.

A week ago, I gave Gordon half my first paycheck in exchange for a visit with Addie in the hospital and an afternoon with Drew.

"Morning, beautiful," Connor says, poking his blond head into my office.

"What are you grinning about?"

He whips a paper out from behind his back. "You, my gorgeous, wonderful friend, have been exonerated. You are no longer being charged with kidnapping."

"What?"

"It's true. The charges have been dropped, and you cannot, will not, be charged again."

We do an impromptu jig in the doorway that causes stares from everyone around us.

"Grab your purse," he says.

"Where are we going?"

"The courthouse. We have one hour to file a petition for emergency custody change, unless, of course, you'd rather wait."

I don't even bother to close the door as I sprint past him and toward the parking lot.

69

The emergency custody hearing is set for tomorrow morning, and Gordon will be served his subpoena this afternoon. Connor assured me this was the only way, but I can't help the feeling of dread that grows with each passing minute.

This is an ambush, and all my weapons are in place.

Gordon has no idea Mr. Rousseau is going to testify or that my mom and dad will be there and that my mom's hoping to tell the story about Martha's butchering.

Connor says our strategy is twofold. First we'll destroy Gordon, then we'll prove I can provide a stable environment for the kids. Michelle has agreed to be a character witness if I need her, and Harris has provided an affidavit affirming my secure position at the firm and my economic stability.

I've tried to plan it right. Bob's taken Drew and Max camping in the mountains, so Drew's safe and out of reach. Gordon only has Addie tonight, and I'm counting on the fact that he won't leave without both of them.

All my ducks are in a row, but as soon as Gordon is served, there's no predicting what he'll do. My parents and I are staying at a hotel tonight, and Connor is going to stay at Pete's.

The bear is about to be poked.

70

Gordon arrives at court looking rabid. He carries Addie on his hip like she weighs no more than a sack of flour. She wears her Cinderella nightie and has on only one slipper. Her thumb is in her mouth, and she looks tired and ill, which she is. Her chemo treatment was only three days ago.

I start to stand to move toward her, but Connor's hand on my arm settles me back into my chair.

Gordon smashes through the swinging gate that separates the audience from the participants and sits down with Addie in his arms. He doesn't have a lawyer with him, and I wonder if he plans to represent himself.

My side of the courtroom is half-full, his is empty. Gordon doesn't seem to notice. The only person he sees is me, his eyes savage.

"It's okay," Connor whispers. "You're safe."

For how long? This moment, the next five, a day, a week?

"All rise, the honorable Judge Morrison presiding."

I stand awkwardly with my extra load, and Gordon does the same, Addie listlessly sucking her thumb against his shoulder.

The judge is a birdlike woman with a lazy eye and teeth that slant to the right, but she has an intelligent face, and I'm relieved to see she's not at all taken by Gordon as a lot of women are.

"Be seated."

Judge Morrison whispers something to the bailiff, and the bailiff walks to Gordon's table.

"Is there someone who can watch the child for you?" the man asks with a southern drawl and soft voice that belies his enormous linebacker size.

My mom speaks up from behind Gordon, who has started to shake his head.

"Gordon, give her to me. I'll watch her."

I feel Gordon wanting to say no, but also calculating the risk of such a move. My mom looks exactly like what she is—a doting grandmother, concerned for her granddaughter.

Everyone's eyes watch.

To my astonishment, Gordon stands, and with a gentle kiss to Addie's cheek and a pained look on his face I feel to my bones, hands Addie over the balustrade. Addie melts into my mom's softness as my mom coos softly in her ear and pats her bald head.

"Your Honor," my mom says, "do you mind if I take her home to rest?"

"You are?"

"The grandmother."

The judge rifles through some sheets on the bench. "Any objection, Mr. Kane?"

Again Gordon's cornered, and I catch a glimpse of Connor beside me. His smile is that of a Cheshire cat, and I realize this was orchestrated. If Gordon says no, he'll look uncaring, and if he says yes, he concedes my mom's not a threat, making my parents the ideal backup plan for custody if Gordon and I both destroy each other and the judge doesn't want either of us to raise our children. Insisting Connor represent me was a good choice, even if divorce isn't his specialty.

"No, Your Honor, that would be fine."

"Good. Then let's proceed."

I hear my mom's thighs swishing as she walks away with Addie.

"Where's Mr. Rousseau?" I whisper.

Connor looks behind us. "Where's Frank?" he repeats to my dad, who's directly behind us, and I hear my dad stand and hobble away.

Connor presents a compelling opening statement outlining the main points of our assertion that sole custody should be granted to me and that a restraining order needs to be issued against Gordon. He talks almost twenty minutes, and even to me, my resume as a professional woman is impressive, overshadowing my reputation as a mom, which is sparse. He follows with his argument against Gordon and the reason we've petitioned for a restraining order. Connor does a brilliant job portraying Gordon as the Jekyll and Hyde husband he is, and even though the story is mine, I'm caught up in his narrative. The problem is, no matter how well Connor delivers the argument, our case rests solely on the abuse. In every other respect, Gordon's been an outstanding father. And since this is a he says/she says hearing, the only objective evidence we have that proves Gordon's not who he pretends to be is his abuse of Claudia.

I feel Gordon's blood pressure rising as Connor talks, and I'm amazed by his restraint. He sits motionless, silently seething at his table.

When it's his turn, he nearly topples his chair as he leaps to his feet.

"Your Honor." His voice is smooth, and only I know how violent he is at this moment. "The accusations against me are nothing but a bunch of lies, designed with the sole purpose of undermining my parental rights. Listen carefully and you will see there's not a shred of evidence to support them. My ex-wife is unstable. She's been hospitalized and medicated for her condition, and unfortunately refuses to accept that it's not in the best interest of our children for them to be raised by her. Three months ago, she kidnapped them, and our daughter nearly died from her neglect. Listen to the facts, Your Honor, and you will see this petition for what it is, an unstable woman's desperate attempt to win back her children, a right she justifiably lost because she's not well."

"He's good," Connor says under his breath beside me, and I want to cry.

Where's Mr. Rousseau?

Connor calls me as the first witness.

He leads me through our marriage chronologically, hitting on the overall abuse, as well as a few specific episodes including the near-fatal choking. We decided against having Drew testify to what he saw that night. I'm unsure how much Drew witnessed, and it would be too easy for Gordon to discredit an eight-year-old's testimony or argue that the ideas were planted in his impressionable young mind. Plus, I was scared to death to put Drew in that position, both for the damage it would do to him to testify against his father and the subsequent damage Gordon would do to him if we didn't win.

So the only evidence of Gordon's abuse against me is my own testimony and a few medical records that corroborate a chipped tooth, several cracked ribs, and a broken wrist that, at the time of care, I claimed were caused by mishaps.

I always imagined if I ever confronted Gordon with the abuse, I would be fierce and angry. Instead, I'm so ashamed that I can barely lift my head to hear the questions, and my answers are so quiet, several times I need to repeat myself. I testify as though the fault is entirely my own, and Gordon was only a bit player—the executioner—while I'm the one who caused it, could have prevented it, allowed it to go on.

By the time I finish confessing the truth about my marriage, I'm completely spent.

"Ms. Kane, do you need a recess?" the judge asks.

I shake my head, determined to finish, afraid to stop for fear I'll lose my courage to start again. I take a deep breath and try to straighten my defeated posture, though it slumps back to beaten almost immediately.

Connor takes his time before asking the next question. He shuffles papers and stares for a long time at his notes, giving me an extra minute to collect myself.

"Just a few more questions," he says.

I nod, knowing the next questions are the most important ones.

"So you left?" Connor asks.

I nod, then realizing I need to speak up, say, "Yes."

"Without the kids?"

For the first time, tears escape, a single vein of wetness down each cheek. Connor hands me a tissue. In the past month, I've realized the critical mistake I made that caused all the awful things that happened after. I left without a plan and without Addie and Drew. My impulsivity led to everything else, including Jeffrey's death. I knew what Gordon was capable of. Yet, in a single moment of irritation, over the most banal of things, money, I made the decision to leave.

Connor continues; he tiptoes around the DUI and Jeffrey's death to ask me about taking the kids.

"Did you kidnap your children?"

I shake my head and answer, "No." We rehearsed this line of questioning, and it's stronger than my other responses. "I took them because I was scared for their safety and my own. I still am."

Connor leads me through the phone call with the insurance agent that led me to believe Gordon was going to kill me.

"I didn't know what else I could do," I say. "I couldn't leave them behind, and if I stayed, he was going to kill me."

The questions are carefully crafted not only to prove I fled because I was justifiably scared, but also to protect me. If I die, Gordon will now be the prime suspect.

I risk a glance at the defense table. For the first time, Gordon looks concerned. He wasn't aware I knew about his attempt to extend my life insurance policy.

Connor leads me quickly through the six weeks we were on the run and Addie's illness.

"Do you still believe you're in danger?"

"At the moment, I'm pregnant, so I don't think so. Gordon's never abused me when I've been pregnant." I feel Gordon's eyes drilling into me. "I've also removed him as the beneficiary from my insurance so there's no longer any financial motive." I'm relieved to say this, to communicate to Gordon that killing me won't benefit him other than for revenge, which judging by his expression is plenty of motivation in itself.

"Are you the reason your daughter's sick?"

I answer, "No," but my head is nodding. "I should have taken her in sooner," I wail, horrified by my outburst, but unable to control it. "I thought it was the flu. Honestly, I did, but yes, I also knew it was more...never cancer...cancer never occurred to me; she's only four. You saw her; who looks at their little girl and thinks she has cancer? But when I think about it now, I must have known. The flu doesn't come and go for weeks. I should have taken her in sooner, and I knew it, but I also knew if I took her to the doctor, we'd be found out." I'm fully sobbing now, and Connor is handing me tissue after tissue as he gently tells me we're done and asks the judge for a recess before the cross-examination.

I stumble from the stand, and Connor leads me into the hallway, his arm bolstering my shaky legs.

"You did great," he says. "The judge believes you."

"What about the Addie part? I didn't take her in soon enough."

He wraps his arm around me and kisses my head. "It's not your fault," he says. "The judge was practically crying with you. She must be a mother."

I nod and breathe deep, feeling slightly better about my testimony.

"Now comes the tough part," Connor says.

Gordon stands twenty feet from us, his eyes fixed on me, the message of his glare absolute—*I will kill you for this.*

Connor's phone rings. He turns me so I'm not facing my peril as he answers it. He says a few, "craps, shits, and God damn its," and hangs up.

"What?"

"That was your dad. Mr. Rousseau's not coming."

"What?"

"Claudia's threatening to kill herself if he testifies against Gordon. He's been on the phone with her all morning. His wife just called the Honolulu police, and they're on their way to arrest her on a fifty-one-fifty, involuntary confinement, but until they get there, he's afraid to hang up."

The blood drains from my face. Everything I just did was for nothing—splaying my dirty laundry and my shame for everyone to see, signing my death warrant—none of it will matter. Without Mr. Rousseau's testimony, Gordon's going to win. Claudia confessed to her father, in a rage, told him she didn't care if Gordon hurt her, that she loved him and wanted to go back. Without Mr. Rousseau, it won't matter whether the judge believes me or not because without his testimony, it's exactly what Gordon said, a bunch of unsubstantiated accusations—my word against his.

"Hang in there," Connor says. "It's not over yet."

But it is.

71

Gordon destroys me on the stand. I can't look at him, and I know it looks like I'm lying, instead of what it is, which is that I'm terrified.

I see it in Connor's face as I step from the stand; I failed. We failed.

He calls Michelle as a witness, and she paints a nice picture of me since I've returned, but when Gordon crosses her, the picture of the mother I was before isn't nearly as pretty.

"Your Honor, we need more time," Connor says.

"I'm sorry, counselor, unless you have more witnesses..."

The doors to the courtroom slam open, and two old lions, Mr. Rousseau followed by my dad, storm through.

"Your Honor, we'd like to call Mr. Frank Rousseau to the stand," Connor says.

My eyes leak as I mouth the words "thank you" across the length of the courtroom. My dad is still my hero—my wonderful, wounded knight in shining armor. He gives me a thumbs-up and a lopsided smile, then hobbles to sit behind me as Mr. Rousseau marches to the stand.

Mr. Rousseau's eyes fix on Gordon as he describes the wounds he witnessed on Claudia. Unlike me, he's not intimidated, and he has no intention of backing down.

And when Gordon cross-examines him, both men's hackles rise, and Mr. Rousseau annihilates Gordon with his own lies.

"You hit her, beat her with your fists, cracked her ribs," he seethes. "She's five-feet-nothing, you son of a..."

"Mr. Rousseau," the judge admonishes.

Mr. Rousseau leans back, tight-lipped and furious.

"I did no such thing. You're making up lies because you don't want me with your daughter," Gordon barks. "Claudia would never say I did those things."

"Mr. Kane," the judge interrupts again, "I'll remind you, as your own attorney, it's your job to ask questions, not to defend yourself."

Mr. Rousseau launches forward again, right to the edge of the box, leaning over like a caged animal trying to get at a piece of raw meat. "And you think she made up the bruises. Marks so deep the blood vessels around them had burst."

"And, Mr. Rousseau, please, constrain your answers to the questions you're asked."

"If I did those things, why'd you have to drag her away? She didn't want to leave me. You forced her, sent her away, threatened her inheritance."

"You sick bastard." Mr. Rousseau leaps from his seat, and the bailiff quickly steps between him and the stairs that lead from the stand.

"Mr. Rousseau, please. One more outburst like that and I'll hold you in contempt."

Mr. Rousseau reluctantly returns to his seat, his pulse pounding in his temple.

"I have proof, Your Honor," he says, his voice hissing through clenched teeth.

Connor looks at me quizzically, and I look back.

"Mr. Rousseau, this isn't how it works. Either Mr. Enright or Mr. Kane needs to ask you for the evidence, but if neither side has any objections..." Her eyes are entirely on Gordon. "In the interest of expediency, perhaps we should see what you have."

Connor is nodding as Gordon stares like a cornered cat at the iPhone Mr. Rousseau's pulled from his breast pocket.

"Mr. Kane?"

"Whatever he has is a lie."

"Well, perhaps we should take a look at it and then decide. Any objection?"

Gordon reluctantly shakes his head.

"You need to speak up for the record."

"No, Your Honor. No objection," he answers tightly.

Mr. Rousseau fiddles with a few buttons and hands it to the judge. Connor and Gordon both move to the bench, and the judge turns the device for them to see.

"There are eight photos," Mr. Rousseau says. "I took them the day I brought Claudia home. She was extremely agitated so our doctor gave her a sedative. She doesn't know I took them, and because of that, because I don't have her permission, because I know she wouldn't give me her permission, I had hoped I wouldn't need to show them. I can only pray someday she'll forgive me."

"This is your daughter?" the judge asks.

"This is bullshit," Gordon barks. "You have no proof I did that."

"Mr. Kane, you will watch your language in my courtroom." And something in the judge's voice has changed. Her words are laced with disgust.

And my stomach jumps with hope.

"Those photos are doctored; they're not real. She didn't have those bruises when he took her from me," Gordon says.

Mr. Rousseau stares at his hands, his chin shaking back and forth against his chest. "I wish they weren't real, and I wish, damn me to hell, that they weren't of my daughter." His voice rasps with emotion. "But I swear, with God as my witness, that they're as real as the pain I feel when I look at them and that they are of my daughter."

Connor submits a sworn affidavit from Officer Gregg Lackey testifying that the bruises are real and were on Claudia when he and Mr. Rousseau picked her up from her home as well as an affidavit from the Rousseau family doctor testifying that Claudia had multiple contusions on her body as well as what he speculated was a cracked rib consistent with a beating.

It takes only fifteen minutes for the judge to return from her deliberation.

"All rise."

When we're seated again, she begins. "Mr. Kane, not only does this court deem you unfit as a parent, it finds your conduct reprehensible. If it were within the power of this trial to have you arrested and charged with assault and battery, I would do so and have you locked up for a very long time. As it is, all I can do is invoke the full jurisdiction of this court in order to keep you as far away as possible from your wife and your children. Therefore, sole custody is hereby granted to the petitioner, Jillian Kane, and I'm issuing a restraining order prohibiting you from any further contact with your children and your wife. Mr. Kane, I urge you to seek professional help, and perhaps with counseling, the issues of the restraining order and visitation rights can be revisited down the road. But until then, I'm ordering you to stay away from them."

The gavel bangs against the wood, the judge leaves, and Connor is hugging me.

He thinks we've won. But I know the truth. We've just taken away the last thing that was keeping Gordon sane.

Beware of the person with nothing to lose.

72

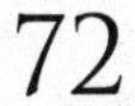

It's been a month since the hearing, and life has resumed some sense of normalcy.

Drew started school at Anneliese's and is shocking us all with how well he's doing. Like a light switch has been flicked, he actually tries, and in the subjects he's interested in—science and history—he excels. His class is small, only eighteen kids, and most of the day is spent applying the ideas being taught—chemistry through experiments, anatomy through calisthenics, history through skits that reenact the past.

The school is housed in an old monastery, which gives me some peace of mind for security. Once the school day begins, the gates close, and I don't need to be concerned about his safety.

Gordon's constantly on my mind.

No one's seen or heard from him, but I know he's not gone. I live waiting for him to appear or for the kids to disappear.

Today's a happy day. Addie finished her last chemo treatment two days ago, and this afternoon we will be leaving the fifth floor for the last time. It's been three months since she was diagnosed.

We celebrate wearing masks because her immune system is

too weak to ward off germs. Her room is crowded with balloons, stuffed animals, and people. Michelle, Max, and Bob are there. So are my parents, her nurses and doctors, and me and Drew.

The celebration is short. The chemotherapy's left Addie with barely enough energy to smile, but this is the last one. And from here on out, the old Addie will start to return.

We made it. All that's left is for us to be grateful, hopeful, and to pray.

My parents drop us at the house and continue on for a dinner out. Frank Rousseau and his wife are taking them to dinner to celebrate Addie being finished with her treatments.

I punch in the code for the alarm to the house.

My dad had a security system installed the week before I filed for the emergency custody hearing.

Addie's in my arms, her legs awkwardly wrapped around my large belly, and Drew carries her Tinker Bell suitcase.

Drew sets Addie's suitcase beside the door and runs into the study to play Xbox. I slide off my sneakers and freeze. Beside the door, my mom's gardening shoes, my dad's loafers, my mom's sneakers, and the sandals I wore earlier in the day face me in a precise line, toes pointed out.

"Drew," I snap.

"What?"

"Drew, come here, now."

"Mom, I'm playing."

"Drew, now!"

My screech must have gotten his attention because, though he looks annoyed, his head pokes out of the study. "What?"

I gesture with my head to the shoes. He steps up beside me, looks at the neat alignment of the toes, and I see him swallow as his body shifts closer to mine.

A light shines softly from beneath the kitchen door, and I can't remember if I simply forgot to turn it off.

"Come on," I say, and we back out of the house.

∞

I stare at my parents' home through my neighbor's window. It's silent. The kitchen light is on; the rest of the house is dark.

Finally, Gregg arrives. It's his night off so he's not in his uniform. He wears his gun in a holster over his T-shirt and jeans.

"I'll check it out," he says, and I hand him my keys.

I watch as the lights turn on one by one and as his shadow passes in front of the windows. Each second I wait for an explosion.

Ten minutes later, he's back.

"All clear," he says.

But it doesn't matter what he says or how many times he says it, Gordon was there, and I know he'll be back. He was in the house.

I carry Addie, and Gregg walks with Drew.

"You gonna be okay?" he asks when we get to the door.

I nod, but I know we're not.

My choice is to run and hope he doesn't find us or to stay and hope that, when he comes, I'm ready.

"Want me to stay?" Gregg asks. "I can either camp in my car or sleep on the sofa."

"Thanks, but we're okay for tonight." It's tomorrow or the next day or a week from today I'm worried about.

He gives me a wooden hug, endearingly sweet in its awkwardness. We're like bumbling, uncomfortable friends who don't know each other very well, but have a bond like that of soldiers who have served together in battle.

I close the door behind him. "Stay here," I say to Drew, who sits beside Addie, who's asleep on the couch.

Gregg assured me the house is empty, but it feels possessed.

My nerves prick at every sound as I creep toward my dad's study.

It's so quiet.

I push open the door and jerk as it squeaks.

The room is empty. I peek behind the door and peer under his desk, then from the safe, retrieve Sherman's gun.

I edge past the dining room, my heart thumping in my ears, the gun heavy in my hand.

Drew's eyes follow me.

Each step on the stairs is a different note, and I try to stay near the edge to silence the symphony.

Outside the door of my room, I wait, listening—the only sound, my blood beating in my chest.

Somewhere in the neighborhood a dog barks, and my heart jumps.

The floor groans as I reach for the knob.

An empty room.

I bend to see under the bed.

I check the empty bathroom, then my parents' room and the kids' room. No one is there.

73

It's been two weeks since Addie's last treatment, and her strength is returning along with her hair, which is now straight and soft as down. Her white blood count is good, so she no longer wears a mask, and for the first time in three months, we don't need to be paranoid about germs.

Tonight we're going to San Onofre beach to join a dozen other families for a night of surfing and fire pit cooking of hot dogs and s'mores.

Addie bounds into the living room, her red skirt flaring around her white thighs. A rhinestone headband winks on her almost hairless head, and my heart fills with so much love I think it's going to explode.

"Wready?"

Drew emerges on cue, his board shorts so low on his hips they seem in danger of sliding down, and he reminds me of Paul.

My dad's going to sit this one out. Although he walks better now, sand is an obstacle better left for those who haven't had a stroke.

"Bye, Pops," Addie says, and plants a kiss on my dad's cheek.

"Bye, Sicle," he says. "Have fun." Since the kids have moved home, my dad's taken to calling Addie Sicle, and she's shortened Papa to Pops because they go together—Pops-Sicle. It cracks Addie up every time. And he never makes the mistake of calling Drew anything but Hawk.

Addie slides on her sandals.

"Your shoes are on the wrong feet," Drew says.

Addie looks up at him confused. "But I don't have any othewr feet."

And my mom and I bust up laughing. Our laughs are the same and blend together in perfect harmony, and every time we laugh together, which lately has been often, I wish it hadn't taken so long for us to share it.

It's a beautiful night, still and chilled. A grinning moon bathes the beach in a soft, yellow glow. The heavens, an enormous indigo umbrella punctured a million times with a pin.

My mom and I unload our beach chairs, blankets, and cooler, and the kids take off into the sand. The smell of charcoal and meat drift past my nostrils, and my stomach rumbles.

People have short-term memory—either that, or they're very good at faking it. Our night at the beach is surrounded by complete acceptance.

I owe a great deal of this to Michelle, who, without being overbearing, keeps a watchful eye on me and my clan to make sure we're included.

"I'm not a boy," Addie says to a kid who's a foot taller than her. Addie's hands are in fists on her hips, and her legs are set in defiance.

"Look like a boy to me, a boy in a skirt," the kid says.

I try to push myself from my beach chair, but my pregnancy slows my progress significantly.

"Who you calling a boy?" Drew gets there first. He's the same height as the antagonist but much thinner.

"What's it to you?"

"That's my sister."

"Well, she looks like a freak."

Drew attacks, his fists flailing, but it lasts only a second before it's broken up by several dads, with no damage done.

I pull Drew to me as the mother of the other boy glares and marches her son in the other direction. Addie's beaming.

"You showed him," she says.

At nine o'clock, we're partied out, and we pack up our gear and head home full of hot dogs and marshmallows.

I park in the driveway, and before I step from the car, I know something's very wrong. The sprinklers spray, and puddles pool around the heads that pop from the lawn like android groundhogs spinning to look for their shadows. I turn off the water and push open the front door. It was unlocked, and the alarm wasn't set.

My mom's behind me carrying Addie, who's asleep on her shoulder.

"Pops?" I call.

I scan the first floor, and my mom sets Addie down and searches upstairs.

The answering machine blinks. I hit play.

"Grace, it's Jan. Don't freak out. Nick's fine. A neighbor took him to the hospital. He was having some chest pain. I tried calling your cell, but there was no reception. He's at Mission Hospital, and they're running some tests. He needs to stay the night."

My mom grabs the keys from my hand and is out the door.

I close it behind her, lock it, and set the alarm.

74

I wake with a start and walk barefoot down the hall, aware before I even get there that they're gone.

I look in the closet, peek my head into the bathroom, check the kitchen. By now, my heart's throbbing, and sweat has pooled in the hollow of my neck.

After my mom left, I locked the door and set the alarm, but he was already in the house. It was the mistake he was waiting for.

I call Gregg, then my mom, then nobody.

They're gone.

75

Time passes, the seconds throbbing by with the relentless pulsing of my heart, moving in lurches and lulls, passing just the same.

I miss them every day and always.

Snapshots of memories, an endless reel of moments spinning through my head. I remember holding Drew in my arms, his tiny fingers curled around mine, the rustle of his breath, the heat of his small body. I think of Addie and the time we found a piece of purple sea glass when she was a toddler, a rare day of just the two of us, her diaper sagging with water, her white belly, her giant laugh. Snippets, a dozen, or maybe a hundred; moments frozen in my brain, playing in an endless loop of torture.

Every week, Gregg updates me with the non-news of the search for Gordon and the kids. The police theorize he's left the country. My mom and dad believe we'll never see him again.

Only I know he's not gone. He's waiting. There's still unfinished business, and he won't leave until it's done.

I live in constant fear.

Like a ticking time bomb, as my stomach grows and the baby's kicks get stronger, the threat looms larger.

I responsibly care for the life inside me. It's a tedious exercise of obligation—I eat to nurture it, walk to insure its health, and take my vitamins—the routine a groaning monotony, a single track of elevator music played just for me.

My parents suffer the same malady of despair. We wait for this baby to arrive, wanting it but not wanting it, none of us brave enough to open our hearts again.

This child is doomed. I have no more chance of protecting it than I did of protecting Addie and Drew. Gordon will claim what's his, then perhaps he will kill me, or perhaps he will realize he already has and leave me be.

It's hard to believe how much has changed in nine months. It seems longer than all the other time I existed put together. Little League games, my job, our home—it was at least a lifetime ago.

Yesterday was Addie's fifth birthday.

I wonder how they celebrated.

Gordon was always big on birthdays—grand celebrations with inflatable jump houses and balloons and hired princesses or magicians. I wonder if this year was different or if he still managed to throw Addie a big bash.

The baby kicks, bringing me out of my reverie. It's time. I gather my backpack from the table. In it is my wallet, my phone, and my gun.

Gordon believes this baby is his.

76

I'm two weeks overdue, which is why labor's been induced. The baby doesn't want to come out, and I can't blame it. I wish I could return to the womb where it's dark and warm and safe and everything is taken care of.

I've been given an epidural, so I feel nothing—the physical now matches the emotional.

"Jillian, it's time to push."

I do as I'm told. My mom stands beside me. My dad's in the waiting room.

An hour later, the baby's out and hollers a healthy wail.

"It's a boy," the doctor exclaims.

My mom and I say nothing. Our thoughts are the same. We miss Drew.

Ten minutes later, the nurse holds a blue-swaddled bundle toward me. I turn away.

"She's tired." My mom excuses me and holds out her arms for the child.

It's been two hours since the baby was born.

Through the window, the sun cuts a ribbon across the ocean and I stare at the glare until my eyes blur.

My mom's gone to the cafeteria to get some food. The baby sleeps in the bassinet beside me.

The cradle is acrylic, and through it, I look at my son. He doesn't look like Addie or Drew. He's dark like his father, and his chin is square. His name is Jeffrey Paul Cancelleiri.

His small mouth opens and closes in a weak attempt to root, then settles back to sleep. I watch him breathe. One hand escapes the swaddle, and the little fist pumps in victory. His nose wrinkles.

The sun is gone, and the window is gray.

He roots again, this time with more determination, his fist waving, searching for something to hold, searching for me.

I hit the button for the nurse.

Nothing happens.

He gets more frantic, his mouth glubbing, his head craning sideways.

I hit the button again.

The nurse pokes her head in.

"He needs to be fed," I say.

"So feed him."

I shake my head.

"Well, I can't. We've got two deliveries." And she's gone.

Jeffrey's other hand escapes, and he reaches out of his blanket, both hands waving. He's still not crying, and I'm proud of his stoicism. He's like his father; I bet Jeffrey wasn't a crier.

Panic starts to fill his face and mine.

I can't do it. I don't want to do it. Where's my mom? The bottle and the formula sit on the table beside the door, a mile away. My breasts ache.

I push my sore body up. "It's okay," I say. "Your grandma will be back real soon, and she's going to feed you."

My voice puts him over the edge. He wails with a cry that defies his seven pounds. It's the roar of a lion and I'm jolted into action.

Before I know what I've done, I've lifted him from his cradle, opened my gown, and he's nestled into the crook of my arm, suckling contentedly.

He's beautiful. Stunningly, painfully beautiful, and tears stream from my eyes and soak into his blanket.

"Looks like you've come around," the nurse says from the doorway, and I realize I've been duped. There were no deliveries.

77

My mom and dad have gone home for the night, and Jeffrey and I are alone.

He's in his bassinet, and I'm staring at him sleeping.

When the door opens, I turn, expecting to see the nurse. Instead, silhouetted in the frame is Gordon, his features obscured in shadow as he glances at Jeffrey, then back at me.

My arms move toward Jeffrey, and my mouth opens to scream, but it's all too slow. A pillow is over my face, Gordon's weight bearing down on me as I choke on the cotton, and my arms flail, banging against the sides of the bed.

I feel the buttons on the rail and frantically press them, hoping one will bring a nurse. My air is draining so fast that it's shocking how quickly I'm going to die, and with so little protest.

I want to fight, but I can't. The pillow presses so hard against my face, it doesn't allow for any hope of salvation, Gordon pinning it against me, not uttering a word or a prayer, simply standing above me, holding me down, waiting for me to die.

The world fades, blackness settles, and my brain begins to

shut down. I lay limp, my body surrendering. Then suddenly, the pressure releases and I'm gasping for air as light blasts into my brain and oxygen fills my lungs. Spots dance in my eyes and, through the dizziness, I see Gordon shove the nurse out of the way and run out the door. The tail of a blue blanket trailing behind him.

I suck in a breath as I look at the empty bassinet, then wrench myself from the bed, grab the backpack I brought with me, and stumble after him screaming, "Call security. Stop him."

The elevator door closes, and I run to the stairs. Obstetrics is on the third floor. I feel blood dripping down my legs, and I know I've ruptured my stitches. My mind spins with wooziness, and I will my shaking legs to hold me, gritting my teeth and concentrating on moving forward, praying my body won't abandon me completely.

Jeffrey. The thought propels me forward.

I reach the first floor and run toward the exit.

A security guard faces off against Gordon; both have guns drawn.

"Set it down," Gordon says. "Put it on the ground and let me walk out the door."

The man's maybe twenty-five and probably just got out of the army. Chances are he was a cook or a mechanic; he doesn't look like a fighter. He begins to crouch, his weapon lowering.

"No," I yell, my momentum hurling toward them. Gordon turns, and everything moves in slow motion—my finger on the trigger, the blue blanket turning toward me. I'm aiming low. The bullet will hit high.

I want to stop it, but like so many things, it's too late. I can only regret the decision I've made.

The sound is instant and deafening, ricocheting and resonating and stopping time. Gordon turns, surprise then fear on his face as he twists sideways, not to avoid the shot, but to take it, to cover Jeffrey. He stumbles with the impact and lurches again as he turns back toward me, the gun in his hand rising then falling as he crumbles to his knees. His mouth opens, but no words come out. Then the gun clunks to the floor, and he topples sideways, his shoulder cradling the baby's delicate head.

Jeffrey tumbles from Gordon's arm and begins to cry. Gordon blinks once, reaches for him, then his eyes settle on me and he dies, his eyes open, a vacant stare on his face like Jeffrey's, but not. Gordon is not in pain, not tormented or concerned with saving himself, his expression peaceful and so full of devotion that, despite my hate, it wrenches my heart.

He would die for them, would kill for them... turns out, I was willing to do the same.

A nurse holds me as I slump against her and the gun is being taken from my hand by the security guard. Another nurse lifts Jeffrey from the floor. Already he's stopped crying and contentedly sleeps swaddled in a safe embrace, blissfully unaware of his role in saving me, of saving Addie and Drew, of destroying the man who would have loved him and raised him as his own.

I'm helped into a wheelchair, and as I'm pushed toward the elevator, the security guard talks rapidly into his phone. "No, I don't think she planned it. Yes sir, he had a gun..."

Did I plan it?

I knew Gordon would come for Jeffrey. I packed the gun. I knew killing him was the only way. Every night since he took Addie and Drew, I lifted that gun in my mind; most of the time it was in the chapel of the hospital, regret lacing my envisagement, the blast echoing in the hollow, holy chamber as Jesus watched.

"My children?" I mumble numbly as I'm wheeled forward.

"Your baby is here," the nurse says.

"My other children, Addie and Drew. He had them."

The nurse kneels. She's an older woman with kind eyes. "How old? What do they look like?"

I give the description, and she conveys it to the security guard, and a moment later, as she helps me back into my bed, the man appears and tells us Addie and Drew were found in a car in the parking lot. They're fine, and my parents are on their way to get them.

"Rest now," the nurse says.

Rest now. It's been ten years since I've rested without fear. I've forgotten what it feels like. I lift Jeffrey from his bassinet and cradle him in the rook's nest of my arm. His tiny lips latch on to my breast, and I close my eyes. *I'm here, little man—you, me, your sister, and brother—we're all here.* And I rest.

78

Today's my birthday. I'm forty-one.

The celebration is a quiet one with my parents, Addie, Drew, and Jeffrey, and it's the happiest and the saddest one I've had in ten years. So much has happened.

My dad and I have begun to rebuild our collection of statues. We have five now, and my gift from him today was the sixth, my favorite, the one with the singing man with the Fu Manchu.

Addie and my mom baked a carrot cake using carrots from our garden, and Drew gave me a bouquet of sunflowers and a book by Stephen King. He remembered me talking to Fred about these things.

Jeffrey looks like his father and not so much like his brother and sister, who both grow to look more like Gordon every day. Addie's smile is his smile, and sometimes Drew will do the most ordinary thing, tilt his head, fold his hands in church, and it's as though his father never died.

Gordon's been gone almost three months, but he's still always on my mind.

I haven't learned to think of him as dead yet. Like an amputee, I feel him all the time. I still jump at the sound of footsteps when I'm asleep, and my heart skips when the scent of a particular deodorant or soap crosses my path.

The gunshot blasting through the fluorescent hallway of the hospital toward Jeffrey resonates so often in my mind that it's part of the rhythm of my life, another tattoo etched on my soul that molds and shapes me.

My conscience is haunted. I know now that in all of us exists a lion and a lamb. My violence is deeply buried, hidden beneath strata of fear, morals, and compassion, but it exists. And with absolute certainty—a clarity not blurred by time or altered by yearning—I know, at the moment I pulled the trigger, my hatred was more than my love.

I knew Gordon held Jeffrey. Gordon knew it as well. One of us pulled the trigger, the other sacrificed himself.

I look around me. I owe him so much. He died for Jeffrey. He saved my dad. He's the reason I have Addie and Drew.

Tyger! Tyger! Burning bright; In the forests of the night.

What immortal hand or eye, dare frame thy fearful symmetry?

In all of us, there is evil, and in some of us, there is good.

A NOTE FROM THE AUTHOR

Dear Reader,

What if...? The two most provocative words in the English language, cause for endless contemplation and reflection, and the inspiration for *Hush Little Baby*. I'd like to start by saying that I am married to a wonderful, kind, not-abusive-in-any-way man. Like Jillian and Gordon, we have two children, a boy and a girl, and we live in the beautiful town of Laguna Beach, California. My life is good. But...*what if?*

What if my husband wasn't as wonderful as he appeared? This exact real-life scenario provided the premise of the novel. A friend of mine was going through a divorce. Until she separated from her husband, the two seemed like the picture of happiness, not too dissimilar from me and my husband. But the story she told over drinks one night of the abuse and cruelty she endured behind closed doors was so frightening it made me wonder how many other marriages are not what they appear.

The curveball came about a month later when we went out again and my friend's story had changed, the tale altered and now with glaring inconsistencies from the earlier version that caused an alarm to blare in my brain. *What if she was making it up?* Custody of the kids was at stake. Could she be setting her husband up? For over ten years, I'd known her husband as a stand-up guy, the baseball coach who never yelled, the neighbor who happily carted your Christmas tree home in his truck, the kind of guy who always showed up and did his part. Yet, how quickly I dismissed all that based on a story over drinks; how quickly everyone dismissed it, so easily accepting that he was abusive and dangerous.

So I got to thinking how easy it is to sabotage a life, that if my husband set out to destroy me, to preemptively strike before I realized what was going on, he could do it. He knows my weaknesses, my failings, my vulnerabilities. If he had the inclination, he could easily undermine my reputation and portray me as unstable or a bad mother, ensuring that if we divorced, he'd get custody of the kids.

My friend loves her children above all else, three beautiful boys. At the time they were four, nine, and twelve, and their futures, as well as her own, hung in the balance. To this day, nearly three years later, I don't know if she was telling the truth or manufacturing lies. Either way, her story was a captivating cautionary tale that made me wonder how far someone might go to keep their spouse from getting custody of their kids, and then, if the kids were in danger, real danger, how far the other spouse might go to get them back.

My life is good. My husband's a good father. I'm a good mother. Our universe orbits around our son and our daughter, and either of us would do anything...*anything*... to protect them.

What if...? The words are chilling, don't you think?

I hope you enjoy reading the novel as much as I enjoyed writing it.

Sincerely,
Suzanne

READING GROUP GUIDE

1. Consider Jillian as a mother. Do you think she's a good mother? Do you sympathize with her? How about at the start of the story? At what point do your sympathies begin to change (if they do)? Do you think most mothers compare themselves to other mothers and worry about inadequacy? Is this more common among working mothers?
2. How do you think the marriage appears from the outside? How do you think the world perceives Jillian? Gordon? Do you think all of us portray an external image different from the reality behind closed doors? If so, how did this story make you feel about that?
3. What do you think would have happened had Jillian stayed in the marriage? Do you think she left primarily because she was scared, because he destroyed the statues, because of the kids becoming aware of the abuse, or because Gordon wanted to borrow money from her retirement fund?
4. Do you sympathize with Gordon at all? Had he married a different woman, do you think he might have been different?
5. How did you feel about the incident of Drew torturing the toad? Why do you think he did it? Do you sympathize with him? Do you think he did it to test Jillian as a mother to see if she'd protect him, or because he's like his father? Do you think Jillian handled it correctly?

6. Jillian has an affair with Jeffrey. Do you sympathize with this or find it reprehensible?
7. Do you believe Gordon killed Jeffrey based on the circumstantial evidence ("Shotgun deaths are brutal," and Gordon using Jillian's name when she confronts him with the accusation)? What if it turns out Gordon didn't actually kill Jeffrey? How does that change your perception of everything that happened after?
8. Do you blame Jillian for Jeffrey's death? Do you think she irresponsibly put him in danger? How do you feel about her not reporting his death or telling the police her suspicions?
9. The wedding ring Gordon gave Jillian turns out to be a fake. Do you think his love was as well? Always? Why do you think they got married in the first place?
10. Gordon and Paul were opposing forces, one a cop, the other a convicted criminal; one controlling, the other not. How did Jillian's time with Paul change her and make her more capable of dealing with her issues?
11. When Jillian was at the Flying Goat, she was a fish out of water. Do you think she could have ultimately been happy there?
12. How do you feel about Jillian getting pregnant by Jeffrey, then keeping the baby to protect herself, knowing she couldn't provide a good life for it? How do you feel about her not telling Gordon the baby was not his, knowing the baby was in danger and that Gordon was going to come for it?
13. Had Addie not gotten sick, how do you think the story might have played out?
14. In what way do Jillian's parents contribute to her staying in her marriage? Do you think she made the right choice re-

turning to Gordon after she left the first time? Do you think she should have returned to live with her parents when she came back from Washington, knowing this put them in danger?

15. Sherman McGregor was a mentor to Jillian. Do you think his story was a cautionary tale that relates to Jillian's choices? If so, how?
16. How do you feel about Claudia? Did you have sympathy for her? Do you think Jillian should have sympathy for her?
17. William Blake's poem, "The Tyger" was mentioned in the story as well as an Aesop's fable. How do you think these stories foreshadowed Jillian's own fate?
18. An underlying theme of the story is whether good and evil exist in each of us. Do you believe evil exists only in some or that it exists in everyone and is exposed based on circumstance?
19. Jillian decided not to kill Gordon in the hospital, realizing that was not the way to fix things, but ultimately she shot him in the end. Does this mean evil prevailed or was she justified in killing him? Would your opinion change had Gordon not shielded the baby and the baby died instead of Gordon?
20. How did Jillian's character evolve throughout the story? Do you think her values or perspective changed?
21. Who was your favorite character? Why?
22. Movie time: Who would you like to see play each part?